"I'm a [barcode: D0379154] *fix."*

Sebastian followed her gaze—and his heart shuddered at the sight of the mistletoe.

"My lord, I do believe I owe you a kiss."

Blood throbbed in his veins at the sound of her silky smooth voice. She could *not* kiss him. He was adamant. For eight years he'd stood fast to escape the girl's kisses. He would not flounder now; give her reason to believe he cared for her in an un-brotherly fashion.

"But you and I are friends," she said next, eyes slanted in demure innocence. "And it wouldn't do a'tall if I kissed you on the lips . . . instead I will kiss you where you've never been kissed before."

Other **AVON ROMANCES**

Coming Soon

And Don't Miss These
ROMANTIC TREASURES
from Avon Books

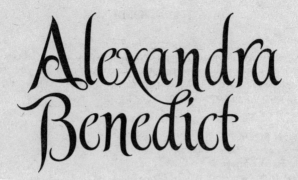

Alexandra Benedict

Too Scandalous to Wed

AVON

An Imprint of HarperCollinsPublishers

This is a work of fiction. Names, characters, places, and incidents are products of the author's imagination or are used fictitiously and are not to be construed as real. Any resemblance to actual events, locales, organizations, or persons, living or dead, is entirely coincidental.

AVON BOOKS
An Imprint of HarperCollins*Publishers*
10 East 53rd Street
New York, New York 10022-5299

Copyright © 2007 by Alexandra Benedikt
ISBN: 978-0-06-117043-0
ISBN-10: 0-06-117043-7
www.avonromance.com

First Avon Books paperback printing: September 2007

Avon Trademark Reg. U.S. Pat. Off. and in Other Countries, Marca Registrada, Hecho en U.S.A.
HarperCollins® is a registered trademark of HarperCollins Publishers.

Printed in the U.S.A.

10 9 8 7 6 5 4 3 2 1

To my parents, with everlasting love and gratitude.

Too
Scandalous
to Wed

Chapter 1

London, 1821

"**G**ood heavens, Henry, you're still in your drawers!"

And Henrietta Ashby was going to stay in her drawers until she figured out the ideal dress to wear—much to the dismay of her mother, Lady Lara Ashby.

"I'll be there in a minute, Mama."

Distraught, the elder woman proclaimed, "But Henry, the guests have already arrived!"

Henrietta wasn't interested in the guests below . . . well, she was interested in one particular guest, hence the crucial decision she had to make.

"Which one, Mama, the pink or the peach?"

Lady Ashby fluttered her fan in quick succession. "Henry, can't you ever make up your mind?"

Unfortunately, Henrietta could not. She had a penchant for disorder and a tendency to waver over every decision. Alas, it was not her fault she had such a flighty disposition. Truly, it wasn't. Henrietta was the youngest offspring of Baron Nicholas Ashby, and, as such, the most pampered of the lot. She also served as the baron's surrogate son, thus the nickname Henry.

You see, the baron had a brood of children—all girls! Desperate for a male heir, he had christened his *fifth* daughter Henry, and like any indulgent papa, the baron catered to his "son's" every wish and whim without complaint. Though there was no property to inherit or title to come into, that did not stop Henrietta from acting the part of the doted-upon son and heir. The only trouble with being Henry was the freedom to do as she pleased without a thought to the consequences.

"I think I'll go with the pink," said Henrietta.

"Fine." Lady Ashby sighed with impatience. "I want you below in five minutes!"

The door thudded closed.

Jenny, the poor chambermaid, blanched at the command, not that Henrietta noticed. She eyed the rose silk ruffs and heart-shaped neckline and thought: *It's perfect!*

The peach frock went flying through the air, skewered on a bedpost. Discarded and forgotten, the dress dangled in neglect like so many other wisps of fabric scattered across the bedroom floor.

Musing, Henrietta glanced around the cluttered space. "Now for the mask."

She went over to the bed, tossed the weekly gossip papers aside—she'd been reading the juicy tidbits earlier in the day—and sifted through the many scattered headdresses, looking for the best match.

With a pleading look in her eyes, the young chambermaid lifted a bejeweled headpiece. "Will this do, miss?"

Henrietta eyed the glittering adornment. "Yes, that will do."

Jenny whistled a sigh of relief and quickly ushered her mistress to the vanity. It took a little longer than five minutes, but soon Henrietta was all decked out in a resplendent evening gown of shimmering rose silk and a lovely jewel-encrusted mask to match.

She twirled in front of the full-length mirror, inspecting her reflection. The frock complemented the auburn glow of her hair and deep brown hue of her eyes to perfection.

If this doesn't draw his notice, I'm going to scratch out his eyes.

With that encouraging thought in mind, Henrietta thanked her maid.

Jenny started to tidy up the room.

"Never mind that," said Henrietta. She took Jenny by the hand and shooed her out the door. "Cook needs help in the kitchen, I'm sure. You can clean the mess later."

Jenny sighed and skirted off. "Yes, Miss Ashby."

A spring to her step, Henrietta made her way down to the ballroom. Baron Ashby's annual masquerade ball was fast becoming a tradition. The third so far, it was first initiated at the behest of

Lady Ashby to help find her youngest daughter a mate. With four sisters already wed, Henrietta was the last of the brood to get leg-shackled. Spinsterhood was fast approaching, and that, of course, put Lady Ashby in near hysterics.

But what Mama did not realize was Henrietta's determination to resist every suitor save one—Viscount Ravenswood.

Henrietta's heart pinched at the thought of Ravenswood. Even his name made her shiver right down to her toes.

Oh, love was such a pesky affair! For eight long years she had dreamed of Ravenswood, ever since his younger brother Peter had married her eldest sister, Penelope. *Eight* agonizing years, and still the blasted man thought of her as a charming chit, nothing more.

Henrietta had a mind to clout the viscount for his mulishness. She wasn't a lass of twelve anymore, but a passionate woman of twenty with a need for one equally passionate man. And if the vexing lord would only stop thinking of her as a spirited imp, she could finally take her rightful place as the next Viscountess Ravenswood. She wasn't getting any younger, didn't he know?

The ballroom loomed ahead.

Her steps more refined, Henrietta gracefully moved to the arena's threshold. She paused under the arched entranceway and scanned the array of twirling dance partners. Her eyes skipped over the feathered headdresses and looked beyond the crystal chandeliers and polished marble statues of Roman gods, searching for Ravenswood.

"Good evening, Miss Ashby."

She bristled. He was the only one in the family who didn't call her by her nickname. It annoyed her beyond words, his willful refusal to grant her even *that* small level of intimacy.

Slowly she turned around to confront the towering figure of masculine energy.

Henrietta let out a little gasp at the sight of Ravenswood. He was decked in striking sable black attire, the white ruff of his cravat set high in an elegant knot at the center of his throat. A thick throat. A strong throat. One that made Henrietta wonder where a peer like Ravenswood would get such corded muscles.

But soon thoughts of "where" turned to thoughts of "who cares" as something squirmed in her belly. A moist heat that dazzled her senses every time she stood near the man. He was immaculate in apparel; only his sable black locks were a bit untidy, a few stray curls draped over and around his red silk mask.

Heavens, he was stunning! Oh, why hadn't she brought along her fan? It was overwhelming, the heat radiating from Ravenswood.

"Good evening, Sebastian." Voice unsteady, she called him by his Christian name. He would *not* deny her that familiarity, at least.

Sebastian quirked a smile at her lack of deference, but otherwise did not remark on her failure to call him "my lord."

"And how are you this evening, Miss Ashby?"

His voice was deep and measured, and it made her heart thump loud and fierce.

"I'm very well, Sebastian, thank you," she squeaked. "And you?"

"I'm quite well, Miss Ashby."

Oh, she wanted to tweak his tongue and get it to say her first name! "I'm so glad to hear that."

The viscount folded his hands behind his back, the breadth of his chest exposed to her eager eyes. And, oh, that spicy scent of Eau de Cologne! The rosemary and lemon made Henrietta positively light-headed.

It was a deuced bother, being in love with such a man. He was much too cavalier; it always put her at a disadvantage . . . well, not this time. This time she had on *the* perfect dress.

Her pulse throbbed. It throbbed even harder when he drawled in that oh-so-husky voice, "You look lovely this evening, Miss Ashby."

"Thank you, Sebastian."

For just a moment, his smoldering blue gaze dropped to caress the swell of her bosom, and Henrietta thought her heart would break through the breastbone.

It's working, she thought. *He's finally going to see me as a grown woman!*

Her hopes soared even higher when he leaned in so achingly close to whisper, "I think you have outgrown your frock, Miss Ashby."

Oh, curse him! Was that all he could say? What about *You look bewitching*? Or *I must claim the next dance*? *Anything* but an overprotective, brotherly remark.

She wanted to rail at him. She bit her tongue instead.

Forcing a smile to her trembling lips, she said, "Have I really?"

The richness of his voice tickled her skin. "I suggest you run back to your room and fetch a chemisette."

And with that, he bowed and walked away.

Henrietta just stood in the entranceway, utterly dumbfounded. A chemisette! She had draped her body in the softest of silk—and all but exposed her bosom with the low cut of her neckline—and he told her to cover up!

She was going to wring his neck. Why, every other gentleman at the ball was gazing at her in admiration. Why couldn't *he*?

"Bloody hell," she muttered in the same vein as her best friend, Mirabelle Hawkins. Things were not getting off to a good start.

And that discourse! Could she have said anything more mundane?

Drat!

Why couldn't she find her voice when in the presence of the viscount? Why did her flesh tingle and her heart patter and her mouth grow dry? Why couldn't she flirt effortlessly like that wench across the room ogling *her* Ravenswood?

Henrietta let out a soft snort, then turned away from the spectacle. She hated to see Ravenswood converse with other women—pretty women. It downright made her heart hurt.

Taking in a deep breath to ease the tightness in her limbs, Henrietta made her way through the throng of guests and headed for the lemonade bowl. She needed a cool refreshment.

She also needed the company of her dearest chum, Mirabelle Hawkins. The two women were kindred spirits. But alas, Mirabelle's family was in the most dreaded of all professions—trade—and while Henrietta did not give a whit about her best friend's familial roots, Mirabelle did. The young woman was quite aware of the stigma upon her head, and she did not wish to besmirch Henrietta's reputation by maintaining an obvious friendship. And so Henrietta could not even invite her best bud to the masquerade ball—and she thus had to suffer the sting of Ravenswood's dismissal alone.

A tap on the shoulder diverted Henrietta's attention, and she set her glass of citrus fruit aside. "Oh, hello, Cat."

Catherine Smith was an amiable acquaintance. A shy girl, she lacked the spirited character Henrietta longed for in a chum. But she was a sweet debutante, eager to please. Henrietta had asked a favor of her, to help her woo Ravenswood. She was about to inquire after Catherine's progress in the endeavor—when she noticed the rose pigment marking the young woman's throat. Was the girl blushing?

"Is something the matter, Cat?"

Catherine stuttered.

"Cat, I can't understand a word you're saying."

The girl paused, took in a deep breath, then said, "I spoke with Ravenswood, just like you asked me to."

Henrietta blinked. "When?"

"Tonight. The ball's been under way for more than an hour, Henry."

Heavens, was she that late? Henrietta brushed her astonishment aside and fixed her gaze on Catherine. "Well, out with it, Cat. What happened with Ravenswood?"

The girl knitted her fingers. "I-I mentioned your name and remarked on your pretty eyes and—"

"Yes, I know what *you* said. We rehearsed the monologue last week. But what did *he* say?"

"Oh, he was quite in accord about your eyes, and all."

"But . . . ?"

"Well, you s-see." Catherine glanced at the polished ballroom floor. "He was so nice and we talked about all sorts of things."

"Things?" Henrietta reared her head back. "What sorts of things?"

"Nothing of consequence. The beautiful summer

weather, the approaching end of the Season, the retreat to the country . . ."

Henrietta wasn't a soul to practice patience. Lord
knew, she didn't have much restraint when it came
to her temper, either. And Catherine was beginning
to gnaw at what little equanimity she had left.

Setting a hand over the girl's fidgety fingers,
Henrietta encouraged, "Yes, Cat?"

Catherine looked up and sighed. "I think I'm in
love with Ravenswood."

Henrietta blinked again. It took her all of two
seconds to gather her stunned thoughts.

"Why, Cat, you little hussy!"

Henrietta snatched the wide-eyed girl's mask,
and in a fit of feminine pique, plucked each and
every feather from the frilly headpiece. She cared
not a jot that she was standing in the middle of the
sumptuous ballroom, amid a throng of masquerad-
ing guests, and causing a bit of a stir. Nor did she
heed Catherine's whimpers. All Henrietta minded
was the ghastly declaration young Catherine had
just uttered, causing her mind to whirl and colorful
spots to dance before her eyes.

"I say, unhand me," Henrietta protested, as a
hand suddenly pinched her wrist and yanked her
roughly away from a sniveling Catherine.

Dragged to the other side of the ballroom and
shoved behind a potted fern, Henrietta glared at the
masked female with obvious ire.

"What the devil is the matter with you?" Indignant, Henrietta demanded, "Who are you?"

At that moment, the mysterious female lifted her feathered headdress.

Henrietta gasped. "Oh, Belle!"

Henrietta flung herself at Mirabelle Hawkins, her very dearest friend in the whole wide world. The horrible downward spiral of the evening immediately brightened, as the two girls hugged and hopped in glee—and let out a few feminine squeals to boot.

Henrietta had not seen her chum in almost a year. Gracious, it had been too long! Though studious in her letter writing, Mirabelle had not come to Town to visit. And Henrietta had missed her terribly . . . so what was Mirabelle doing here? Henrietta had not invited her to the ball. Was the woman in some sort of trouble?

Discarding Catherine's tattered mask, Henrietta removed her own bejeweled headpiece. "What's the matter, Belle? Are you hurt?"

"I'm all right." Mirabelle took in a rather shaky breath, indicating otherwise, then pointed to the shabby mask on the shiny ballroom floor. "What was *that* all about?"

Her temper rankled once more, Henrietta made a moue. "Oh, Cat's a conniving little witch."

"Cat?"

"Catherine . . . never mind." Henrietta waved a

hand. "The girl *was* my friend up until a minute ago."

"What happened?"

"Catherine was supposed to tweak Viscount Ravenswood's nose and get the man to notice *me*. She wasn't supposed to set *her* cap on him." Henrietta huffed. "As if Ravenswood would ever flirt with a mousy little thing like her."

"Viscount Ravenswood?"

And that was all the encouragement Henrietta needed to vent her frustrations. The story poured forth—every vexing detail.

All the while, Henrietta stared at Ravenswood from across the room. He wasn't with the wench anymore, but conversing with Papa—listening to Papa—for he was far too busy glaring at her to say much of anything to Baron Ashby.

The viscount surely thought her tiff with Catherine inappropriate. Well, a pox on him. If he wasn't so pigheaded about his true feelings for her, they'd be married by now, and Henrietta wouldn't have to fend off other hopeful maids vying for the viscount's hand.

In the end, Henrietta puckered her lips and said, "I'm going to have to do something scandalous to get Ravenswood's attention."

"Scandalous?" echoed Mirabelle. "You mean like wearing a *very* revealing gown?"

"Can you believe it?" She glanced down at her dress. "Rose silk, deep ruffs, a heart-shaped neckline, and still the dratted man won't *look* at me. He tells me to put on a chemisette; the impudence. I'm not a debutante."

Mirabelle quirked a smile. "It is a bit too charming, shall we say?"

"Don't you start that, too." Henrietta glared at her chum with reproach. "Besides, your dress is just as risqué . . . I say, isn't that my dress?"

"Yes, well, I had to sneak into the house and borrow the dress to come and talk with you. I didn't bring along my dancing clothes, you know? I didn't know you were having a ball!"

"Oh, that's right." Henrietta pushed Ravenswood to the back of her mind and returned her attention to Mirabelle. "Why are you here, Belle?"

"I'm stranded."

"What do you mean? What happened?"

It was a sharp inhale, born of pain. Henrietta could sense it. Despite the joyful reunion, there was an aura of melancholy surrounding her beloved chum. Henrietta had never seen the woman like this, so bereft of spirit.

"Tell me, Belle."

The soft coaxing did the trick, for Mirabelle confessed, "I'm a fool, Henry. I very nearly gave my heart away to a rogue."

"Ooh, really?"

Henrietta had a certain fondness for rogues herself, so dashing and sensual—and infuriating at times.

"Really," said Mirabelle. "I even thought I could

share a life with him." Then sullenly: "But I was wrong. I can't be with him."

"Why, Belle?"

"I just can't have him. Trust me, Henry."

"I do, Belle." Henrietta patted the woman's hand. "Hush. It's all right."

"It's not all right, Henry. I was with the rogue, here in London . . . but then I had to get away from him. We had a fight; he doesn't care for me."

Henrietta wasn't so sure about that. Mirabelle had a wild and wonderful spirit. She was beautiful, too. The man would have to be daft not to care for her, even a little.

Her mind a whirl, Henrietta could just imagine it: a lovers' quarrel. Mirabelle disappearing in anger . . . her secret beau giving chase through the winding streets of London. Perhaps he was still out there, looking for her? Oh, how romantic!

"But now I'm stranded, Henry. And I have to get back home to my brothers."

Henrietta was snapped from her reverie. Brothers? Oh, that's right. Mirabelle was an orphan. She had four brothers—all sailors—looking after her. Henrietta didn't know much more about the family. She had never met the Hawkins brood. And she was mighty peeved about that. She wanted to be a part of her best friend's life. But she had to maintain a clandestine friendship with Mirabelle.

It was all a deuced bother, obeying social norms. Why, Henrietta would gladly introduce her dearest chum to the rest of the *ton*. Mirabelle was handsome and witty—and the *ton* would be envious. That, and her best bud's lack of riches and a title, made social acceptance a fanciful dream. Alas, Mirabelle was right. Better to keep their friendship secret—for now.

"Say no more." Determined to assist her chum in any way that she could, Henrietta said, "I know where Papa keeps a stash of coins hidden from Mama."

"Thank you." Mirabelle smiled in appreciation. "I'll send the money back to you as soon as I get home, I promise."

"Oh, rot! What's a few farthings between friends?"

After all, Mirabelle had saved her life more than a year ago! Well, sort of. Desperate to escape yet another would-be suitor, Henrietta had fled from the townhouse by scrambling out a second-floor balcony and down a tree, only to snag her foot on a gnarled twig! Stuck in such a compromising pose, she had started to panic, but then Mirabelle had come along—a true guardian angel with her tawny gold locks—and offered to help.

With surprising agility, Mirabelle had scaled the tree and set Henrietta's foot loose, and together they'd clambered for the safety of Mother Earth—until Henrietta had slipped. Both girls had landed in a heap of crisp fall leaves. After such a spectacular tumble and a hearty laugh to boot, the duo had become instant friends. The very best of friends.

Clasping her dearest bud by the hand, Henrietta wondered, "Are you going to be all right, Belle?"

"I think so." Mirabelle sniffed. "Henry, I know he's an undeserving rogue, but still . . ."

Henrietta offered her a thoughtful look. "Still what, gel?"

"It hurts," Mirabelle whispered.

A look of understanding passed between the two women.

"Oh, Belle!" Henrietta gave her a tight hug. "Don't I know it."

Chapter 2

Sebastian Galbraith, Viscount Ravenswood, eyed the little hoyden skirting across the dance floor and tsked. The chit was determined to ruin herself, wasn't she? Tearing apart Catherine's mask and then dashing off the dance floor, her skirts flying. Didn't she care about her respectability? Didn't anyone else?

"Leather tips!" The baron beamed. "Can you believe it, Ravenswood? Leather tips at the end of cue sticks. Why, it's ingenious. It will revolutionize the game of billiards, I daresay."

No, it looked as if no one else was sensible to Henrietta's antics, least of all the doting Baron Ashby. It seemed the task of admonishing the minx would have to fall upon Sebastian. Well, she was akin to a sister. Perhaps he should do his "brotherly" duty and scold the chit? No one else was going to discipline her, it seemed. Besides, he didn't want the girl to end up a spinster, wasting her youth pining over him while simultaneously discouraging the suit of every other eligible bachelor with her wild behavior. It just wasn't right.

Resolved to corner the vixen and give her a sound talking-to, Sebastian turned to the baron and said, "Will you excuse me, my lord? I have a matter to attend to."

"Quite. Quite." And without missing a syllable, the short and rotund baron fixed his gaze on the unsuspecting gentleman to his other side, and resumed his narrative on the innovations in billiards.

Sebastian slipped off the dance floor. Out in the corridor, he removed his red silk mask and headed through the house, searching for the elusive Miss Ashby.

A soft "oof" and "drat" soon tickled his ear, and he paused before the baron's study.

Carefully he opened the door and quirked a brow.

The shifty little witch was perched on an ottoman, her toes spiked, reaching for the top shelf of the baron's bookcase. She pinched and swiped at something just out of her reach, and Sebastian used her moment of concentration to quietly slip inside the room.

He closed the door and leaned against the barrier, gaze intent on the curious creature.

At last she huffed in satisfaction and removed a small purse from its hiding spot.

"Pinching from your poor father?"

Henrietta shrieked and tottered on the ottoman.

He stiffened, about to leap forward to stop her fall, but she grabbed the shelf for support and quickly regained her balance.

He eased the corded tension in his muscles and rested against the door once more. But *she* shot him a look of pure murder.

"Borrowing, I'll have you know."

The pink cherry spots dotting her cheeks told him otherwise, but he refrained from further comment. He was here to upbraid her about her scandalous behavior. Sermons on thievery would have to wait.

"Why did you attack Catherine?"

"*Catherine?!*" She almost choked. "You call me . . . but you call her . . ." She fisted the blunt in her palm. "My tiff with Catherine is none of your concern."

Still perched on the ottoman, she stared down at him, a fire in her ginger brown eyes.

Such a little hellion. A pretty little hellion, even with her rosy lips pursed and slender brows pinched. But she was too thin in Sebastian's opinion. And she had a dreadful sense of fashion, with her primped russet-red locks and fluffy pink frock. Her décolletage was far too low, too. Young girls should not be showing so much bosom.

"I beg to differ," was his terse retort. "I am part of this family, Miss Ashby. If you cause a scandal, it reflects poorly upon all of us."

She snorted. "What scandal? I plucked a few feathers from Cat's mask, that's all. It will hardly make the *Times*."

"You did more than pluck a few feathers; you put the girl to tears."

"Cat deserved it." And then under her breath, "It's all your fault, anyway."

He lifted a brow. "What was that?"

"Never mind." She stepped off the ottoman. "Cat is fine," she said in defense of her boorish manner.

Sebastian shot her a dubious glare. "What did the two of you quarrel about?"

"Nothing of consequence." Boldly she moved toward him. "Now if you will excuse me."

"Not yet, Miss Ashby."

He'd hoped the darker timbre of his voice would instill in her the significance of the subject matter, but it only made her lashes flutter.

He sighed. When was the minx going to give up her foolish childhood fancy for him? He was stumped. He never touched the girl. He always called her Miss Ashby. Frankly, he played the part of the utter dud. One would think she'd have lost interest in him by now.

Well, he had to set the mulish girl right. She really should be married with a brood of squalling brats by now.

"I lied, Miss Ashby."

She blinked. "About what?"

"I'm not concerned with the family's reputation, but yours."

She took another bold step forward—and thrust out her bosom. "Really, Sebastian?"

He wanted to laugh. Her adorable attempts at seduction amused him. If it wasn't in the chit's best interest to marry a respectable bloke, he'd keep her around as a quaint diversion. "Miss Ashby, you must find yourself a proper husband."

A curt bob of the head. "I absolutely agree with you."

Not me, he wanted to clarify, but said instead, "And if you continue in this outrageous manner, you'll be ruined."

"Yes, ruin me."

He quirked a brow. "What?"

"I mean, I will *not* be ruined." Flustered, she blinked a few times. "You exaggerate, Sebastian. Now I have a very pressing matter to attend to, so if you will please step aside."

She lifted her gloved hand to push him out of the way, but before her fingers brushed his arm, he moved away from the door.

He could have sworn he'd heard a whimper of disappointment at her not being able to touch him, but she quickly skirted from the room.

Alone, and thwarted, Sebastian let out a frustrated breath. He moved over to the baron's desk and poured himself a tipple.

He wasn't the only bachelor in Town, didn't she know? Why set her cap for him, and not some other, more agreeable gentleman? Why the stubborn refusal to give up on him?

He downed the spirits. He had to get away from

the girl, take a sojourn. Stay out of the incorrigible chit's sight for a few months. The mainland would do him good, he thought. Give him an opportunity to have a bit of sport. Henrietta might find herself another mate in the meantime. He could hope.

Sebastian vacated the baron's sanctuary and made his way back over to the ballroom. Having failed to inquire further about the money Henrietta had filched from her father, he now searched over jewel-encrusted heads for the little imp, determined to see what sort of mischief she had gotten herself into now.

He spotted said imp by the terrace doors, leading a fair-haired nymph by the hand.

Sebastian smiled. Now there was a woman with curves just begging to be fondled. The nymph was a sultry vision, her gown far too snug—as if it was a size too small for her—leaving nothing to the imagination. It fact, it looked a lot like one of Henrietta's fluffy dresses.

In any event, Sebastian's wicked inclinations sallied forth at the seductive sight, and he found himself perusing the lovely, fair-haired creature in every detail.

But his lazy daydream was shattered by the appearance of a dark-haired devil. A scoundrel, just like him. It was easy to spot a fellow rogue, and when he moved—thundered—toward Henrietta, Sebastian's primal instinct was to trounce the bounder.

Sebastian was already cutting through the crowd,

intent on whisking Henrietta away from harm, when he stopped. The bounder didn't want Henrietta. He paused long enough to kiss her gloved hand, then swiftly ushered the fair-haired nymph back out onto the terrace.

Ah, a lover's tiff. Sebastian could appreciate a fiery quarrel. He'd had many such spats himself. What he could *not* appreciate was the daft chit's determination to follow the heated couple out onto the terrace. Friendship and loyalty and other such rot aside, Henrietta had no business getting involved with the bounder and his passionate ladybird. And unless the bounder had a penchant for an audience, Henrietta was apt to get brushed aside—violently.

The reckless minx!

Sebastian wove through the throng of dancers, tamping the alarm that had sprouted in his breast. He reached the terrace edge—and stilled.

As expected, the bounder and fair-haired nymph were locked in an amorous embrace, but what was *not* expected was the innocent Miss Ashby's apparent fascination with the couple.

Sebastian moved to the shadows, behind a bush. Well hidden, he observed Henrietta fanning herself with her mask, gazing in awe at the groping couple.

Why, the naughty little vixen. He'd never pegged Henrietta for a voyeur. And when he heard her longing voice—"I'd give my baby toe to be kissed like that"—he couldn't help but smile.

After a few quarrelsome words with the bounder—and another fiery kiss—the fair-haired nymph relinquished the blunt.

Ah, so that's what Henrietta had needed the money for, to give to her friend. But the fair-haired nymph didn't need the blunt anymore. It was returned to Henrietta. It looked liked the quarrelling lovers had reconciled, for the couple absconded to the garden edge just then, disappearing from sight.

Only Henrietta's cry, "Bye, Belle! Let me know how it all works out," was heard, followed by a sigh. "Oh, how romantic!"

Sebastian couldn't resist. He stepped out of the shadows and approached the quixotic chit.

"Is it romantic?"

Henrietta started and whirled around. Drat! He was upon her again. And *again* at the most importune time. First he'd cornered her in the library. Now he'd trapped her on the terrace . . . while she was gushing very private reflections.

Oh dear, how much had he overheard?

She lifted her nose a notch in feigned confidence, all the while trying to keep her knees from quivering. "Yes, Sebastian, it is very romantic."

"To be carted off like a sheep at auction?"

She gasped. "No! To be whisked away in a moment of passion."

He cocked an amused black brow.

Oh, did he have to be so sinfully handsome? Did he have to make her breath catch and her mind go blank and her heart roar in her ears?

"So what would *you* consider to be romantic?" she said.

He shrugged. "Did I say I was romantic?"

"You flirt with every skirt." *Apart from me*, she thought sourly.

"About the weather, Miss Ashby. I love to talk about the weather."

Henrietta bunched her fists. Did he think to make her think ill of him with that paltry fib? Convince her he was a dull sort and not worthy of her affection?

She withheld a snort. Well, he'd have to do better than that. She was much too determined to have him as her husband to heed his constant—and misguided—attempts at sabotage. She knew the man's *true* feelings, even if he was too mulish to admit them.

It was a good thing Henrietta had such a headstrong disposition. She was fated to be with Sebastian. And one day, the man was going to thank her for her unwavering fidelity . . . though perhaps not today.

"Never mind," she said, rather irritably. "You would never understand."

"You're right . . . and I certainly wouldn't give my baby toe for something so scandalous as a kiss."

Humor glittered in the dark blue pools of his seductive eyes before he bowed and swaggered back into the ballroom.

Heavens, he had heard her girlish confession! Henrietta didn't know whether to perish from shame or clock the scoundrel over the head for his impudence.

Insufferable rogue! Why couldn't she have set her cap for a more amiable gentleman?

Because only Ravenswood makes your heart pinch in expectation of a touch . . . a kiss.

She sighed. It was so true. Only Ravenswood disturbed her dreams and ruffled her temper and made her want to do the most inappropriate things to capture his attention.

And yet, everything she *had* done to make an impression on the rogue had failed. What was she going to do to get the viscount to admit his true feelings for her?

Henrietta pressed her lips together, deep in thought.

It was clear she needed help. A teacher of some sort. But whom could she ask for assistance? Her sisters?

Henrietta mulled that over for a bit, then decided against the idea. She might have four elder sisters, all married, but her kin were too prim and proper to offer advice on tempting a mate. And her dearest chum had just reconciled and run off with her beau, so she couldn't ask Mirabelle for counsel. So where could Henrietta go to learn the art of seduction?

There wasn't a school out there for aspiring flirts. What was she to do?

"Drat!" she muttered.

Lips twisted in consternation, she pondered her next move.

Just then a bright star sallied across the midnight sky . . . and it must have dropped an idea into Henrietta's head, for she gasped then, a wicked thought coming to mind.

"The weekly gossip papers!" she whispered. "That's it!"

She remembered the infamous story now; she had read all about it over morning tea.

Filled with hope, Henrietta took in a deep and satisfied breath. "I'm going to show you *scandalous*, Sebastian."

Chapter 3

"**I**'ll not hear another word, Jenny!"

The distraught maid slumped against the cushioned squab with a whimper.

Henrietta returned her attention to the moonlit landscape, tamping her own misgivings into submission.

She had done everything to preserve her reputation: brought along a chaperone, hired a hack to transport her to the city's boundaries. She had even dressed in plain, unsightly garb and sported a hooded mantle to conceal her identity.

What could possibly go wrong?

Wringing her fingers in her lap, Henrietta tried to convince herself this really was the best—the only—choice she had. If she even uttered the word "husband," Sebastian blanched. If she tried to touch him, he recoiled. If she bared her bosom, he rebuked her for it. One would think the man had no regard for her.

But Henrietta knew that wasn't true. She thought

back to a time, about four years ago, when the whole family had gathered in the country for a christening. One of Henrietta's nieces was to be baptized, and Henrietta was late for the ceremony. Rushing to get to the foyer and join the rest of the waiting family, she had knocked over her mother's most cherished vase: a gift from Grandmama. Henrietta was sure to get the strap from Mama—Papa never disciplined her—but then Ravenswood had come along and accepted the blame for the mishap, saving her hide.

Henrietta sighed at the fond memory. The viscount cared for her, she was sure. He was just too stubborn to admit it.

But Henrietta had to get him to confess his true feelings. And after last night's disastrous masquerade ball, it was apparent a more drastic measure was needed to grab the willful viscount's attention.

Her heart cramped at the dreadful recollection. In the wee hours of the morning, after every guest had gone, a thoroughly fagged Henrietta had set off to bed, when Sebastian had made a ghastly announcement:

"I'm off, Miss Ashby."

"Yes, good night Sebastian," she'd murmured, yawned, and mounted the steps.

"See you at Christmas."

Christmas!

She'd whirled around. "What do you mean, Christmas?"

"Well, I've decided to go on a trip, Miss Ashby."

She'd tried to keep the panic out of her voice, but had failed miserably. "Where?"

"Truthfully, I've no idea. But I'll be gone a few months, so take care, sister."

And with that, he'd made a curt bow and sauntered away, leaving a perplexed Henrietta atop the steps, mouth agape.

It was then she'd realized, however scandalous her intentions, she *had* to go through with her plan. Soon Sebastian would see her but once a year. And then not a'tall. Soon he would be lost to her forever.

Henrietta bunched the fabric of her skirt between her fingers. So absorbed with her thoughts, she hadn't noticed the bend in the road. But the stately dwelling that soon appeared did capture her attention, and she quickly forgot her woes to stare at the grand house, a castle really, with its spire rooftops and stone façade. It was reminiscent of the royal chateaux she'd seen in French paintings, classic in presentation and design, with rows of tall glass windows, all reflecting a brilliant glow of candlelight.

Henrietta had never been to Paris herself. Oh, she had always longed to go, but the war with France had prevented the excursion. Even though the continental strife was now over, she still preferred not to visit the foreign land—not alone, anyway. She hoped to go on her wedding tour one day with her future husband—Viscount Ravenswood.

Henrietta eagerly pressed her nose against the

glass in admiration and fervid anticipation. If Madam Jacqueline didn't help her, she was doomed.

The hack rolled to a shaky stop.

Three servants in bright yellow livery promptly appeared, each young and devilishly handsome—and very attentive. One opened the carriage door, one produced a stepping stool upholstered in quilted silk, and one offered his white-gloved hand in gentlemanly support.

A giddy Henrietta stepped out of the carriage, accepted the offered hand, pressed her slippered foot to the cushioned ottoman, and marveled at the well-orchestrated attendants.

She had to admit, this was not the kind of reception she'd expected from Madam Jacqueline, so warm and inviting. According to the gossip papers the woman was a reclusive curmudgeon, grieved by the loss of her notorious charm and beauty. Henrietta was pleased to learn it all a fabrication. Already nervous, she'd dreaded meeting such a frightening being. Now the rendezvous might even be agreeable.

Jenny stepped out of the carriage next before the door was closed, the footstool quickly confiscated, and a sweeping gesture made toward the wide open entrance.

"This way, mademoiselles," said a footman.

Henrietta skirted inside, her maid right behind her.

An attendant approached to remove Henrietta's mantle, but here the gallantry would end, for Henrietta pinched the ribbons at her throat, unwilling to relinquish the garment.

"You are safe, mademoiselle," assured the footman. "Please allow me to take your cape."

Hesitant at first, Henrietta soon loosened her grip on the stays, and the hooded cloak was whisked away.

It was then her eyes beheld the majesty around her. She had been to many balls in many prestigious homes. She had attended court and dined in country splendor. But she had yet to encounter the likes of a Scandinavian ice palace in the heart of English society. Why, it was a scene from a northern fairy tale, she was sure. A Valhalla, of sorts, fit for a Viking god or warrior.

The walls gleamed like ice, bedecked in white silk splendor. Even the grand staircase in the center of the foyer was carpeted in pearl white textiles. A silver chandelier dangled beneath an arched domed ceiling, proudly displaying about a hundred flickering candle lights. More candelabras sat poised on elegant, smoke gray marble side tables, while baskets of creamy white rose petals filled the atmosphere with a heavenly scent. There was even a white bearskin rug under Henrietta's toes, and she let her pampered feet sink into the soft, warm fur.

Jenny was evidently unimpressed by the spectacle, for she tugged at Henrietta's sleeve and hissed, "Miss Ashby, I really think this isn't—"

"Oh, hush, Jenny."

Henrietta wasn't about to turn back now. She had sneaked out of the house, flagged a passing hack, endured the uncomfortable and clandestine journey into the surrounding countryside, and she wasn't leaving until she'd acquired *some* practical knowledge to help her win Ravenswood's hand.

A footman stepped forward and extended his arm. "If you please, mademoiselle."

The two remaining servants circled Jenny, hindering her attempt to follow.

"Madam Jacqueline wishes to see you alone, mademoiselle," said the footman. "Your maid will be well looked after, I assure you."

A bit wary, Henrietta nodded. She smiled at an anxious-looking Jenny, vowing, "I'll be back soon."

Jenny appeared ready to protest, but was quickly ushered away by the attendants.

Meanwhile, Henrietta was escorted through the ice palace to a nearby salon.

It wasn't so much the grandeur of the salon that dazzled Henrietta, as the total turnaround of decor. By stepping over the threshold, she'd departed the pleasures of a Scandinavian ice palace and traveled thousands of miles east to the mystic Orient.

The footman gestured to a dark red divan. "Mademoiselle."

Henrietta settled against the rich cushions. A small fire crackled in the hearth, the smoldering warmth deflected by an exquisitely embroidered Japanese screen.

"Sherry, mademoiselle?"

The silver goblet, shaped like a tiger's head, was delivered into her hand, but Henrietta was too nervous to drink the offered refreshment, so she set the goblet on the lacquered table in front of her, trimmed with ivory ornamentation.

"Madam Jacqueline will be with you shortly."

And with that, the footman bowed and quietly vacated the room. A good thing, too, for Henrietta needed a private moment to gather her wayward thoughts.

Heavens, what had she gotten herself into? The more time she spent alone in the peculiar wonderland, the more she wondered if perhaps Jenny hadn't been right. Perhaps this wasn't such a good idea, after all.

But then thoughts of Ravenswood entered her mind: how the dratted man treated her like a rebellious pet, and she dismissed her qualms outright. She would not spend the rest of her years pining for the man. She would spend the rest of her years as his wife. And she needed Madam Jacqueline's assistance to accomplish her goal.

Henrietta stifled a gasp as the wall gave way—well, a paneled door in the wall—and a figure emerged from the secret nook.

A rather small figure.

Draped in flowing silks of Oriental design and sporting a turquoise turban to match, the woman, not more than three score and five years, was an eclectic mix of cultures, and not very pretty at that.

Oh, it was not the years marking her features that made Henrietta think so, but the hard slant of her jaw, the wide breadth of her nose. Such attributes made Henrietta wonder if she had ever been pretty, even in youth. Though there was something unique about her eyes, a most unnatural shade of mist green. A very captivating pair to be sure. But still, *she* was England's most renowned courtesan?

Henrietta crinkled her brow. "Madam Jacqueline?"

The small woman settled on a divan opposite Henrietta, her jewels winking in the candlelight. "As you see."

Throat a bit parched, Henrietta partook of the sherry. "Ah, thank you for agreeing to see me."

"I must admit, I was surprised to receive your letter."

Not nearly as surprised as Henrietta was to meet the notorious courtesan. According to the gossip papers, Madam Jacqueline had so enamored a Russian prince, he'd all but made her his royal bride, to the outrage and near revolt of St. Petersburg. She had charmed a French duke so terribly, he'd put a pistol to his head when she'd broken off the affair. And then there was the tale of the ruined Italian noble, so bewitched by Madam Jacqueline that he'd surrendered his entire fortune to her. Or so the stories had claimed. And Henrietta was most curious to know if these stories had been fabricated, too.

"It is all true, Miss Ashby."

Henrietta yelped and placed her fingers over her mouth. Heavens, had she sputtered her thoughts *aloud*?

No. Wait. She had done no such thing. Then how . . . ?

"You are a witch?" said Henrietta, disquieted.

The woman laughed, a deep and husky sound, oddly soothing to the ear. "Some might think so, but I assure you, I do not dabble in the black arts."

"But you read minds."

"Nonsense, child. I read faces. And you are thinking, *How can this small, plain, and extravagant woman be the famous Madam Jacqueline?*"

Henrietta did not confirm the woman's astute observation, for she felt that rather rude. Instead she said, "I need your help, Madam Jacqueline."

"Yes, you mentioned that in your letter. Do go on."

Henrietta blushed.

Oh, out with it, silly. It's why you're here!

But every word was strangled as Henrietta tried to make her desire clear. Just how did one go about asking for such intimate help?

"Well, you see, I need to learn how to . . ."

"Seduce a man?" said Madam Jacqueline.

"Yes!"

Henrietta sighed. With Madam Jacqueline's talent for observation, Henrietta might not have to voice her bashful thoughts too often. A boon she was most happy about.

The woman cocked her head, a brilliant emerald at her bust flashing in the firelight. "Miss Ashby, do you know what I am?"

Henrietta nodded sagely, thinking, *It's why I've come to see you!*

"And what am I?" said the woman.

"Well, you're . . . a . . ."

Henrietta pondered her answer. Was "courtesan" the proper word? Or would the woman be offended by the term? Henrietta couldn't imagine so, but still, she really needed Madam Jacqueline's help, and she didn't want to say anything that might upset—

"I am a philosopher, Miss Ashby."

Henrietta blinked. "Pardon?"

"A philosopher," she said again. "Men of great wealth and power visit me to ask my advice. I inspire men, Miss Ashby, where their wives have failed."

"Oh," said Henrietta. She hadn't considered Madam Jacqueline in *that* kind of light.

"And who do you wish to inspire, Miss Ashby?"

Henrietta's heart throbbed at the thought of him. "Sebastian."

"And how do you intend to inspire Sebastian?"

"Well, I'm not really sure," she admitted dolefully.

"Hmm." The older woman cast her a critical eye. "Do you intend to bat your pretty lashes at him until they fall off?"

Affronted, Henrietta said, "No." Then belatedly realized she *had* been doing that a lot of late.

Madam Jacqueline's eerie ability to read faces quickly picked up on the fib. "You will never win his heart like that, Miss Ashby."

All the years of frustration and anguish bubbled to the tip of her tongue, and Henrietta let out a desperate plea, "Then *how* will I win his heart?"

"You must be his friend and his lover."

Drat! She didn't understand the first thing about being a good lover. She couldn't even get Sebastian to kiss her! And friendship? After eight years the man still treated her like a child. How would they ever become friends?

Crestfallen, Henrietta slumped her shoulders forward, whispering, "I don't know how to be either."

"There are ways to learn."

Henrietta's eyes brightened. "Does this mean you'll help me?"

The woman perused her for a thoughtful moment. "I will."

Her heart filled with hope. "Oh, thank you, Madam Jacqueline!"

Madam Jacqueline reached for a leather-bound book on the small round table next to the divan. She opened the tome to a random page and set it before

Henrietta. "To begin, tell me about the couple in the picture."

Henrietta leaned forward for a better view, balked, then slammed the book closed.

Good Lord, did lovers actually do *that*?

Madam Jacqueline quirked a painted brow. "You will start by going through the entire book, Miss Ashby. You will stare at every page, and stare and stare again, until you can look at the pictures without blushing . . . until you want to engage in those very acts with Sebastian."

Henrietta's heart thumped terribly loud. She didn't know if she could do such a thing!

But one look at Madam Jacqueline's wise and charismatic gaze, and she understood she didn't have a choice. If she wanted to seduce Sebastian, she had to learn to be both his friend *and* his lover.

"Yes, Madam Jacqueline, I'll do as you say. And I'll pay you for your teaching."

If I survive the lessons. Heavens, what a mortification this was going to be!

"I have no need of your money, Miss Ashby."

Henrietta's brow furrowed. "Then why are you doing this?"

The woman smiled, a very charming gesture. "I wish to pass along my wisdom. I feel it a terrible thing to waste."

Chapter 4

The manor house, nestled amid snowy mounds, stood prominent against the winter land. Smoked curled from each of the six chimneys, and in the fading afternoon light, the candle flames, sparkling from each of the glazed windows, gave the home a warm and inviting glow.

Sebastian reflected upon the quaint country dwelling—and the quirky family that hibernated within. Five months ago he had quit England for the mainland. It'd been an agreeable trip, filled with gluttony and sinful pleasures. But all good things must come to an end. Five months ago he had severed all communication with the Ashbys, hoping the youngest and most willful of the brood, Miss Henrietta Ashby, would set her cap for a more deserving gentleman. Now he'd returned to see how his plan had fared.

The sleigh slid to a stop, the sleigh bells chiming, announcing Sebastian's arrival. He was wrapped in bearskin to keep warm and tossed aside the fur, stepping out of the cutter.

The butler greeted him at the door, helped to divest him of his greatcoat, collected his hat and gloves.

Sebastian looked around the country house. Everything seemed the same, he thought. The inlay side table to his left. The ornate mirror to his right. All the same. And yet something was out of place . . .

Sebastian didn't have a chance to reflect upon the oddity, though, for he soon heard the proverbial voice, a baritone timbre, and he turned to find the baron shuffling toward him, arms outstretched.

"Ravenswood, my good man, how delightful to see you again!"

Sebastian offered his hand in greeting. "Thank you for the invite, Lord Ashby."

"Nonsense, my boy, you are family. Family, I say. The Yule festivities would not be the same without you."

Sebastian nodded in appreciation. "How are you, my lord?"

"Oh, the same, Ravenswood. The same. A few pounds heavier, a few white hairs shorter."

The viscount quirked a smile. For all the baron's foolery, he was a charming old fellow. "I'm glad to hear it, my lord."

"We've missed you these last five months, we have." The baron gestured to the study door. "Come, Ravenswood. Join me for a drink."

Sebastian cocked his head in acquiescence.

The baron beamed and led the way. As Sebastian trailed the rotund man, he once more reflected upon the nameless oddity that had plagued his senses. The chairs, the pictures, all seemed to be in the right spot. So what was it then? What was amiss?

"The hounds."

The baron looked over his shoulder. "I beg your pardon, Ravenswood?"

"Where are the hounds, my lord?"

"In the kennel, I'm afraid." He sighed. "Lady Ashby ordered the poor boys out of the house after one . . . er, decorated her favorite rug. The boys are not allowed back inside for the rest of the day. Punishment, you know."

Ah, so that's what was wrong. No hounds. Sebastian knew there was something missing underfoot . . . No, wait. That wasn't it, either.

Sebastian inspected the house as he moved through it, searching for . . . a little hoyden.

That's it! That's what was missing. Henrietta.

Where was Henrietta?

Sebastian furrowed his brow. She was always the first to greet him. For the past eight years, without fail, she had bounded up to him in salutation before he'd set both feet inside the house. It was the only time she was ever *on* time for anything.

Sebastian perused the empty foyer once more. "I say, Baron, is the *whole* family here?"

"Quite. Quite." The baron ushered him inside the

study. "You are the last of the guests to arrive. So good of you to join us, Ravenswood."

Sheltered inside the study, Sebastian settled in a comfortable armchair and inquired, "Is the family well, Lord Ashby?"

"In capital health, my dear boy."

Odd. If Henrietta wasn't ill and tucked away in bed, then where was she?

The baron made his way over to the bookcase and collected a decanter, filling two glasses with a splash of brandy.

"So tell me, Ravenswood, how was the mainland? Drab compared to our mighty England, I daresay."

It was nothing of the sort, but the viscount wasn't about to admit that. He accepted the drink with a nod of thanks. "Quite right, my lord."

Resting his heavy frame in an opposite chair, the baron plunked his feet upon the ottoman with a sigh.

Sebastian stared at the door, waiting for it to open, anticipating Henrietta to come fluttering in, all out of breath and professing apologies for being tardy in her welcome.

But she did nothing of the kind.

Perhaps the girl was wed and thought nothing of him anymore? Now *that* was an agreeable thought.

Taking a sip of brandy to warm his belly, Sebastian wondered, "And how fares the youngest Miss Ashby?"

"Henry? Capital. Capital. The darling boy is such a pleasure."

Sebastian grimaced at the "darling boy" bit. The baron, so determined to have a son, brooked no argument that Henrietta was, in truth, a lady and thus needed to be reared accordingly. A deuced nuisance it was, too, for had Henrietta been raised as a proper young miss, she'd be married by now, instead of hounding him.

"I've been gone so long, my lord," said Sebastian. "Tell me, has there been any cause for celebration here at the house?"

Like a wedding, perhaps?

"Oh yes!" the baron cried. "A happy event indeed."

Splendid! The girl was married. No more adoring looks or scandalous quips to combat. Sebastian could rest easy now, be free of the smitten chit.

"I have leather-tip cue sticks!" The baron clapped his hands together. "Isn't it grand? We must play a game of billiards, Ravenswood."

Not exactly the good news Sebastian had been hoping to hear.

With a sigh, the viscount tried another tactic. "My lord, about Miss Ashby?"

"Yes, Ravenswood."

"Is the girl fond of anyone?"

"To be sure, Ravenswood. To be sure. The dear boy's fond of many folks. He's got a most generous heart, I daresay."

Sebastian took another swig of brandy, and since

subtle conversation was not the baron's forte, asked outright, "My lord, is the girl engaged yet?"

"Rot!" cried the baron. "Henry's got more sense than to get himself leg-shackled. Nasty business, I say. Drives a poor chap into hiding."

Sebastian glanced around the cramped reading nook. A dusty nook, filled with heavy tomes. It was the only part of the house reserved for the baron's exclusive use.

The viscount sighed in disappointment. "Yes, nasty business."

The baron gave a curt nod. "One needs a strong disposition to be riveted. An authoritative voice, a firm hand. Now I have such a disposition and can weather the storm of matrimony, but dear Henry is a most delicate boy, and I feel better suited to a quiet life at home."

"Quite right, my lord." Sebastian downed the rest of the brandy. "But is the girl interested in a gentleman?"

"Interested? My Henry?" The baron looked at the ceiling. "Why, I don't think so."

"Are you sure, my lord?"

"Oh yes, quite sure. Why, I'd hear all about it from Lady Ashby if Henry had a beau. Now back to my cue sticks . . ."

The viscount turned his thoughts to more pressing matters. The girl was still unattached, was she? He had underestimated her stubbornness. Well, then he'd just have to go back to the mainland.

Traipse through the Parisian underworld and consort with the Italian demimonde. It was an infernal bother, visiting all those lovely Spanish wenches, but he was a gentleman, and as such he had a duty to disabuse Miss Ashby of her girlhood fancy. He had no choice, it seemed, but to return abroad to cavort with more foreign beauties—after Christmas, of course. He wasn't a total degenerate. He did adhere to some religious observance.

"Please excuse me, my lord." Sebastian stood up. "I would like to rest before dinner."

"Capital idea, Ravenswood! The butler will show you to your room."

Sebastian moved to the door. "I will see you at dinner, my lord.

"Yes, of course, my good man. At dinner."

And with that, the baron promptly closed his eyes and went to sleep.

Sebastian quietly vacated the study and made his way through the familiar passages. He didn't need the butler to show him to his room. He had occupied the same bedchamber for eight years whenever he called upon the family. He knew his way around the house very well.

Sebastian mounted the steps, making his way to his room. He was going to rest for a bit, then dress for dinner.

But he was still baffled. If Henrietta wasn't even engaged, then why hadn't she come down to say hello?

* * *

"You're leaving after the holidays?"

Sebastian glanced at his flabbergasted brother. "That's right, Peter."

"But you just returned home, Seb. Why the rush to run off again?"

Because Sebastian needed to part from a certain incorrigible hoyden . . . who happened to be late for dinner—as usual. Not that the family seemed to mind. Accustomed to the girl's tardiness, the brood had simply immersed themselves in the freshly cooked fare, an empty chair left for Henrietta at the far end of the rosewood dining table.

Sebastian sliced open the broiled fish. "I have a rather pressing matter of business to attend to on the mainland."

Peter snorted. "You mean you have a pressing itch in your—"

"Peter," Sebastian drawled. "Mind your manners at the dinner table."

Peter shook his head. "I don't understand you, Seb."

"Oh?" He quirked a brow. "And what don't you understand?"

"Why you have to go abroad to attend to 'business,'" Peter whispered. "What the deuce is the matter with English wenches?"

Sebastian chuckled. "Nothing a'tall, brother. I just need to go abroad. Trust me."

The other man sighed. "Well, we're here till

Twelfth Night, so let's make the best of what little time we have together . . . Did you hear the baron has leather-tip cue sticks? We should play a game of billiards, Seb."

"I suspect we will, Peter."

Sebastian scanned the amassed company. The "we" included the baron and baroness, and *all* the Ashby sisters and their respective spouses. Sebastian didn't really get along with the other gentlemen, though; too prudish for his taste. He only got along with his brother, really. And the baron, of course. Sebastian just wasn't the sort of man to make friends easily or engage in platonic pleasantries. He was more of a flirt. A seducer. And after the death of his parents from consumption almost ten years ago, he'd immersed himself in more unsavory pursuits.

"By and by," said Peter, "why are you here? I'm bound to the family till death, but you've no familial obligation. Unless, of course, you want the last of the sisters for yourse—"

"Finish that thought and I'll stab this fork into your hand."

Peter chuckled, well aware of his brother's plight with Henrietta. "And spatter blood all over Lady Ashby's fine linen tablecloth? Heaven forbid."

"Then I suggest we let the matter rest."

"Sound advice, but I feel I must warn you, Seb, you might have to settle down one day, however foul the idea."

"Rubbish."

Sebastian was never going to tie the marital noose around his neck. What the devil for?

"The estate needs an heir," said Peter.

"Yours will do just fine."

An airy sigh from Peter. "While nothing would please Penelope and me more, you know very well it might never come to pass."

It was a rotten truth, and Sebastian knew it. The three other Ashby sisters were already mothers—their seven brats, thank the heavens, tucked away in the nursery—but Penelope had yet to have a babe, much to the sorrow of both her and her husband.

"The duty might fall upon you yet, Seb."

Bloody hell. Still, Sebastian wouldn't dwell too much on the ghastly matter. Penelope was not yet thirty, while Sebastian was already thirty-six and too jaded to even contemplate marriage. There was still plenty of time for the young woman to produce an heir. He needn't fret about the dreadful responsibility. Not yet anyway.

From across the table, Penelope offered him a warm smile. "Tell us, Ravenswood, has the fashion in Paris changed much since the spring?"

"Most assuredly," he said with a flirtatious wink. "But I must admit, I paid little attention to the vogue."

"Oh lud!" from the other sister, Roselyn. "Why couldn't you have been more of a dandy, Ravenswood, and heeded the trends?"

Sebastian bowed his head. "It was dreadful of me, I know."

Next Cordelia chimed, "Did you happen to notice the more fashionable colors, Ravenswood?"

"Pink, I believe."

"Pink?" Tertia, the last of the sisters, wrinkled her brow. "Surely not, Ravenswood. Pink was last season's color. You must be mistaken."

But before Sebastian could offer another opinion, Henrietta appeared.

Sebastian bristled.

The chit paused in the doorway, her head held high, her shoulders set back. A charming smile touched her lips; a playfulness winked in her eyes. After a brief delay, she entered the room with uncanny confidence, her rich, auburn locks in a whimsical twist, tendrils bouncing by her ears.

What had happened to the girl?

A few cordial greetings drifted from the table, but otherwise the gathered party made no particular gesture or remark to reflect upon Henrietta's baffling transformation. Was the family so distracted by hunger? How could they just sit there in perfect harmony and not gape at the little hoyden skirting across the room?

Skirting? No, she wasn't skirting. She was . . . swaying. Artfully so. The soft and rhythmic rustle of her petticoats tickled his ears as she swished this way and that. Good God, the girl had hips!

"Henry, my boy," the baron shouted in jovial salutation. "How good of you to join us."

Henrietta pressed her lips to her father's brow—her round rump arched ever so slightly. "Good evening, Papa."

A peculiar spasm gripped Sebastian's heart. What the devil was the matter with the girl's voice? So deep, husky even, the inflection steady. Did she have a cold?

Sebastian watched, transfixed, as an attending footman helped Henrietta into her seat. With a flick of the wrist, she unfurled her white linen napkin and set it across her lap. A meal was placed before her, and she set to work on gracefully devouring the fare—without so much as glancing his way.

"Well, Ravenswood?"

Sebastian snapped his gaze back to Tertia. What were they talking about again? Paris? Clothes? Colors? That's it! "Blue, I believe."

Peter choked.

Tertia lifted a delicate brow. "I should purchase a blue mare, Ravenswood?"

Sebastian frowned. "We're not talking about the Parisian vogue?"

"No, Ravenswood," said Tertia. "Ponies. For my Edward's fifth birthday. We were talking about the best breeds."

"My apologies, sister."

Sebastian was back to glaring at Henrietta. Good

God, the girl was huge! Two dress sizes bigger, he was sure. What's more, the astute cut of her rust brown frock made sure to highlight those striking curves. And damned if she hadn't sprouted a figure worthy of notice.

"What do you think, Ravenswood?"

Blast it! Not again. What was it this time? Birthdays? No, breeds! "I believe a Shetland is the best choice."

Tertia coughed. "I most certainly will *not* serve horseflesh at my Eddie's birthday dinner!"

Sebastian stifled an oath.

"Devil take it, Seb," his brother leaned in to whisper, "whatever is the matter with your ears?"

His ears might be faulty, but there was nothing the matter with his eyes. "Look at her, Peter."

"Who, Seb?"

"Henrietta, you fool!"

Peter did as he was told. "What about her?"

"Are you daft? Don't you notice something different about the girl?"

Peter crinkled his brow. "No, not really. Then again, you've been gone five months, Seb. I'm sure we all seem a bit different to you."

"*You* are tryingly the same, brother." Sebastian glanced at Henrietta, then back at Peter. "Can't you see the change in her?"

Once more, Peter peeked down the rosewood dining table. And once more he affirmed, "There's nothing the matter with her, Seb."

Sebastian sensed his temples throbbing. "She's twice her normal size!" he hissed.

Peter choked again. "Good heavens, Seb, are you mad? She's nothing of the sort."

"Look closely."

"I *have*. She's hardly half a stone plumper, and more'n likely due to the heavy winter garb she's wearing."

"Rubbish, the girl is . . ." So lushly curvaceous, Sebastian's fingers twitched in a most wicked way. "What about the way she eats?"

"What the deuce is the matter with the way she eats?"

Well, for one, she was savoring her meal far too greatly. The way she slowly licked her lips after each bite made Sebastian's breath hitch.

"Seb, are you feeling all right?"

Sebastian looked at his brother, confused for the first time in a long time. There was something dreadfully wrong with Henrietta. Why was he the only one who noticed?

Chapter 5

A gentle snowfall showered the earth. Henrietta stared into the distant night, dragging in deep, cold breaths to steady her throbbing heart. She had done it! For five months she had rehearsed the art of flirting. For five months she had practiced every lithe movement in the mirror, read aloud to train her voice, and tonight the time had come to put all her hard effort to work.

Oh, it had been a wretched wait for Ravenswood to appear! She had paced her room, her belly in a whirl, her rug threadbare from abuse. And then the sleigh bells had chimed, heralding his arrival—and she'd paced some more.

Never show too much affection.

It was one of Madam Jacqueline's cardinal rules. And so Henrietta had stewed in her bedchamber, awaiting the dinner bell. Even then she'd delayed her entrance to the dining room for maximum affect. And it had worked. Splendidly, in fact. She'd sensed Sebastian's dark gaze on her the entire time.

Henrietta was so giddy she could giggle. It was over, the first test. Madam Jacqueline had taught her well. Henrietta had the strength, the skill to go through with the rest of the seduction. And she intended to make Ravenswood hers forever.

"Good evening, Miss Ashby."

Oh, that rusty male voice! How she had missed it. Heart thumping loudly, Henrietta gathered her features and turned to find the most devilishly handsome man in creation sauntering toward her.

She couldn't help but sigh. Inwardly, of course. Madam Jacqueline had instructed her on the art of looking composed even when one didn't feel very collected.

Henrietta smiled and curtsied. "Good evening, my lord."

Sebastian paused dead in his tracks at the appellation "my lord." Another one of Madam Jacqueline's basic rules: take away the familiar until the man longed for it back. She would not call him Sebastian again until he implored her to.

The moment of shock over, the viscount resumed his steady march. Snow crunched softly beneath his booted heels. He came to a stop just short of her arm's reach, a light dusting of snowflakes clinging to his hair, his coat. The tiny white puffs even settled upon his thick and sooty lashes, and Henrietta found herself quite mesmerized by the charming sight.

"How are you this evening, Miss Ashby?"

Her smile broadened just a bit. Madam Jacqueline

had been right. A rake like Ravenswood would pick up on her subtle sexual signals. She hadn't believed it true. The man had never noticed her obvious attempts at seduction. How would he ever heed the obscure ones? she had thought.

But a patient Madam Jacqueline had explained to her the power of a subtle courtship. The thrill a man obtained from picking up "the scent" and then partaking in "the hunt," as she'd put it. Henrietta need not change her appearance or manner in any wild way, the courtesan had said. Just a tweak here and there. A few extra pounds to give her figure the right curves. A more throaty voice to invite salacious daydreams. And a confident stride to attract attention. Enough alteration to draw Sebastian's notice without disturbing the equanimity in the household. After all, she didn't want her parents, her sisters to see what she was doing. Only Ravenswood.

"I am well, my lord. Just enjoying the winter air. It's so crisp and refreshing, wouldn't you say?"

"Yes, indeed," he murmured.

He was staring at her. Hard. Trying to decipher the puzzle she had become with those avid blue eyes of his. But he would never learn the true lengths to which she had gone to capture his heart. He'd wring her neck for sure if he ever found out.

"How was your voyage abroad, my lord?"

"Quite pleasant, Miss Ashby." He perused her briefly, his hot gaze ever so warming. "In fact, I intend to return to the mainland after Twelfth Night."

Her heart shuddered. "Really, my lord? We shall mourn the loss of your company."

Drat! He was running off again, and she wasn't daft enough to believe his desertion had nothing to do with her. Well, she was just going to have to seduce the mulish man by Twelfth Night then.

"And you, Miss Ashby? How have you fared these last five months?"

"Very well, I daresay."

According to Madam Jacqueline, it was not so much what one said but how one said it that mattered. And Henrietta made sure to keep her voice steady and low, even under the viscount's probing glare.

"Then you are not ill, Miss Ashby?"

"I am in perfect health, my lord. Why do you ask? Do I look ill?"

He paused. "You look . . . different."

"Oh?" She quirked a brow. "In what way?"

"I can't quite put my finger on it, Miss Ashby."

I'm sure you can't, she thought impishly. And she intended to keep him perplexed for a while more. If she flirted too firmly, he would guess at her intentions and dash off before Twelfth Night. She didn't want to spend another five months stewing at home while he gallivanted about the mainland. Certainly not.

She dipped her eyes to his booted toes. In a coy voice, she said, "You know me so well, my lord."

"Then something *is* amiss?"

"Alas, I'm afraid so." Eyes lifting to meet his once more, she whispered, "I have a secret."

"And will you share it with me, Miss Ashby?"

"Only if you promise to never breathe a word of it."

He nodded slowly. "I promise on my honor as a gentleman."

Henrietta peeked from side to side, then said, "I'm having an affair."

Sebastian stopped breathing. She could tell by the scarcity of icy breath escaping his lips.

But soon the icy clouds started forth once more—through his nose. "I don't think I heard you right, Miss Ashby."

"It's dreadful, I know." She sighed, a gloved hand to her heart. "I'm heartily ashamed of myself."

His voice was taut, stiffly so. "And with whom are you having an affair?"

"Why, with Mrs. Quigly's pastries, of course."

He blinked. "What?"

"Our new cook, Mrs. Quigly, is a wonder in the kitchen." Henrietta twirled her eyes. "Her pastries are divine. I must admit, I've developed an unhealthy fondness for sugared cakes."

Sebastian didn't say anything for a moment. Instead he rubbed his lush lips together, deep in thought.

Henrietta, enraptured by the subtle display of movement, had to whisk her gaze back up to meet the viscount's. Though her heart was thudding in her breast like a drum, she fixed a playful smile to her lips to conceal her fluster.

"You are teasing me, Miss Ashby."

The rugged drawl of his voice did wonderful things to Henrietta. Delicious shivers rolled over her in rhythmic waves. How she longed to hear that deep and sultry voice by her ear! To feel the warm breath of his words caress her skin.

Henrietta took in a sharp breath to steady her wayward thoughts. "Of course I'm teasing you, my lord. What is a little harmless banter between friends?"

And since she'd never teased him a day in eight years, she could understand the man's bewilderment.

Sebastian lifted a sooty brow. "Friends, are we? Pray tell me, Miss Ashby, what will we do as friends?"

"Why, we will do as every other couple engaged in friendship."

"Unfortunately, I do not have many friends, Miss Ashby, so I will need your guidance in this matter."

She counted off her gloved fingers. "Well, we shall share each other's company and tease one another. Oh, and we shall confide in each other our deepest and darkest secrets."

"Like a penchant for pastries?"

She quirked a grin. "Precisely, my lord."

"I see." His smoldering gaze touched her like a hot iron poker. "Well, since we are friends, Miss

Ashby, do you have any other deep and dark secrets you'd like to impart?"

The scoundrel was trying to unsettle her with that piercing stare of his; muddle her thoughts, make her slip up and say something to betray her *real* secret. Well, she had an ideal countermeasure for just such a wily move.

Taking Madam Jacqueline's advice to heart, Henrietta thought about one of the many wicked images in the courtesan's naughty book of pictures that she had come to memorize, even desire. An image of a naked couple, their limbs intertwined, their lips in very intimate places. And then she looked at Sebastian's lips. Let her eyes rest on the soft, full pair as she delved deep into her fantasy.

After a few decadent moments, she lifted her gaze to meet his penetrating stare, and smiled. "No more confessions tonight, Lord Ravenswood." She let the words roll off her tongue, then curtsied. "Pleasant dreams."

Skirting around him, Henrietta all but skipped off the terrace. If she hadn't bowled him over before, she'd bowled him over now. Madam Jacqueline had been right. Again. Think a naughty thought and it'd show in your eyes. Something a true rakehell would never miss.

Sebastian stood on the terrace, staring at the vast winter wonderland. As the minutes ticked by, he looked more and more like a man of snow. He should really get himself inside where it was warm. But he did nothing of the sort. In truth, he didn't feel the cold. He didn't feel much of anything—but for a smoldering spark burning deep in his belly.

Had the little hoyden just leveled a most sinfully wicked stare his way? Sebastian was sure the answer was an unequivocal no. All common sense indicated Henrietta a whimsical chit and nothing more. Which meant *he* was totally daft.

Bah! He was just tired was all. The journey to the Ashby country home had taken a few grueling hours. He was imagining things. Fatigue was the culprit for his wayward thoughts.

A sinfully wicked stare, indeed. He snorted. The chit didn't know the first thing about being wicked. She was far too innocent.

Sebastian took in a deep and measured breath. One thing was for certain, though. There was something very different about Henrietta. He sensed the change in her. Why, the girl had actually called him by his title! He'd all but tripped upon hearing the appellation. In *eight* years she'd never referred to him as anyone but Sebastian. And for some bizarre reason, it was strange to hear her call him "my lord."

And what was this deuced nonsense about friendship? Did the girl still want to marry him or not?

Something was definitely amiss. There was one conundrum after another. Like what the devil did Henrietta mean by teasing him like that? An affair with pastries. Had all that sugar gone to the girl's head? The sweet tooth did explain one anomaly, though. That plump and curvy figure. Hips! The girl actually had hips! Lush and oh-so-round . . .

"Bloody hell," he growled and quickly vacated the terrace. The cold was seeping into his brain, making him imagine all sorts of absurdities. Still, he doubted a warm fire would put his senses to right. He had a quandary on his hands.

Pleasant dreams? Not tonight. Not for a great many nights. Not until he debunked the mystery of the curious Miss Ashby.

Chapter 6

"**G**ood heavens, she married a duke!"

"Who married a duke?"

Startled, Henrietta folded the letter in her hands. She looked up to find Sebastian poised in the door frame, shoulder slumped against the ornate wood paneling. Thick arms folded over his strapping chest, legs crossed at the ankles, he perused her, a drowsy glint in his otherwise clear blue eyes.

Oh, had the handsome viscount not slumbered very soundly? Had a certain temptress, mayhap, haunted his dreams?

"Good morning, my lord." Biting back her grin, Henrietta stood and reached for the still steaming teapot. "Tea?"

Sebastian sauntered into the breakfast room. My, he looked splendid. All decked out in regal day wear. Tight and clinging day wear. The muscled form beneath the layers of clothing was hard to miss. Ever since her lessons with Madam Jacqueline, Henrietta had come to admire the masculine figure. And Sebastian's was a specimen worthy of more intimate study.

"Thank you, Miss Ashby," he said, and took a chair opposite her. Black curls a bit disheveled, voice a smoky drawl, he was too sinfully handsome for words.

Henrietta set the teacup on the table in front of him and returned to her seat. Needing a distraction, she unfurled the letter once more, and said, "I've just received a missive from my dearest chum, Mirabelle."

"Is she the one from the masquerade ball?"

"The very one."

He whistled. "She married a duke, did she?"

"The Duke of Wembury! Oh, but I didn't get to go to the wedding. Drat!"

At least she didn't have to keep her friendship with Mirabelle a secret anymore. That was one good thing. Mama would be positively agog to learn that her daughter was now friends with a duchess!

Sebastian slowly sipped his tea, eyes intent upon her. "Why didn't you go to the wedding?"

Henrietta shivered under his smoldering gaze and looked back at the note. "It was a simple ceremony, Mirabelle writes. Only family attended. But I've been invited to the castle for a visit."

"Will you go?"

"Of course I will."

But there was still Ravenswood to seduce, she

thought. The viscount was staying at the house until Twelfth Night. If she went to visit the duchess, she was going to lose a few days with the viscount . . .

"I shall postpone the trip until the spring," she said. "I shall write to the duchess today to inform her."

"Why wait so long?"

Keeping her voice light and airy, she said, "Oh, I have a few other matters to attend to here at the house."

Sebastian shrugged. "I didn't take Wembury for the leg-shackling sort."

Henrietta's eyes widened. "You know the duke?"

"Of him. He was dubbed the 'Duke of Rogues' long ago. At one time, he even belonged to my club. Before I was a member, though."

"What club?"

A dark shadow passed over Sebastian's eyes. "A gentlemen's club," was all he said on the matter. He took another sip of tea before he resumed. "About two and a half years ago, though, after the death of his brother, Wembury disappeared from the world. And now he's back? And riveted at that? Shocking."

"Well, it seems the duke's reformed his ways."

"A scoundrel can never reform his ways, Miss Ashby."

She quirked a brow. "Is that so?"

"Oh yes." He reached for a pastry on the table. "It's impossible to rid oneself of wicked intentions. A thief will always be a thief. His fingers will always itch and burn to pinch one thing or another. And a man so scandalous as to be dubbed the 'Duke of Rogues' will always be a rogue, I'm afraid."

Henrietta's fingers itched and burned to do a little pinching of her own. Only she wanted to pinch that willful lip of his until it bruised.

Was he going to use that tired old line on her: once a rake, always a rake? Rot! If *she* could transform from whimsical to wanton, then surely one could go from rake to respectable.

But before she could argue her point, Sebastian parted his lips to partake of the pastry, and all irascible thoughts deserted her.

A warm heat invaded her belly, spread through her every limb. At the decadent sight, Henrietta scratched out the image of the pastry from her mind and put herself in its place. And at the thought of Sebastian doing to her what he was doing to that pastry, her whole body started to quiver.

"Miss Ashby, are you all right?" He reached for a napkin to wipe his fingers, staring at her curiously the whole time.

Henrietta had to fight really hard to find her voice and keep it from squeaking. "I'm quite well, my lord. I assure you." She took a moment to gather her wits, then said, "You don't think a man can reform? Why is that?"

He shrugged. "Some of us are born good, Miss Ashby. And some of us are not. It's the natural way of the world."

She screwed up her face. Where the devil did he get that idea from? But before she could ask, he said:

"You're up early this morning."

Her curiosity stifled, she fibbed, "I always rise early."

He wrinkled his brow. "Do you? I remember you rising closer to noon."

So true. And it was a bloody wretched business getting up with the cocks. But she'd no time to diddle away in bed while Ravenswood was in the house. She had until Twelfth Night to achieve her goal, and she was going to put every waking minute to good use.

"There's just so much to do today, my lord."

"Such as?"

Such as seducing you, she thought impishly.

"Well, there's the skating party to organize," she said. "My sisters and I have decided to take the children down to the pond for an afternoon of sport. I do hope you brought along your skates, my lord."

"I'm afraid not, Miss Ashby."

She waved a dismissive hand. "No matter. You can borrow Papa's skates. He doesn't use them anymore."

"Thank you for the offer, but I must decline."

"Rubbish! Why else would you come all this way to visit if not to enjoy the merry company?"

He gave her a dubious look at that. Was she being too forward? Well, she had to get the dratted man to the frozen pond somehow. She was going to employ a new tactic today: scent.

Scent was *the* strongest aphrodisiac, according to Madam Jacqueline. And Henrietta wholly agreed. Why, just standing next to Sebastian and breathing in the rich waft of rosemary and lemon had always made her woozy.

Anyway, she'd coaxed from her brother-in-law the name of Sebastian's favorite perfume. And it was time to put that knowledge to good use.

"Come, Ravenswood, we are friends," she persuaded him gently. "And friends often skate together."

"Do they now?"

"Most assuredly."

He stared at her for a long while, then said, "With the children?"

"And my sisters and their husbands. Even your brother Peter is joining in the revelry. So you see, you simply must attend."

After another lengthy pause, he finally sighed. "I've not skated in years."

"Fret not, my lord, I'll be there to catch you if you fall."

Sebastian landed on his arse—again.

He'd had enough. Taking his lumbering self over to one of the fallen logs, he sat on the makeshift bench and unfastened the leather straps from his boots, discarded the skates.

Feeling much steadier now that he had his own two feet back, Sebastian stretched his hands toward the fire sparking away in a large tin bucket.

As he rubbed his frozen palms together, he let his eyes wander over the icy pond and the crowd of skaters, and settle upon a little hoyden dragging two wobbling sprites along beside her.

With one hand latched on to an unsteady niece and another clamped on to a rambunctious nephew, Henrietta steered the two novice ice dancers, encouraging them softly, her laughter spirited, but kind, when one little rump hit the sheet of ice. And yet she herself looked so graceful among the chaos. In her fur-trimmed cape and matching gloves, she appeared a winter faerie, dancing over the frozen pond.

"What's this?" Peter shouted from the ice. "Have you given up already, brother?"

Snapped from his reverie, Sebastian stared once more at the snapping flames.

Since Peter was already scaling the embankment, there was no reason for Sebastian to raise his voice. "I'm afraid so, Peter. I've lost my touch on the ice."

Peter sat down beside him with a snort. "The only time you've ever 'touched' the ice is with your arse."

"Yes, thank you for the reminder."

Peter knocked his brother's hands out of the way, so he could hog the fire. "What are you doing out here anyway, Seb?"

"Devil if I know."

"You've not skated in years."

"Yes, I know, Peter. I was tricked into the excursion—I think."

"Tricked? By whom?"

"A redheaded minx."

"Henrietta? Be serious, Seb. She's a darling chit and all, but she's not one for skullduggery."

Sebastian was beginning to wonder about that. "Well, if she didn't trick me, then what the deuce am I doing out here?"

Lips parted, Peter looked like he was about to impart some witty words of wisdom, then paused. "You know, I've no idea, Seb. But then again, you are a bit of a mystery."

"How's that?"

"Well, you're here for one. At the estate, I mean. A scoundrel like yourself cloistered amid the very essence of domesticity. It defies reason."

"Can't a scoundrel visit with family?"

"Yes, of course, but *why* would you come to call at this time of year? When every Ashby is gathered in rambunctious familial rapport. It's beyond me."

"Well, then let me solve this mystery for you, brother. I've come to see Henrietta."

Peter brought his frigid fingers to his lips and blew. "Oh?"

"I'd hoped to find the girl wed, even engaged. But regrettably she's still unattached.

"A vexing predicament."

Was that sarcasm Sebastian detected? "It most certainly is vexing. I've spent the last five months in exile, hoping the chit would find herself a mate. All to no avail, I might add. The baron assures me the girl isn't even interested in another bloke."

"So *that's* why you disappeared to the mainland? And that's why you're going back again, isn't it?" Peter chuckled. "My sympathies, Seb. You've a most dire predicament on your hands. What with a beautiful woman chasing you about, and all."

He growled, "You know damn well nothing can come of it."

"Oh yes, perish the thought that a man your age should retire his wicked ways and settle down with a lovely chit."

Sebastian glared at his brother. "What the devil do you mean, 'a man my age'? I've yet to sprout a white hair."

"Listen, Seb, it's worth thinking about—"

"No! It's not."

Peter sighed. "And why the devil not?"

Because Sebastian wasn't about to give up his foul habits. A deviant did not "retire" his wicked ways. Such behavior was an incorrigible way of life, an addiction in the blood. And he happened to *like* his wicked ways, blast it! A fussy wife was sure to dampen his lusty disposition, spoil his sinful pursuits. And he certainly wasn't going to marry an adorable minx like Henrietta, who didn't even spark a bit of arousal in him. "I won't marry the girl."

"Oh, Seb."

Peter looked across the pond, and Sebastian unwittingly followed his brother's gaze.

The viscount caught sight of Henrietta with the children, waving to him. Something snagged on his heart. He quickly dismissed the sentiment.

"Leave it alone, Peter. I don't belong with Henrietta."

An hour later, hungry and tired, the skating party quit the ice and headed for the cozy comforts of home.

Sebastian, too, trailed after the crowd, dodging the children's snowballs—and Peter's. He was about to wallop his pestering brother over the head, when he noticed one member of their group was unaccounted for.

Henrietta.

Sebastian looked back at the pond to find her skating alone. Hands clasped behind her back, her cape fluttering in the breeze, she gracefully twirled on the ice, humming, enjoying the solitude, no doubt.

He turned away to give her peace, when the sharp sound of cutting ice filled his ears.

"Will you join me, Ravenswood?"

Sebastian peered over his shoulder again. Henrietta had skated to the pond's edge, her cheeks flushed with rosy life, her breath icy clouds on her plump red lips. Vigorous exercise heartily agreed with her, it seemed. Even her eyes sparkled like golden syrup.

"I wouldn't be very pleasant company, Miss Ashby."

She let out a husky laugh. Though it was cold, the frigid air making her voice scratchy, Sebastian still sensed a peculiar jolt in the pit of his belly at her smoky chortle.

"Rot, Ravenswood! Besides, you need the practice."

She winked at him. A playful wink that struck a chord of . . . arousal in him? Preposterous. He could not have these kinds of feelings for the girl. It was simply impossible. She was a delightful scamp. Always had been. She had not changed *that* much in five months. Nor had he, surely.

Sebastian looked back at the skating party, now fading dots on the horizon. "Really, Miss Ashby, I think it best if we both return to the house."

"Oh, I'm not ready to retire. But you go on ahead, if you must. Know this, though, you leave a friend vulnerable in the wilderness."

He flicked a brow upward at the wilderness bit, for the house was in perfect view of the pond, but otherwise did not protest. Instead he sighed and rested his sore rump on the frozen log once more. "Then I suppose the duty falls upon me to guard you, Miss Ashby—from the wilderness, of course."

"I like that." With a haughty air, she admonished, "You'll sit there, on that icy lump, rather than skate with me? I warn you, Ravenswood, a friend might start to feel slighted."

"I assure you, Miss Ashby, I've no intention of affronting you."

"I'm glad to hear it." She smiled and moved off again, shouting, "Now put on your skates!"

Why, the bossy little chit! When the devil had she sprouted such an officious disposition? Better yet, *why* had she sprouted such an officious disposition? What was the girl up to?

"Would you like me to come ashore and help you with your skates, Ravenswood?"

"That won't be necessary, Miss Ashby," he all but growled, as he set to work strapping the bothersome skates to his boots once more. Blast it! How the devil had he gotten himself into this mess—again?

With an unsteady air, Sebastian made his way back onto the ice, and quickly found himself surrounded by Henrietta.

"Here," she said. "Take my hand."

And before he could protest, she clasped him by the hand and secured her other palm to his waist.

Sebastian stiffened at the intimate embrace. Never before had the girl touched him in such a way. He'd been so careful in the past to avoid physical contact, not wanting to encourage her misplaced adoration. But now that she had him in her arms, a bewildering warmth seeped through his blood.

"You and I have never danced before," she said, as she waltzed across the ice with him—leading, at that. The impudent chit. "Why is that, Ravenswood?"

Because you've always hounded me for your husband, that's why.

But he fibbed instead. "I'm a very poor dancer, Miss Ashby."

"A poor dancer. A poor skater. Poor company. Do you expect me to believe you flourish at nothing?"

"That's right, Miss Ashby."

"Rot!" Her eyes sparked, a dark fire burning in the bronze pools. "I think you flourish at a great many things, my lord, and I wish you'd share your accomplishments with me. We are friends, after all."

Sebastian glowered at her, not really sure what to make of her request. If only he could think straight. But with the girl's elfin fingers caressing his waist, stirring a fiery storm in his belly, there wasn't much chance of that happening.

Brushing her palm away from his midriff, Sebastian set it atop his shoulder—where it belonged.

Belatedly he realized that wasn't a very wise move, for now *his* hand would have to go on *her* waist. Bloody hell.

"Miss Ashby?" he said with firm purpose.

"Yes, my lord."

And that was another thing. What the deuce did she mean by calling him "my lord" and "Ravenswood" at every turn? It'd been a quaint diversion the first night of his return, but now it was a bloody distraction to hear her call him by his title. He had the feeling the girl was funning with him each time she used the appellation.

"Ravenswood?"

He blinked. "What?"

"You had something to say to me, I believe."

That's right, he did. He had a great many things to say to her. *Why aren't you married yet?* for one. And *What the devil has come over you?* for another. "Is that jasmine I smell?"

"Why, yes, my lord. Do you like it?"

Like it? He could wallow in it. It was his favorite scent. Not that he'd ever told the girl so. Certainly not. It was a mere coincidence she was wearing the one fragrance that could make his head spin.

Devil take it, that's not what he wanted to talk to her about. "Miss Ashby—"

"Do you realize you've not stumbled once, my lord?"

Sebastian reflected upon her words. She was right, he hadn't.

"You are a very good teacher, Miss Ashby."

"Rubbish. You're just not that poor a skater."

No, he was a very poor skater, which made the balancing act all the more mystifying.

"You've misplaced your confidence in me, Miss Ashby."

Slowly she shook her head. "I don't think so."

Sebastian watched the gentle sway of her locks, a dark auburn in hue. Her curls were tucked beneath a fetching fur cap, a few stray tendrils bouncing with each twirl on the ice.

She really did look like a snow faerie, so whimsical and fearless. Her bright eyes gleamed with laughter and life. And for just a moment, he could see himself in the honey brown pools. It alarmed him.

"It's getting dark," she said softly, her russet red lashes fluttering. "We should head back to the house."

She broke away from the embrace and skated to the pond's edge, leaving Sebastian feeling curiously cold in the center of the ice.

Chapter 7

A disgruntled Sebastian made his way through the house and scowled. Henrietta's penchant for tardiness was rubbing off on him, it seemed. He had snored right through breakfast!

Stifling a curse, he stepped into the dining parlor.

"Morning, Seb." Peter was sitting alone in the room, reading a paper. "'Bout time you roused your sleepy head to join us."

Sebastian ignored the quip and poured himself a cup of lukewarm tea. He was hungry, but the serving plates on the table were dusted with crumbs. He looked at his brother.

"Oh, sorry, Seb." Peter rustled the paper. "But you know how it goes: the early bird gets the worm, and all. There might be a few scraps left in the kitchen."

With a sigh, Sebastian set his teacup aside and quit the room in search of the kitchen.

He stifled a yawn. He hadn't nabbed a wink of

sleep the other night, he was so restless. Had the baron changed the bed since his last visit? Sebastian didn't think so; the bed looked the same. But something was keeping him awake.

He moved through the house to the servant stairwell and strutted down the dark steps.

It was a large underground system of tunnels, leading to the kitchen, all lit by candlelight. Sebastian strolled past dish racks and dry sinks, a wine cellar and the cook's bedroom before he happened upon a warm, roasting fire . . . and Henrietta.

She was at a long wood table, her auburn hair twisted in a tight chignon. She was wearing an apron to protect her day dress—and rolling dough.

Sebastian sniffed the air.

Ginger.

She was making gingerbread.

Henrietta picked up a small sack of flour, tipped it, and dumped most of the powder on the breadboard.

She gasped and quickly scooped the extra flour back into the sack, stirring up a white cloud.

"Achooo!"

He shouldn't be alone with the chit; it wasn't right . . . but he was hungry.

"Bless you, Miss Ashby."

She bristled. "Oh, good morning, Ravenswood." She stuffed the rest of the flour into the sack, wiped her powdery fingers across her apron—and smiled.

The warm glow of the fire brightened her cheeks,

the soft dusting of a rosy blush making her all the more winsome.

"What are you doing here, Ravenswood?"

Sebastian stooped to pass under the short door frame. "I'm hungry, Miss Ashby."

There was a look in her eyes, a smoky look. The kind of look a wanton mistress would offer when she was gripped by a *carnal* hunger.

Sebastian blinked. It must be the shadows in the room, fooling his eyes.

"I'm afraid I missed breakfast this morning, Miss Ashby."

There was a wooden bowl on the table, covered with linen. She flipped back the cloth. "Cookies, my lord?"

Sebastian approached the table and peeked into the bowl. "Did you bake the cookies?"

"Just now."

A bit dubious, Sebastian picked up a piece of gingerbread. "Why are you baking cookies, Miss Ashby?"

"Oh, I bake them every year at Christmas."

"Do you?"

She nodded. "For the children in the village."

Sebastian eyed her, then the cookie again. Well, it looked edible.

He popped the spicy treat into his mouth and found it to be . . . "Delicious."

She beamed. "Thank you, my lord. Have another."

"I think I will, Miss Ashby."

One. Two. Three. Four treats later—maybe more—Sebastian's belly was thoroughly filled and satisfied. The chit really was a splendid cook.

"That was very good, Miss Ashby."

There was something shifty about her smile. "I'm glad you think so, Ravenswood." She plunked another breadboard on the table. "Here. You'll need this."

He eyed the culinary accouterment with curiosity. "For what?"

"Well, since you ate all the children's cookies, you'll have to make some more dough."

He blinked. "Miss Ashby, you're not—"

A large bowl landed on the breadboard. "Put in three cups of flour."

Sebastian just stared at her. She wanted him to bake? Cookies?

"Miss Ashby, I don't know the first thing about making cookies."

"That's why I'm here, Ravenswood." She passed him a cup. "Three cups, remember."

Sebastian took the cup and stifled a growl. He had to *work* for his food. How ignoble. If he'd known the price of those blasted cookies, he'd have starved instead.

He divested his coat and rolled up his sleeves.

"You tricked me, Miss Ashby." He dumped the flour into the bowl. "That wasn't very good of you."

"Perhaps I did, my lord . . . a cup of brown sugar next . . . but it's lonely down here; I need the company of a friend."

He humphed and mixed in the brown sugar.

She handed him two small vials. "Now for a pinch of cinnamon and a dash of ginger."

He tossed in the spices. "What happened to your sisters?"

Henrietta worked at her end of the table, rolling a ready batch of dough. "My sisters took the children in the sleighs for a winter trip."

"What about the servants?"

"Tomorrow's Christmas, Ravenswood. The servants get a holiday. Besides, *I* volunteered to bake the cookies."

"And yet here *I* am, helping you."

She grinned. "I really appreciate the assistance, my lord." She took a round tin cookie cutter and sliced up the gingerbread. "If we work together, we'll be done by luncheon."

He paused. "Luncheon? How many cookies do you intend we bake?"

"Oh, a few hundred or so should do it . . . the wet ingredients are next."

She pushed a jug of brown goop his way.

After he'd recovered from the shock of having to make a few hundred cookies, he looked into the jug and grimaced. "What is that?"

"Molasses." She picked up a spoon. "Here. Use this to scrape it out; the molasses is very thick."

Sebastian sighed and poured in the gummy ingredient. The wily chit had hoodwinked him thoroughly. Again. How did he keep getting tricked into skating trips and cooking parties?

But it was hard to be vexed with the girl when there was a dusting of flour on the tip of her pert nose.

"I didn't know you were so generous with the village children, Miss Ashby."

She put the rest of the gingerbread cookies on the iron griddle. "There's a lot you don't know about me, Ravenswood."

"I'm beginning to realize that."

Henrietta picked up the griddle and a scrap of black wool, and sashayed over to the fireplace. She reached inside the hearth with the wool, pulled out the crane, and set the griddle on the S-hook.

She swung the iron arm back over the fire. "That should take just a few minutes."

All the while, Sebastian studied her lithe movement. He pondered her skill in the kitchen and wondered what else he didn't know about the girl.

Henrietta returned to the table and checked on his progress. "Now for the egg, my lord. Try not to get the shell into the bowl . . . on second thought, let me do it." She cracked the egg on the side of the dish and dropped in the yolk, discarding the shell. "Now mix it all up."

Sebastian glanced across the cluttered table, spotted a wooden spoon, and picked it up.

"Oh no!" She whisked the wooden spoon away. "With your hands."

He looked down at the sloppy mixture. "I'm not touching that."

She sighed. "Let me show you, Ravenswood." She took his hands and pushed them into the gooey blend. "Like this."

Sebastian's outrage fizzled the moment she started to work her fingers over his. In deft strokes, she kneaded the dough with him, pushing his hands together, forcing him to press and squeeze the supple compound.

There was something very familiar about the movement of her hands. A pulsing rhythm that warmed the blood in his veins.

Perhaps he should bake cookies more often?

Sebastian could hear her soft breath, a slow beat. Smell the sprinkle of jasmine at her throat. He looked into her eyes as she molded the dough, such a deep toffee brown. Dots of flickering candlelight reflected in the glossy pools.

Sebastian must be standing too close to the fire, for he could feel the flames licking . . .

"Smoke," he whispered.

She flicked her pretty lashes. "What's that, my lord?"

He sniffed. "I think the cookies are burning, Miss Ashby."

"Oh no!" She quickly wiped her fingers on her apron and rushed over to the hearth. With the scrap of black wool, she snatched the griddle from the flames and carried it back to the table.

Henrietta set the griddle on the iron spider and inspected the cookies. "They don't look too bad."

With a knife, she picked up a cookie to check the underside.

Black as pitch.

"Oh dear." She tsked. "I'll feed these to the hounds. We'll have to start anew, my lord."

Sebastian took in a deep breath to dispel the balmy heat in his belly.

Finished by luncheon, indeed.

"Be careful, Henry!" Penelope cried. "You'll burn your sleeve!"

"Give the boy some room," said the baron, and waved a hand. "Step back everyone. Step back."

Henrietta pursed her lips in concentration. She eyed the floating raisin in the fiery bowl—not an easy task in the darkened room—and licked her fingers to moisten the tips.

"Oh, I can't look!" The baroness covered her eyes with a kerchief, but still peeked through the stitching in the fringe.

As swift as she could, Henrietta dunked her hand into the shallow bowl, grabbed the fiery raisin, and popped the brandy-soaked fruit into her mouth, much to the jubilation of the crowd around her.

"Hurray, Aunt Henry!" the children shouted in unison. "Hail to the Queen of the Snapdragon!"

Devilishly pleased with herself, Henrietta mimicked her best royal curtsy. "Why, thank you, my dear lords and ladies."

The baron clapped his hands together and beamed. "What a good show, my boy!"

"Thank goodness that's over with." Fan fluttering, the baroness clutched her large bosom. "Lights!"

The attending footmen whisked about the room, lighting candles, tweaking oil lamps, and stoking the dwindling flames in the hearth.

A bit breathless herself, Henrietta separated from the family and ensconced herself in a window seat, resting her warm brow against the chilled glass. It was Christmas Eve, the parlor a flutter of activity. But she needed a moment of repose. She still had a seduction to orchestrate—and tonight she intended to move the courtship along.

With a discreet pinch, Henrietta assured herself the little velvet purse was still tucked up her sleeve—and had not drowned in the fiery bowl of brandy. It concealed a gift for Ravenswood: one she hoped would warm the viscount to her. Next she peeked at the doorway, and was pleased to see the mistletoe still in place, for it would come in handy later in the night.

With a confident smile, she rested her brow against the window again. Across the room stood Ravenswood, conversing with his brother. Henrietta did not look directly at the viscount. Instead she fixed her eyes on the pane of glass and watched him in the reflection of the room.

He looked so dashing, she mused. And he was watching her closely, she could tell.

But she would not acknowledge his stare. It was another one of Madam Jacqueline's cardinal rules: ignore the man as much as possible. Make *him* come to you.

And it wasn't long before Henrietta's heart fluttered at the movement in the glass.

Ravenswood was approaching.

She scrunched her feet beneath her posterior, making room on the window seat should Sebastian wish to join her. He didn't sit next to her, though. Instead he paused by the window, drink in hand, delft blue eyes perusing her figure in that familiar lanky stare.

"How fare your fingers, Miss Ashby?"

Tingles of pleasure rippled along her limbs at his low and husky drawl. "A bit tender, my lord."

She quelled a shudder when he took the seat next to her. "Let me see your hand."

It was a gruff command, and she all but squeaked in delight to see how much he cared for her. Oh, he loved her all right; she'd suspected it for years. But the mulish man had never made a public display of affection. This was a most favorable boon.

She offered him her hand. Gently he clasped her

palm, and Henrietta all but toppled off the window seat.

With exquisite tenderness, he stroked her fingers, glaring at the flushed flesh as though willing the injury away.

But the slight burning sensation in her hand intensified the more he caressed her, and it wasn't long before the rest of her body was feeling the heat as well.

"Perhaps you should retire as Queen of the Snapdragon?"

It took her a moment to gather her wayward thoughts and reply, "Perish the thought. The children would never forgive me."

He let go of her hand, let it slowly slip between his strong fingers. "I will get you a cold compress, Miss Ashby."

She delved deep into his stormy eyes, shivered at the loss of his touch. "No, wait!"

Sebastian looked back at her. "What is it?"

"Stay, Ravenswood. I have a present for you."

He eyed her curiously. "A present? For me?"

Henrietta removed the small trinket from beneath her sleeve and presented him with the gift. "Here."

Sebastian stared at the satchel with obvious confusion. "What is it?"

She thrust her hand forward in encouragement. "Open it."

Setting his drink aside, he accepted the black velvet purse. For a moment, he did nothing but hold it. But soon he stretched the golden cords and opened the little sack.

Carefully, Sebastian removed the ring and lifted it to the light for a better look. It was a gentleman's ring, crafted from gold, the emblem on the surface a Celtic love knot.

Did he recognize the symbol? She hoped not. She didn't want to frighten him off with a clear show of her affection. But he didn't look alarmed. In truth, he looked very surprised.

"Do you like it, Ravenswood?"

Chapter 8

Yes, he did like it. He liked it very much.

Sebastian slipped the ring over his pinky finger. A perfect fit. "Thank you, Miss Ashby. It was very thoughtful of you."

He'd never received a gift before. Not like this. Not from a woman. It was usually he who did the gift giving, showering a mistress with jewels to keep her content. But he'd never been the recipient of such a gesture himself.

It was a warm sentiment, to be bestowed with a present. Especially if the gift was from a . . . friend.

"I'm afraid I don't have anything for you, Miss Ashby."

"Rot, Ravenswood! We are friends, you and I. And friends give gifts without expecting anything in return."

He looked into her warm brown eyes, so spirited. Such a lovely pair of eyes to match such a lovely soul . . .

Young Edward bounded up to his aunt Henry then, and stole her away for a game of hoodman blind.

Henrietta flashed him a dazzling smile before she took off with the boy, then fastened the blindfold over her eyes and hunched to tickle and tag the children skipping around her.

Sebastian watched her for a time. He pressed the back of his head against the cool glass window, and let his eyes wander in curiosity over the little hoyden.

She was draped in a woolly frock, a rusty red in hue. The apparel matched the sunset shade of her long locks, twisted in an elegant knot, yet contrasted with the creamy brightness of her soft skin.

Sebastian eyed the naked flesh at her neck, her bust. He pictured his lips tasting the tender skin, his tongue licking the sweet scent of jasmine at her throat . . .

He slew the salacious thought at once. He was a villain. A jaded wastrel, through and through. It was just like him to think such a wicked thought, to corrupt the innocent Miss Ashby in his mind's eye.

If only the chit didn't have such a devastating figure: curves in all the right places. He could resist the allure of her smoky drawl then, the soft touch of her faerie fingers . . .

"You look smitten."

Snapped from his reverie, Sebastian snarled at his brother. "Rubbish!"

Peter occupied the abandoned seat next to him, and said, "You have a dreamy look in your eyes."

The devil he did!

"I'm just tired," was Sebastian's curt reply.

But Peter continued with his diagnosis, unperturbed. "A sort of hazy expression across your face." He gesticulated with his fingers. "I've never seen you like this, Seb."

"There's nothing the matter with me."

"Did I say there was anything wrong with you? Having feelings for a woman isn't a malady, Seb, like some might suggest."

Sebastian growled, "I'm *not* smitten with Henrietta."

"Then what do you feel for the girl?"

"Brotherly regard."

"And?"

"And what?"

"Well, I hate to tell you this, Seb, but most men don't look at their sister like she's something tasty to eat."

Sebastian resisted the impulse to crush his brother's throat. "Henrietta and I are just friends."

"*Friends?* Are you daft?"

Sebastian glared at his brother. "And why the devil not?"

"You can't be friends with a beautiful woman. Hell, you can't be friends with a plain woman! There's just something about you, Seb. You have a tendency to rut about with anything in a skirt."

And since Sebastian *was* having such a devilishly hard time stifling his wicked thoughts about Henrietta, he wanted to throttle his brother all the more for pointing out the wretched truth.

Still, Sebastian wouldn't admit to the struggle inside him.

"You're wrong, Peter," he said firmly. "I *can* be friends with Henrietta. I'm sure of it."

And he was.

Really.

Later that night, still unsettled by the conflicting sentiments inside him, Sebastian strolled through the quiet household on his way to his bedchamber.

He fiddled with the ring on his finger, twisting it round and round, thinking of Henrietta.

Five months ago, he had abandoned the chit, hoping she'd find herself another mate. Well, she'd not set her cap for another bloke, but she'd also not pestered him with adoring looks or flaunting gestures, either. Instead, she'd offered him friendship.

Sebastian twisted his lips. He didn't have very many friends. Oh, he'd many partners in debauchery, but none he'd consider friends. He'd certainly no female chums, so he didn't know what to make of his newfound "friendship" with Henrietta.

And where the devil had the whole idea of friendship come from anyway? Five months ago she'd wanted to snag him as her husband. Now she wanted to be his friend? Was he to assume she'd given up on the whole idea of being the next Viscountess Ravenswood? Or was the mischievous chit up to something?

He'd no idea. And he couldn't ask Henrietta outright. She'd only fib if it was a ploy of some kind. One thing was for certain, though. A friend was not supposed to stir the heat in your belly. Peter had been right about that.

Disgruntled, Sebastian turned a corner, passing through an arched entranceway—and smacked right into Henrietta.

Alarmed, he said, "Forgive me, Miss Ashby."

"Oh, bother that." She rubbed her nose in the most delightful way. "It was an accident. Think nothing of it, Ravenswood."

"Did I hurt you?"

She wrinkled her nose. "Not a'tall."

He cut her a dubious stare. That fragile feminine face crashing into his brute form had to sting, even a little. "You've not broken it, have you?"

"Rot!" She sniffed. "I'm stronger than I look."

He had to admire her spirit. Most women would be reduced to tears right about now. Some might even demand reparation: a diamond necklace, for instance. But not Henrietta. He suspected she wouldn't carp even if he'd injured her. And that only made her character all the more mystifying.

"Where were you off to in such haste, Miss Ashby?"

"I was looking for . . ."

"For?"

She looked straight at him. "I was looking for my sisters."

He quirked a brow. "It's after midnight. Your sisters are likely in bed. Which is where you should be, Miss Ashby."

"You're quite right." She waved a dismissive hand. "I'll speak with my sisters in the morning. Good night, Ravenswood."

"Good night, Miss Ashby."

She turned to leave, then paused. "Oh dear."

"What is it?"

She looked back at him, a bright blush dusting her cheeks. "I'm afraid we're in a terrible fix."

Was the girl about to faint? Had she bumped into him a little harder than he'd thought?

Sebastian reached for her elbow to steady her. "Miss Ashby, are you unwell?"

"Oh, I'm quite well, but . . ."

Her lashes flitted upward.

Sebastian followed her gaze—and his heart shuddered at the sight of the mistletoe.

Now where the hell had that come from? Prior to the Yule festivities, he'd made considerable effort to locate all the ghastly foliage in the house so he could avoid it. And that mistletoe had *not* been there before.

"My lord, I do believe I owe you a kiss."

Blood throbbed in his veins at the sound of her

silky smooth voice. And when she started to chew on her bottom lip in that wanton fashion, blood started to pound in other less savory places, too.

She could *not* kiss him. He was adamant. For eight years he'd stood fast to escape the girl's kisses. He would not flounder now, give her reason to believe he cared for her in an unbrotherly fashion. It would only break her heart to learn the truth. He was determined not to devastate her.

"But you and I are friends," she said next, eyes slanted in demure innocence. "And it wouldn't do a'tall if I kissed you on the lips."

Sebastian heard the breath rush through his teeth. Rampant relief filled him. Thank heavens the girl had good sense! For he had not the fortitude to resist a pair of plump pink lips, dusted with the scent of jasmine. He was sure about that.

"Instead, Ravenswood, I will kiss you where you've never been kissed before."

His breath hitched.

So much for the girl's good sense.

It could not be stopped, the fire burning in his belly at her wanton proposal. The rogue within him took an instant liking to the proposition, the more reasonable part of him tossed to the wayside.

Sebastian could do naught but stare, mesmerized, as she reached for his hand.

He bristled, grasping for his wits, about to pull away, when a jarring voice inside him cried: *Devil take it, Seb, let* her *show you where you've never been kissed before!*

And upon that blasted reproof, all thoughts of propriety were stomped asunder.

Slowly Henrietta lifted his hand to her lips. Ever gently, she pulled back the cuff of his sleeve, the fabric scraping over his skin, making him shudder.

Mischief twinkled in her bright brown eyes, and she whispered, "I shall kiss you right . . . here."

Sebastian closed his eyes, the rogue within him groaning in feral satisfaction.

Warm, wet lips kissed, then sucked at his wrist, the rhythmic movement of her mouth reminding him of other sensual pleasures.

"Henry," he breathed hoarsely, trembling under her salacious ministrations.

It was an entreaty, her name. A plea to break away from him, for he had not the power to do it himself. And unless the girl abandoned him this instant, she was going to find herself up against the wall—

Sebastian was startled by the sudden surcease. Limbs throbbing in repressed ecstasy, he struggled to regain control of his mind, his breath, his very soul.

"There now," she whispered warmly, eyes bright with sensuality. "We've not broken with tradition." She smiled. "Good night, Ravenswood."

She sauntered into the darkness of the corridor, leaving him stranded under the mistletoe in abject chaos, for not only had *he* broken with tradition by allowing the girl to kiss him, but he'd done the one thing he'd vowed never to do: call her by her nickname.

Chapter 9

Henrietta burst into her bedchamber.

Heart still throbbing in her throat, she closed the door and sprinted toward the bed. She buried her face in her pillow and let out a squeal of delight. A bit more composed, she sat up and sighed. But the giddiness inside her refused to be tamped, and she giggled again.

He had called her Henry! It was the sweetest sound she had ever heard, that guttural whisper. Every fine hair on her body had spiked to shivering attention when he'd said her nickname.

And she had kissed him! Not on the lips, but still, she had tasted the heady musk of his skin for the first time—and was utterly intoxicated.

Letting out another dreamy sigh, Henrietta flopped back onto her pillow. Her plan was working splendidly. And at a clipped pace. She could not afford to slow down. She could not give Sebastian a chance to reflect and realize that something was amiss; that he should leave the house at once.

But she didn't want to move *too* fast, either, or she might make the man balk and run anyway. It was such a tricky balance to keep.

Yet she needed to be bolder if she wanted to seduce the viscount. She had worked on her friendship with Sebastian, but now she needed to nurture the other part of their relationship, too. She needed to become his lover.

Heart ticking in enthusiasm, Henrietta reached under her pillow and yanked out a black, leatherbound volume: a parting gift from Madam Jacqueline.

And as she opened the book of naughty pictures to a random page, her thoughts turned wily and wicked, as she pondered which of the erotic acts to perform with Sebastian.

Under waning candle glow, she traced her fingers over the sultry images, daydreaming about Sebastian.

She had come to admire the sensuous pictures in the book; she didn't blush to look at them anymore. Each provocative image illustrated a bond of ecstasy between a couple.

Henrietta longed to know that kind of bliss, to share that kind of intimacy with Sebastian. It was a burning need inside her, to be close with the man she loved.

She flipped the page again, and paused.

A romantic illustration seized her imagination: a couple in silhouette, ensconced in a big, comfy chair by a roaring fire. The woman straddled the man, her flimsy night rail rucked up to her waist. Her loose shift exposed a plump breast, too—and the man in the picture looked very eager to taste it.

It was a titillating image, but also passionate. There was a deep, dark look in the couple's eyes. Henrietta could *feel* the intense bond between them. She wanted that same kind of rapport with Sebastian, and she started to feel all warm inside just thinking about it.

The door burst open.

Henrietta gasped and slammed the tome closed, shoving it back under her pillow.

Dazed, she gaped at the entourage pouring into her room: four sisters draped in evening wrappers and curling ribbons in their hair.

The women quickly circled the bed like a swarm of angry bees.

Penelope, the eldest of the bunch, stuck her hands on her hips, and said, "Henry, are you having an affair with Ravenswood?"

Body still hot and tingly from staring at sinful poses, Henrietta struggled to gather her wits and bring her erratic heartbeats under control. Heavens, was she having a nightmare?

"Out with it, Henry," said Roselyn. "Don't idle in bed."

"Speak up, Henry," from Tertia.

"Yes, Henry, do tell us the truth," insisted Cordelia.

Henrietta wanted to plug her ears with her fingers. Drat! How had her sisters spied the subtle courtship? She had been so careful, acting aloof in public and bolder in private.

Baffled, Henrietta said, "Why do you think I'm having an affair with Ravenswood?"

Penelope narrowed her dark brown eyes. "I've just had a little chat with my husband. Peter believes Ravenswood is smitten with you."

Gripped by a profound urge to hop up and down on the bed, Henrietta swallowed her pleasure instead, and said, "Really?"

A snort from Penelope. "My fool husband thinks it absolutely marvelous that the two of you get married."

So did Henrietta. So why the devil didn't her sisters agree?

"I don't understand," said Henrietta. "Why don't you like Ravenswood?"

"We *do* like him." Roselyn folded her arms across her chest in an imperious manner. "But we like him as Penelope's brother-in-law, *not* your husband!"

Henrietta was confused, and wondered, "And why would you *dis*like him as my husband?"

Tertia sighed. "Oh Lord, listen to the fool girl."

"Henry," said Penelope in reproach, "you must see how inappropriate such a match would be."

Inappropriate? That she marry a respectable viscount? The man that she loved? Was her sister mad?

"I most certainly do not," said Henrietta.

"The poor dear." Cordelia tsked. "She's lost her wits."

"I've done no such thing." Henrietta huffed. "I think *you've* all lost your wits. I've loved Ravenswood for years. Why are you scolding me now?"

"Oh, hush, Henry." Tertia wagged her finger. "You don't really love the man. You're just trapped in a girlhood dream."

Henrietta humphed in indignation. "Rot!"

Roselyn sighed. "Fine, Henry. Then tell us, *why* do you love Ravenswood?"

Henrietta could think of a hundred reasons; there were so many memories to draw from. The fall harvest for one. She had been seventeen at the time and very anxious to get her hands on a juicy apple after so many months of wanting. She'd been about to clamber up a tree to fetch said apple, when Ravenswood had appeared. He'd offered to scale the gnarled tree in her stead and had climbed to the tips of the branches to obtain the sweetest fruit for her. Her heart still fluttered at the memory.

"Because," said Henrietta, "he makes my heart—"

"Go pitter patter?" said Tertia.

"Do you get butterflies in your belly?" from Roselyn.

"Or tongue-tied in his company?" said Cordelia.

Henrietta made a moue.

"It's called infatuation, Henry." Penelope folded her arms. "It's not love. Now *are* you having an affair with Ravenswood or not?"

Four piercing stares stabbed her.

Henrietta was stubbornly quiet for a moment, then said, "I'm not."

Yet!

The sisters liberated a collective sigh of relief.

"Thank goodness," from Penelope.

"We've come just in time," said Roselyn.

No, you've come at the most importune time, thought Henrietta, and bunched her brow in consternation. "I still don't understand the sudden disapproval of Ravenswood."

"There's nothing sudden about it, m'dear," said Tertia. "Ravenswood was *always* unsuitable for you. But so long as he didn't return your affection, there was never the danger of a match being made."

"Danger? Unsuitable? What rot!" Henrietta clambered to her knees, eyes level with her sister's. "Ravenswood is a viscount. He is most suitable."

"We're not speaking of titles, Henry." Tertia sniffed in displeasure. "We're speaking of character."

"The man is a rogue!" Cordelia blurted out.

Roselyn pinched her. "What Cordelia means is Ravenswood isn't husband material."

"He'll make you unhappy," said Penelope.

Henrietta glared at all four of her sisters. "I know Ravenswood is considered a rogue, but I've every intention of reforming his roguish ways."

Well, not too much, thought Henrietta, for she happened to like a bit of the rogue within him. Ravenswood was flirtatious . . . sensuous. A reputed rake, he enjoyed the company of a lady. That made him a rogue, true. But the man could make her toes curl. Henrietta quite liked the feeling. And so long as the viscount was faithful to her once they married, he could be as "roguish" as he liked.

"Henry!" Roselyn shook her head. "You can't reform a rogue."

Now where had Henrietta heard that before?

"Especially a rogue like Ravenswood," said Tertia.

"Why especially?" Henrietta demanded.

The sisters all looked at one another.

"Ravenswood is handsome, to be sure, and charming," said Penelope, "but he's also sinister."

Henrietta snorted.

"He is," insisted Roselyn. "The talk about him is scandalous. It's frightening, too."

Henrietta bunched her brow. "What talk?"

"There's talk he's a member of a notorious club." Tertia went on to whisper, "One dedicated to vice."

Henrietta scoffed. "It's all rubbish, I'm sure."

But then Henrietta remembered her chat with

Ravenswood the other day. He had confessed he belonged to a club, a "gentlemen's club." She was sure it was just like any other club, though, where one smoked and played billiards and such. Although Ravenswood had also mentioned her best friend's husband, the "Duke of Rogues," was once a member . . .

Still, the gossip was drivel. If her dearest chum could marry the "Duke of Rogues," then surely Henrietta could wed Ravenswood. The club couldn't be *that* notorious.

It was all just idle gossip, she was sure. The papers were often wrong about such stuff. Madam Jacqueline had been a purported shrew, yet the woman was nothing of the sort. And while it might be fun to listen to scandalous chitchat, Henrietta wasn't going to choose her mate from the *ton*'s society papers! She knew Ravenswood. He was dashing. Wonderful. He was going to make her very happy.

She just had to convince her sisters of that truth.

"No, really," Cordelia chimed, "I've heard the talk, too, Henry. The club is like a den of sin, unfit for respectable company."

Henrietta grimaced. "Rot!"

"Henry, it's true." Penelope lowered her voice. "Peter often laments about his brother; how he wishes Ravenswood would give up his immoral ways and settle down."

Henrietta thought "immoral" was a tad too strong a word for a flirt, but she still defended the viscount with a tart: "Ravenswood *will* give up his 'immoral' ways and settle down." She pointed to her chest. "With me."

Penelope sighed. "Henry, Ravenswood isn't the man for you. You must give up this foolish childhood fancy!"

Henrietta meshed her lips together in defiance. "I intend to follow my heart, sisters."

Four sets of arms went across four sets of bosoms.

"Well, Henry, if your heart is in the *wrong* place, then I suppose the duty falls upon us to protect you."

Henrietta looked at her eldest sister, aghast. "What do you mean?"

But it was Roselyn who enlightened her: "If Ravenswood's got the fool idea into his head that he can have his way with you, then we'll just have to convince him otherwise."

Perish the thought!

"I don't need protecting from Ravenswood," was Henrietta's hasty rebuttal. "He would never hurt me."

"He *will* hurt you, Henry." Cordelia offered her a rueful expression. "You don't know the man a'tall."

"I've known the man for *eight* years!"

"No, Henry, you've *dreamed* about the man for

eight years," said Tertia. "He's not a knight in shining armor."

Something bubbled in Henrietta's throat. A vile lump of pain that was hard to swallow.

Why were her sisters doing this? Petty gossip was no reason to interfere with her contentment. *She* didn't bother in any of their personal affairs. So why were *they* bothering in hers? And so cruelly at that?

Henrietta sniffed. "Why don't you want me to be happy?"

It was a smarting pain, to have her own sisters be so determined to quash all her joy.

"That's just it, my dear," said Roselyn in a more soothing voice, "we *do* want you to be happy. And Ravenswood will *not* make you happy."

Henrietta quelled her sorrow to assert, "*Only* Ravenswood will make me happy. He might show the world his roguish side, but *I* know his heart. He's not a villain, and I won't listen to any more of this rubbish."

Penelope sighed again. "Willful girl."

"Where does she get it from?" wondered Tertia.

"It's all Papa's doing," quipped Roselyn. "He should have taught her to obey."

"Now she'll never listen to reason," said Cordelia.

A nod from Penelope. "Then I suppose we'll just have to take care of this matter on our own."

"No," said Henrietta, panicked.

"We'll make sure Ravenswood stays far away from her," agreed Tertia.

"No!"

"He shan't be allowed to say two words to her," chimed Cordelia.

"No! No! No!"

Roselyn bobbed her head. "It's settled then."

And the four harridans left the room in accord, Henrietta glaring after them, wondering how the devil she was going to get out of this muddle.

Chapter 10

Henrietta had slept in. Drat! She was supposed to spend every waking moment seducing Ravenswood. But last night she'd had the most dreadful dream. It had started out pleasant; she and Sebastian tangled together in the bedsheets. But just when Sebastian was about to slip his hand beneath her petticoat, four ravens had swooped into the room and pecked out his eyes.

Henrietta let out a huff. Troublesome sisters. What the devil did they mean by threatening to interfere in her life? Henrietta wasn't a child anymore. She didn't need a guardian—*four* guardians. All she needed was a few more private rendezvous with Ravenswood.

Oh, lud! Madame Jacqueline had not instructed her on the art of ridding oneself of meddlesome sisters. What was Henrietta to do now?

The parlor loomed ahead. Henrietta could hear the buzz of chatter. She smoothed out her skirt and took in a deep breath to soothe her agitation before stepping into the room.

Even among a crowd, Henrietta spotted Ravenswood with ease. There was something about the man: a magnetic pull that always teased her senses. My, he looked dashing, primped in a marine blue waistcoat and dark breeches, sooty black locks curling at his temples. But it was his eyes that captivated Henrietta. Smoldering eyes that darkened the moment she entered the room.

"Good morning, Henry!"

The four unanimous greetings had Henrietta seething beneath her composed cheerfulness. She was too late. The harridans had circled Ravenswood at the breakfast table. She couldn't get anywhere near the man.

Still smiling, Henrietta tried not to sound too petulant. "Good morning, sisters."

She took an empty seat at the far end of the table, her eyes resting on Ravenswood once more. She could see the fire burning in him. The fire she had ignited the night before with a sinful kiss.

Henrietta shuddered under his scorching gaze. The steel blue of his sexy eyes transfixed her. Made her giddy, too, for she realized then a night apart had not doused the flames of his desire for her. Capital! Now if only she could steal a few moments alone with the viscount to keep that fire burning.

Henrietta inclined her head and smiled. "Good morning, Ravenswood."

But Sebastian had no opportunity to offer a return greeting, for the harridans captured his attention then with a plethora of mindless questions.

"Tell me, what do you think of the French lace at Penelope's sleeve, Ravenswood?"

"How about the exquisite fringe on Cordelia's shawl, Ravenswood? Isn't it grand?"

"Of course, the green ribbon in Tertia's hair is very fetching. Wouldn't you agree, Ravenswood?"

"And let's not forget the chemisette at Roselyn's neck. It's so fashionable, isn't it, Ravenswood?"

Sebastian looked a bit spooked, surrounded by so many demanding females. He hadn't a chance to breathe between answers, never mind look back at Henrietta.

Curse her sisters! They were going to occupy the viscount's every waking moment, become a wall between her and her love.

Henrietta had a strong urge to flick forks across the table at her sisters.

"Here you are, Henry, my boy." In a clandestine gesture, the baron pushed a crumpet on a white linen napkin across the table. "I saved the last one for you. I know how much you like sweets."

"Thank you, Papa." Henrietta gave her father a warm smile. She reached for the crumpet and buttered it, all the while telling herself she would *not* let her sisters disrupt the wonderful progress she had made with Ravenswood. She *would* find time to be alone with the viscount. Her sisters could *not* devastate true love, however much they tried.

Henrietta stuffed the buttered crumpet into her mouth.

"You look weary, sister."

Mouth full, Henrietta glanced sidelong at her brother-in-law Peter.

"I understand you didn't get much sleep last night." He sighed. "I believe I owe you an apology, Henry, for it was I who spoke with Penelope about Seb's . . . attachment to you. I just didn't think she'd fly into a tizzy about it."

Henrietta swallowed the crumpet, her heart skipping a beat. She didn't have time to be vexed with Peter for confiding in Penelope and setting in motion this whole blasted affair. She was only curious to know: "Do you really think Sebastian is 'attached' to me?"

Peter looked at her thoughtfully, almost hopefully. "I do."

A surge of bubbly emotions stormed her breast. It was comforting to know she had an ally in Peter, that at least one member of her family wasn't bent on destroying her chance at happiness with Ravenswood.

"Oh, Peter"—eyes darting across the table, Henrietta peeked to make sure no one was eavesdropping—"what am I going to do? My sisters are dead set against my marrying Sebastian."

He whispered, "I'll help you."

"You will?"

Peter nodded. "It's high time Seb settles down. You're perfect for him, Henry, and he knows it. He's just being stubborn." Peter paused, then: "You do care for him, Henry, don't you?"

"With all my heart," she said.

"Right then." Another firm nod. "I'll take care of your sisters. You look after Sebastian."

But for the present company, Henrietta would have smothered Peter with grateful kisses. "Oh, thank you, Peter!"

"Think nothing of it, Henry. This is all my fault anyway, so I'll right the matter." Peter looked down the table at his brother, then said, "I don't know what you've done to Seb, but he's not looked so smitten in . . . well, ever. So you just go about your way and leave the sisters to me. Oh, and Henry?"

"Yes, Peter?"

"Thank you for caring for him."

She patted his hand. "You don't have to thank me, Peter. The blackguard stole my heart long ago. I didn't really have a choice in the matter."

Peter smiled at that.

"Heavens, look at the time," piped Roselyn. "We'll be late for church!"

The whole table erupted in chaos then.

It was Christmas Day, and the annual Yule service was set to start within the hour.

"Fetch the children!"

"Ready the sleighs!"

Like a herd of horses, the family poured into the corridor and headed for the front door.

Henrietta busied herself getting ready: wrap, muff, fur hat. All the while, she slowly maneuvered herself next to Sebastian. Behind him, really. In the tumult of the household, he didn't notice her standing there.

Henrietta was about to impart some whispered words—to remind Sebastian of the kiss they'd shared the other night—when Penelope whisked by and hooked her arm in his.

"Come Ravenswood." Penelope smiled. "You'll ride with Peter and me."

Drat! Henrietta glared after the departing couple. She didn't know how Peter was going to get her sisters away from Ravenswood, but Henrietta dearly hoped he'd come up with something soon.

Bless Peter! He'd caused such a ruckus in the household, Henrietta was sure to find a moment alone with Ravenswood.

The whole family was in a tizzy because Mama's Christmas bell was "missing." It'd been in Mama's family for more than a hundred years, and it was tradition to ring the bell before the Yule feast.

According to lore, the little porcelain bell blessed the food *and* the family. No one could eat until the bell sounded, so a troop of famished Ashbys were scouring the house, looking for it.

But Henrietta was looking for something a mite different: Ravenswood.

She bustled through the passageways, peeking into the branching rooms. She noted the parlor was empty, but just then a dark head popped up from behind the settee.

Sebastian.

And he was alone!

Henrietta took a moment to fluff her skirts and ease her thundering heartbeat. With as much aplomb as she could muster, she waltzed into the room.

"Any luck, my lord?"

Sebastian stopped dusting his trousers to stare at her, a seductive glow in his dark blue eyes.

Henrietta was having a devilishly hard time keeping her wits about her. For far too long, Sebastian had looked at her with platonic regard. Now each time he glanced her way, a carnal fire burned in his eyes. It delighted her to her very core, his wanton attention, but it also distracted her.

"I'm afraid not, Miss Ashby."

So he was back to calling her Miss Ashby, was he? It didn't matter. She'd have him breathing her nickname again soon enough.

There was a low timbre to his voice. "I can vouch, though, that the Christmas bell is not underneath the settee."

Henrietta busied herself in the room, "searching" for the bell. "Where could it have gone?"

"Perhaps one of the children took it?" he said. "It is a rather shiny trinket, if I remember correctly."

Henrietta peeked inside a vase. "The children pledge on all their toys they did not take the bell." She looked into a tea caddy next. "But with the help of the staff, we should find the bell soon—before we all perish of hunger."

"Miss Ashby?"

She purred, "Yes, Ravenswood."

He bristled.

Drat! She had not meant to sound so wanton.

Coughing into her fingers, she said, "Forgive me. My throat is a bit parched. You were saying, my lord?"

He looked lost for words. In truth, he looked preoccupied with staring at *her*.

Henrietta felt a giddy rush of warm fuzzies tickle her right down to her toes.

"I was going to suggest, Miss Ashby, that you look inside the armoire for the Christmas bell."

"Oh." She skirted to the tall piece of furniture with glass inlays. "What a good idea, my lord."

Henrietta opened one of the glass doors and poked around the shelves, behind the assortment of trinkets.

"You've a parched throat, Miss Ashby?

The fine hairs on the back of her neck spiked.

Sebastian was approaching. She could hear the soft click of his boots, smell the very masculine scent of him grow near.

"I hope you didn't catch chill while you were ice skating," he said.

Confident in Madam Jacqueline's training, Henrietta assured herself she could do this; she could get Ravenswood to kiss her—on the lips this time.

"It's just a little tickle. I'll be fine, Ravenswood."

Shifting through the precious heirlooms in the armoire, she ignored the loud thudding of her heart to ask, "How did you sleep, my lord?"

"Not a wink, I'm afraid."

He was beside her now. She sniffed the spicy scent of cologne. Oh, it wasn't fair to her senses that the man should look, sound, smell so sinfully delicious! It made her attempt at seduction all the more grueling, with the distraction he imposed.

"I'm sorry to hear that, my lord."

"Are you really, Miss Ashby?"

"Why, of course, Ravenswood." She peered behind a figurine. "We are friends, you and I. And friends always want what's best for each other."

"Hmmm."

His warm breath tickled the soft hairs by her ear, making her shiver.

"About our friendship, Miss Ashby?"

Henrietta stopped searching through the armoire and looked at him. "Yes, Ravenswood?"

A storm raged in his sea blue eyes. "Do you really think we can be friends?"

The deep rumble of his voice did very pleasant things to her, arousing things. But she stifled her growing passion to respond, "Indeed, Ravenswood. Why do you ask?"

She was careful to match his low tone, to mimic the brewing desire reflecting in his watery gaze.

"I remember the first time we met, Miss Ashby."

Unfortunately, so did Henrietta. "At Peter and Penelope's engagement party?"

"That's right. You were too young to attend the celebration."

"Yes, I remember," she murmured. "Mama had ordered me to bed."

"But you did not obey."

Henrietta shrugged. "It was a spectacular event. I *had* to see it for myself."

"You almost broke your neck."

"Rot! It was just a little tumble."

But it wasn't *that* little a tumble. Henrietta thought back to that both magical and disastrous night. She had crouched by the top of the stairs, peering below at the dashing guests streaming into the house. And then *he* had entered the main hall, decked in dapper garb of sinister black.

A peculiar spasm had gripped her heart. An omen really, telling her the viscount was special among all the rest. And to get a better look at him, she had poked her head around the banister . . . and lost her footing.

Like tumbleweed, she'd rolled down the steps and landed right at Ravenswood's feet. What a mortification!

"You were fortunate to have survived the accident, Miss Ashby."

"My backside was a bit sore, is all."

But upon mention of her sore backside, something dark, ravenous even, sparked in Sebastian's eyes. A rather naughty look that Henrietta quite liked.

"Why do you bring up the past, Ravenswood?"

"It's just that we've known each other for so long, Miss Ashby. I think of you as my—"

"Rubbish, Ravenswood." She moved closer to him, wanting to slay the pestering thought before it took root. She was *not* his sister. She was his soul mate. And she was going to make the dratted man realize it in a matter of seconds. "Our years together will only strengthen our friendship."

"Will they?"

Henrietta tensed. He touched her cheek with the pad of his thumb, stroking. Her lashes fluttered under his tender regard; her breath hitched.

"They will," she whispered softly. "I promise. Trust me."

His thumb moved to her lips, grazing the swelling flesh in light wisps.

Henrietta could see it in his eyes, his need to taste her. She had a similar longing. It burned and thundered in her veins, the desire to press her mouth to his lush lips.

Her carefully orchestrated seduction was slowly unraveling. She was not supposed to falter under his mesmerizing stare, but the deeper she delved into the glossy wet pools, the heavier she breathed—and the more she thrust her body forward, aching for his touch.

Fingers trembling, Sebastian lowered his head, and breathed, "Henry."

Sweat pooled at the base of her spine, gathered under her breasts. She closed her eyes, her heart throbbing, and parted her lips.

"There you are, Ravenswood!"

Reeling, Henrietta smacked her head against the open glass door of the armoire. She clutched her breast in an attempt to quell her rampant heart-beats.

Ravenswood looked no less harried, combing a shaky hand through his curly mane, nostrils flaring.

Penelope and Roselyn flanked the viscount, each hooking a hand—perhaps "claw" was a better word?—around his arm.

Penelope flashed a dazzling smile. "We've come to escort you to luncheon, Ravenswood."

"The Christmas bell's been found," said Roselyn. "It was hiding in the kitchen, by the fire. One of the hounds must have put it there."

And so Ravenswood was snatched away, like a

hapless mortal kidnapped by mischievous faeries.

Henrietta could do naught but stare after him, willing her heart to stay lodged in her breast. Heavens, what a fright! She bloody well had to remember to lock the door next time she tried to kiss Ravenswood.

"Come, Henry!" Penelope sang from the doorway. "Luncheon awaits."

Henrietta scowled at her sister. So close. She had come so close to tasting Sebastian's sweet lips.

Drat!

Chapter 11

Sebastian stood by the library window, staring into the black beyond. Insomnia plagued him. He'd not nabbed a wink of sleep since his arrival four days ago. And it was getting to him, the restlessness. He thought of Henrietta more and more. In very ungentlemanly ways.

Snowflakes flicked across the pane of glass, a mesmerizing flurry. He watched the little white dots dance and whirl, trying to banish the image of Henrietta from his mind. But the willful chit refused to go. She pouted her lips at him, so flush, so tempting to taste.

Sebastian moved away from the window. With a disgruntled growl, he poured himself another glass of port. Dash it! Trapped in a house with a family to drive one mad. First the peculiar Miss Ashby teased and tantalized his senses. Now her sisters behaved in the most baffling manner, peppering him with idle questions, following him around the house.

Sebastian rubbed his brow. Twelfth Night seemed an eon away.

The creaking hinges disrupted the viscount's musings.

"Forgive me, my lord. I didn't mean to disturb your privacy."

Sebastian bristled. She was stunning. Billowing russet red locks glowed in the firelight, hugging the curves of her shoulders, her breasts, her well-rounded hips. She was dressed for bed in a flimsy night rail, butter yellow in hue, tucked beneath a thick woolly wrapper. Such a wild temptress, exposing a scandalous patch of skin: her bare toes!

"What the devil are you doing here, Miss Ashby?"

Sebastian was having a deuced hard time purging the whimsical chit from his thoughts without her prancing about so scantily attired. Not that he was in a more fitting form of dress, clad in breeches and a wrinkled linen shirt. Why, the two of them looked ready for a night of passionate lovemaking.

Bloody hell.

She stepped deeper into the library, her voice smoky. "I could ask you the same question, my lord."

He perused her supple figure. Even beneath the bulky wrapper, her curvy form was evident.

Sebastian gritted his teeth, tamping the wanton stirrings in his belly. But it was hard to dismiss the chit's plump and oh-so-provocative curves. His fingers burned to trace the shapely outline of her figure, to divest her of that woolly wrapper . . .

"I couldn't sleep," he said, a bit strangled.

"Neither could I." Sashaying over to the bookcase, she skimmed her fingertips along the leather-bound volumes. "I've come to fetch a tome. Some light reading might help put me to sleep."

Staring at her delectable arse was definitely *not* going to put him to sleep, so Sebastian set his port aside and made a move toward the door. "I will leave you to your book reading, Miss Ashby."

She whirled around. "No!"

He quirked a brow. "No?"

"I mean, please don't leave on my account."

He made a curt bow. "Good night, Miss Ashby."

"Ravenswood—ouch. Dash it!"

His heart pinched at her cry of distress.

Quickly he turned around to find her clutching the back of a chair for support, her expression pained.

He hastened to her side. "Miss Ashby, are you all right?"

"I'm fine," she gritted out. "Just stubbed my toe on the chair leg."

"Come here, you foolish girl." He moved to her side and scooped her in his arms. Blast it! Did she have to feel so devilishly good against him?

Tamping the snarling hound of lust in his belly, Sebastian whisked her over to the settee and set her down.

He knelt beside her. "Let me have a look."

He captured her foot in his palm. It was such a small foot. A wonder it could cause her so much pain.

He stroked the big toe, swelling slightly. "Can you wiggle it?"

Chewing on her bottom lip, she said, "I think so."

The toe twitched

"It's not broken." He let go of her foot, for it was causing him an absurd amount of pleasure to touch her in such an intimate place. "Where are your slippers, Miss Ashby?"

"I couldn't find the pair. It was dark in my room."

"Of course it was dark." He glanced at the mantel clock. "It's well after midnight. Why didn't you summon your maid?"

She snorted. "And wake the poor girl at this hour?"

"It's the girl's duty, Miss Ashby, to serve you and your whimsical needs. That's why you pay her."

"There's nothing whimsical about my getting a book to read."

"It's very whimsical when you insist on traipsing through the house at such an ungodly hour."

She sniffed in defiance.

He glowered at her. "Well, Miss Ashby, after a *sensible*, barefooted jaunt to the library, how do you intend to return to your room? You can hardly walk."

And *he* wasn't going to carry her. The three steps

to the settee he'd taken with Henrietta in his arms
had stirred a fire in his belly he was still struggling
to douse. Carting her through the house was going
to leave him a pile of cinder before he ever reached
the chit's room.

"Then I shan't go back," she said.

Up went a dark sable brow. "Oh?"

"I'll just stay here for the night."

"In the library? Alone?"

"Any why not?"

"I can think of one very good reason," he growled.

"Such as?"

"Such as an aghast footman stumbling upon you
in the morning. You're half dressed, Miss Ashby."

"Rubbish." She fluffed her wrapper, a bit more of
her flimsy night rail peeking through the part in the
woolly fabric.

The muscles in his groin hardened.

Sebastian tried not to look at the delicate arch of
her ankles and the soft swell of her calves, both vis-
ible through the translucent shift, but the wicked
rogue within him was adamant about taking in the
provocative sight.

"I just need a blanket and I'll be fine," she said.

He blinked, dispelling the vision of her wanton
legs. "And I suppose the duty falls upon me to fetch
you that blanket? While your maid sleeps soundly
away?"

Her lashes fluttered. "Would you mind, my lord?"

He pressed his lips together. The little hoyden always flirted with impropriety. Was she really going to stretch out on the settee in her undergarments? Blast it! Of course she was. She was just the kind of rash chit to do such a thing. At least a blanket would cover her dainty toes.

Disgruntled, Sebastian hoisted himself to his feet. He spotted a coverlet across the room, draped over a chair back, and set out to recover it.

He returned to the settee.

"Thank you, my lord."

He unfurled the blanket and draped it across her form, sorry to see so many delectable curves disappear. No! He was not sorry to see the curves covered. He was grateful to be spared from further temptation. Really, he was.

"You're welcome, Miss Ashby."

She clasped her hands together in her lap. "Will you fetch me a book, Ravenswood?"

"You still want to read?"

"A little, yes."

He sighed and headed for the bookcase. The girl was making him restless. He itched to touch her. To peek under that woolly wrapper . . .

Sebastian took in a deep breath. He was a bloody fool.

He reached the bookcase. "Anything in particular, Miss Ashby?"

"Shakespeare."

His finger paused on a tome. "You read Shake-speare?"

"Voraciously."

He located *Sonnets* and pulled it from the shelf. "Really?"

"You look surprised, Ravenswood."

"I admit, I am, Miss Ashby." He moved back to her side and handed her the volume. "It was years ago, but I remember the family attending a production of *Hamlet* at the theater." He crouched beside her again. "And you very loudly proclaiming: 'Shakespeare is a dull, old wart.'"

Even in the dimly lit room, he noted the blush dusting her cheeks.

"I'm afraid your memory is a little rusty," she said. "It must have been one of my sisters."

"Perhaps you're right, Miss Ashby," he murmured. "Enjoy your reading. I hope it brings you sweet dreams."

She clasped his hand. "Will you read it to me?"

Sebastian stared at the elfin fingers caressing his meaty palm. Such soft fingers, stirring the heat in his belly with each deliberate caress.

He shuddered.

"Please, Ravenswood." Her forefinger whisked across his knuckles in faerie strokes. "Be a dear friend and read a little to me?"

Thoughts deserted him. He could not come up with an excuse to refuse her request.

How the devil did he keep finding himself in these predicaments?

"Very well, Miss Ashby." He sighed and collected a nearby chair. He took the book from her hand and opened it to a random page. " 'My love is as a fever, longing still . . .' " Sebastian closed the book. "On second thought, I don't think this is a very good idea."

"Rot, Ravenswood!"

"Really, Miss Ashby, I should go." He set the book aside. "It's late."

She placed her hand on his knee this time. "Ravenswood, is something the matter?"

Yes! The wrapper had parted the moment she'd leaned forward, exposing even more of the fluffy night rail—and the plump swell of one breast. Funny how he'd never noticed her breasts before, always shoved together in a confining corset. But now the drop and natural curve of the supple flesh seemed so enticing. His fingers twitched to part the wrapper even more; to mold the lush breast to his hand.

"Well, Ravenswood?"

Henrietta started to rub his knee, deft strokes exciting the rogue within him.

He gripped her hand with the intent to remove it from his leg, but he squeezed it instead. Not hard. A firm hold to make sure she couldn't pull away. And then he did the most ridiculous thing: he brought her wrist to his lips and kissed it.

Chapter 12

Henrietta didn't want to move the seduction along too quickly. It was a risky move, for she might frighten Sebastian away. But with four sisters threatening to devastate all her plans, she didn't have a choice in the matter. Time alone with Ravenswood was precious, and she had to make every private moment count.

And so she'd intended to put to good use one of Madam Jacqueline's seduction tips: if all else fails, feign injury. A man can never resist rescuing a damsel in distress. Only, in her haste to stop Ravenswood from leaving the library, Henrietta really *had* stubbed her toe.

But despite the pain throbbing in her foot, a different kind of throbbing gripped her heart . . . her loins.

With bated breath, Henrietta watched Sebastian lift her wrist to his lips. She thought her heart would stop, the anticipation was so great.

And when his warm mouth tickled her skin, sending shudders of pure delight scampering along her limbs, she closed her eyes and sighed in total fulfillment.

Soft lips moved over her wrist in feathery kisses. He flicked his tongue over her thumping pulse, then gently sucked at the sensitive spot, making her shiver and coo.

He was doing to her what she had done to him the other night. And he was very good at it! Henrietta ached inside to hold him. So many years of longing had culminated in this erotic moment. But Sebastian was determined to be a tease.

Slowly he pushed up the sleeve of her wrapper, pressing kiss after warm kiss to each patch of skin he uncovered.

When he reached the hollow of her elbow, and his dark locks grazed her tender breast, her heart thundered even more, the wild beats deafening echoes in her ears.

"Ravenswood," she whispered, and stroked his curly black hair, beckoning him closer.

He obliged her.

Shifting from the chair, he moved to the edge of the settee.

The dark fire in his eyes forewarned of heady passion. Her sisters had advised her he was a dangerous man. But Henrietta was too aroused to quail under the viscount's scorching look. Besides, she trusted the man. However much he desired her, he would never hurt her. She was faithful in her belief.

Sebastian trailed a finger along the parting in her wrapper, widening the woolly garment.

Her breathing deepened.

"You're not a little girl anymore, are you, Henry?"

He whispered the words, a dark timbre.

Henrietta placed her palm over his hand, and in a shaky voice said, "No, Ravenswood, I'm not."

She pushed his hand to her beating heart, the swell of her breast fitting into his large palm.

He lifted his eyes, such a stormy pair of eyes. "Do you want me to touch you here, Henry?"

Henrietta was having a devilishly hard time keeping her voice steady. Months of training with Madam Jacqueline had prepared her to flirt, but she'd yet to feel a man's hand on her body. That Ravenswood was the first to caress her in such an intimate way made the moment all the more wonderful—and made her all the more giddy.

"Yes," she whispered, taking in a shuddering breath. "Touch me."

His fingers splayed to take in the entire mound of her breast. He cupped the flesh in his sturdy palm, and gently squeezed.

Henrietta closed her eyes and dipped her head back, thrusting even more of her aching breast into his masterful touch.

Heavens, what a delicious torment!

"Oh, Ravenswood," she breathed, her nipple puckering under his languorous caress. "Don't stop."

Sebastian kissed her throat, the spicy scent of him filling her lungs.

"Say my name, Henry."

She gasped when he nipped at her neck, then soothed the bite with the flick of his hot tongue.

Henrietta shivered. "Kiss me."

He lifted his lips to graze hers ever so softly. "That's blackmail, Henry."

"A fair trade," she whispered instead, breathless.

Pulse throbbing, Henrietta waited for his reply.

Sebastian delved deep into her eyes, probing. His fingers still rubbed her breast in tantalizing motions, making her head spin and her belly dance. But it was a kiss on the lips she wanted more than anything else in the world.

His hand moved away from her breast. "Say my name first."

Henrietta wanted to whimper at the loss of his balmy touch, but she soon sucked in a sharp breath when his hand started to rove to other more intimate places.

Sweat gathered between her breasts, her knees trembled, as he slipped his hand beneath the blanket and under her night rail.

The rogue!

Henrietta stared, mesmerized by the hand rubbing along her leg.

"Say it, Henry."

Robust fingers caressed her calf, making the blood pound in her head—and other places, too.

The flesh between her legs started to throb. A moist heat gathered at her apex. Henrietta didn't want to say his name. She was more curious to see where his hand was going to end up.

He nuzzled her cheek. "Say my name, Henry."

Her lashes fluttered at the heady sound of him.

But she quickly cried out at the sudden firm pressure between her legs.

She trembled and ached under the deft strokes of his thick fingers tickling and teasing the oh-so-sensitive folds of flesh.

"Say it, Henry," he beseeched again. "Say my name."

A finger slipped deep inside her wet passage.

"Oh, Sebastian!"

She almost choked on the words, the pleasure was so intense.

He kissed her then. A hard kiss that pinched her breath and made her dizzy with delight.

Moisture pooled in her eyes, between her fingers. She cupped his cheeks in fervid desire, drinking in the rich taste of him, the spicy scent of him.

"Say it again," he breathed, and thrust a second finger inside her wet passage.

She groaned. "Sebastian."

"And again," he said roughly, pumping his fingers deep inside her, kissing her between commands.

She sensed he wanted her to make up for all the

times she'd called him by his title. And she would gladly oblige him.

"Sebastian!" she cried again, and again, and again.

Between hot kisses and wanton strokes, Henrietta sensed a deep, thrumming tension winding in her belly. The pressure was so great, demanding release, she wanted to scream. She didn't dare, though. Instead she groaned, telling Sebastian she was on fire, that she needed to be doused.

Blessedly, his fingers worked their magic.

The muscles in her womb shuddered, the spastic pulses taking away the tight knot of thrumming need, dazzling her senses.

Henrietta couldn't move. She was a blissful lump on the settee, so sated, so full of joy.

Sebastian didn't seem able to stir much, either. And it was a long, breathless while before either one of them could say a word.

He kissed the tip of her nose softly. "I think you owe me something, Henry."

Dazed, Henrietta said, "Thank you?"

He chuckled. A deep, rumbling sound that made her feel all fuzzy and warm.

"I appreciate the gesture, Henry, but it's not what I had in mind."

She wrinkled her brow. "Then what?"

He gave her a roguish smile. "I do believe you owe me your baby toe."

"Oh." She *had* made that promise the night of

Papa's masquerade ball, hadn't she? Well, if the man wanted her toe, he deserved it. She stuck her bare foot out from under the blanket. "Take it. It's yours."

He looked at the foot, bent down, and kissed the baby toe.

Henrietta smiled, devilishly pleased with his romantic gesture.

"Come." He scooped her up in his arms, blanket and all, and collected a candle. "I'll take you back to your room."

With a sigh of contentment, Henrietta rested her head against the groove of his neck and closed her eyes.

It'd been perfect, the kiss. Everything she had ever dreamed. She was now surer than ever that Ravenswood was her mate in life. And after tonight's passionate encounter, she was just as sure he'd ask for her hand before Twelfth Night.

Chapter 13

～～∽⌒∽～～

Sebastian set the light aside before he placed Henrietta on the bed. In the sultry shadows she looked a wanton sight. Hair rumpled. Eyes moist. Lips plump, still swollen after a sinfully delightful kiss.

His body throbbed with impotent lust. He ached to touch her; to finish what they'd started in the library. But he fisted his palms instead. He couldn't ruin the chit. He'd have to marry her then. And he damn well wasn't going to do that!

He bent down to buss her brow. "Good night, Henry."

She cupped his face in her soft palms and squeezed. "You don't have to go, Sebastian."

He was tempted. So very tempted by her seductive offer.

It baffled him, the intensity of his desire for her. He was a jaded wastrel. How could an innocent flower bewitch him so? There was something about Henrietta that inflamed the darkest recess of his soul. Her innocent beauty, her goodness, engaged him. Made the rogue within him stand up and take notice.

Sebastian settled on the bed beside her. He stroked the long and silky strands of her auburn hair scattered across the bedspread. In the candlelight, the russet locks glowed like the fiery streaks of a sunset. Her eyes, too, blazed in the smoldering light, perusing him with heady passion.

"You're so beautiful, Henry."

She lifted her lips to his. "So are you." And kissed him softly.

Sebastian closed his eyes with a faint groan. He slipped his hand beneath her head to support her, fingers curled in her rich mane, giving her freedom to ravish his mouth. She tasted so sweet, a lemon-scented, soapy perfume. He breathed in the citrus fragrance, let it tease and enchant his senses.

"So beautiful," he breathed against her lips. "So good."

She opened her mouth for him. He slipped his wicked tongue between her teeth, stroking her. And when she moaned, a deep, feral moan, blood rushed through his veins, pulsed in his head, and pounded in his groin.

"Oh, Sebastian."

He deepened the kiss. He wasn't going to bed the girl. Really, he wasn't. He'd bring the kiss to surcease. Soon. He just wanted to taste her a little longer; to feel the warmth of her body. It both soothed his soul and rankled his lust, to have her pressed beneath him, writhing in sensual pleasure.

"Touch me," she bade.

Sebastian groaned again. Did she have to sound so sexy, his little despot? How was he supposed to wrest himself away from her if she beckoned—ordered—him to touch her? He damn well couldn't resist such a sultry invitation. And he was beginning to think she knew it.

Enchanted by the bewitching minx in his arms, Sebastian stroked her waist, rubbed her plump hip.

Henrietta cupped his hand and pushed it down. "Touch me lower, Sebastian."

The look of lust in her eyes made the blood pound in his cock. He was shaking, deuce it! Shaking like a virginal mooncalf. Henrietta was just so warm and sweet and so full of passion. He could stay in her arms forever. It was true bliss . . . It was a frightening thought.

Sebastian fixed his eyes on Henrietta's flushed features. He didn't dare look down, as she raked the train of her night rail over her knees. He'd lose every last ounce of resistance, he was sure. Instead he let her guide his hand to the moist crevice between her thighs; let her steer his fingers over the folds of her feminine flesh in any way that she wanted.

Sebastian dropped his brow to hers, pressed his lips to hers, breathing in the wanton sounds of her desire. He was sweating and trembling. He wanted nothing more than to tear the blasted shirt off his back, unfasten the buttons of his trousers, and slip between Henrietta's warm and creamy thighs.

"Henry, you vixen."

He kissed her hard, stroked the petal-soft skin between her legs at her behest.

The sweat dripped off his brow. He ached to bury himself deep inside her. It burned within him, the need to bed her.

In the passionate tussle, Sebastian's hand moved under her pillow—and knocked something hard.

He fingered the peculiar item. "What is this?"

Breathless with desire, but still curious, he yanked the heavy object from its hiding spot.

A book.

Henrietta reached for it. "No, Sebastian!"

In the struggle, the tome landed on the bedside rug—and opened.

Sebastian bristled.

There, under flickering candlelight, was an image of fornication.

Dazed, Sebastian sat up. Lust still raged in his groin, but the bewildering picture spread out at his feet captivated him.

He picked up the book and moved away from the bed. Taking in deep and steady breaths to soothe the desire in his belly, he leafed through the tome.

But erotic picture after erotic picture flipped before his eyes—and inflamed his passions even more.

"Where did you get this, Henry?"

She sat up, hair and wrapper rumpled, eyes wide.

She curled her legs under her chin, and pulled the blanket up to her knees. "Well, I . . . um . . ."

"Tell me!"

She flinched.

He quickly regretted his clipped tone. But devil take it, he was stunned. *What* was the girl doing with such a wanton tome?

"It was a gift," she said, breathless.

The lust still thrumming through his veins ebbed away, a simmering rage coursing through him instead.

"A gift?" A profound need to snap the impudent man's throat overwhelmed him. "From who? Tell me, Henry. Are you having an affair?"

"No!"

"Is he trying to seduce you? Give me his name. I'll kill him."

"There is no one, Sebastian. I swear."

He was breathing hard, ragged. "Then *who* gave you the book?"

"Madam Jacqueline."

She whispered the name. A woman's name.

Sebastian's mind raced. He had heard that name before. But where? And then it came to him. "The courtesan?"

Henrietta nodded.

"But why did you accept a gift from a prostitute?"

"You don't understand. I went to see Madam Jacqueline. I needed her help."

"For *what*?"

Silence.

"Out with it, Henry. Are you enceinte? Is that why you went to see the prostitute? To get rid of the babe?"

Her fists pounded on the bed. She hissed, "How dare you, you stubborn blackguard! You know there isn't anyone in the world I want, but you!"

It was a blow to the gut, the revelation. Sebastian looked back at the book; to a picture of a woman straddling a man, dominating him . . . seducing him.

Nonplussed, Sebastian lifted his gaze to Henrietta. She had studied the book. It was evident in her very manner. She had looked at the pictures, over and over again, dreaming up ways to bewitch him.

But still, she had refined her sexual allure in a short period of time. Even looking at sinful pictures was not enough to shape her seductive ways so quickly. She'd had a teacher.

His nostrils flared. "Tell me why you went to see Madam Jacqueline."

"Sebastian," she said more softly, "I needed her to teach me how to . . ."

"Say it, Henry!"

She huffed. "How to seduce you."

There it was, the dreaded truth.

"You tricked me," he breathed, even more bewildered. He had abandoned his home, drifted across the mainland for five months, all in the hope of breaking his bond with Henrietta. And *she* had plotted and schemed to seduce him the entire time he was away.

"No, Sebastian." She tossed the blanket aside and clambered to her knees. "I wanted to be with you. I just didn't know how else to get you to notice me."

He growled, "You mean you didn't know how else to trap me into marriage?"

A rush of memories flooded his head. It was all a ruse: her shapely hips and artful looks and whispered words. A bloody sham to enchant him. And she had risked her reputation, the fool girl, to learn the art of seduction. To leg-shackle him!

He slammed the book closed. "All that rubbish about friendship."

"But I did mean it, Sebastian. I *do* want to be your friend . . . and your lover."

He shuddered to hear her say the word "lover." She was a charming mess, her hair mussed, her wrapper askew. He could see the round curves of her breasts, her hips beneath the flimsy night rail. Such a titillating sight, designed to entice him. To trap him—the poor, wicked viscount—into matrimony with the one thing he couldn't resist: sex.

Disbelief roiled in his belly. Wretched grief, too. Henrietta had betrayed him. He'd believed her the last good soul on earth. What tripe! He should have known there was no such thing as an innocent heart. After all, he spent much of his time cloistered amid the dregs of humanity. He understood the fickle human heart, the wily will. And Henrietta was as devious as any other charlatan.

"You're just like all the other scheming flirts of the *ton*," he said.

"Sebastian, please." She crawled off the bed and limped to the bedpost, clutching it for support. "I did this for you."

He sneered, "For me?"

"Dash it, we belong together!"

"No, Henry, we do *not* belong together. We will *never* belong together."

She huffed. "Sebastian, I know you're angry, but listen to me."

He threw the book across the room. It collided with the fainting couch, the thud muffled.

"I've heard enough." He was fighting hard to keep his temper in check. One roaring word and he'd have the household at the door. Then he'd *have* to marry the conniving chit. "I'm leaving, Miss Ashby."

"Sebastian, wait!"

He thundered toward the door, opened it, then hastened into the corridor. It was late, so the passageway was deserted.

He headed for his room, his mind a whirl. He was such a bloody ass! How had he let the sly little chit beguile him like that? She had so wholly bewitched him, he'd kissed her after an eight-year hiatus. Slathered his lips over her, groped her, shoved his fingers in her . . .

Sebastian paused. He slumped against the cold wall and took in a sharp breath. He was a disgusting wretch. The girl might be a scheming flirt, but she was still an innocent. He had fingered the tightness of her sheath . . . and cupped the dewy folds of flesh at her apex, the moist curls.

He shuddered at the erotic memory, and pushed away from the wall. He should not have tainted the girl with his vile touch. He should not have put his hands or his filthy mouth on her. And he definitely shouldn't have enjoyed the encounter so much.

Sebastian raked a shaky hand through his tousled hair. He had to leave the house. Pack his bags and never look back. He would go to his club. Relieve himself there of the burdensome lust Henrietta had provoked. He was a fool for having touched the girl. But he was an even bigger fool for letting the scheming flirt charm him so.

"I will never forgive you for this, Henry."

Chapter 14

"**M**adam Jacqueline, I've ruined everything!"

Henrietta slumped against the cushioned divan, too distraught to even notice the courtesan was wearing her night rail and was still tucked away in bed.

Tears gathered in Henrietta's eyes. Sickness roiled in her belly. She'd not nabbed a wink of sleep, so troubled by last night's stormy row. The fury in Sebastian's eyes haunted her still. The hurt, too.

She had to set things right. She had to make Ravenswood understand she was not just another fawning young miss, looking for a brilliant match. She loved him, the blackguard! So much so, her heart ached at the thought of losing him.

"Good morning, Miss Ashby," said the courtesan.

It was a drab morning, so like the gloominess in Henrietta's heart. She looked up to say so, when she noticed the decor in the boudoir, all scarlet red in hue. Drapery . . . rugs . . . silk wallpapered walls. All red. And then there was the bed. A bright red satin bedspread with flowing chiffon curtains framing the four walnut posters. It was a big bed. And a small Madam Jacqueline was cozy under the covers, sitting up and reading a newspaper.

"I'm sorry," said Henrietta. "I didn't think you were still in bed. The footman assured me I could come right up to speak with you."

Madam folded the newspaper in her lap and put it aside. "You are welcome, Miss Ashby. Now tell me, what seems to be the trouble?"

Henrietta groaned, "Where to start?"

Madam Jacqueline patted the bed. "Come and sit by me."

Henrietta obeyed. She sat down at the foot of the bed, facing the courtesan.

Madam was draped in an elegant white night rail with rich embroidery. Her hair was hidden beneath a regal white turban, a brilliant diamond wedged snug in the center. The pale apparel only highlighted her eerie mist green eyes, which captivated Henrietta the moment she settled next to the woman.

"What's happened, Miss Ashby?"

"It's Sebastian," she sobbed. "He hates me."

It was a crushing blow to the breast, to say the words aloud.

Madam Jacqueline eyed her shrewdly. "Why do you think he hates you?"

Henrietta took in a shaky breath before she recited the entire wretched tale.

"If only he'd never found the naughty book of pictures," she said in closure, wiping the tears from her eyes.

The courtesan tsked. "I warned you not to be too zealous, Miss Ashby."

"I know," she said quietly. Ardent emotions frightened a man into retreat. So to find such a book in *her* room, to hear such a scandalous confession from *her* lips, that she had tried to seduce him, must have bowled Sebastian over. "How do I set things right, Madam Jacqueline?"

"Tell me, did Sebastian suspect you were seducing him before he found the book?"

"No, he looked so surprised when I told him."

"Then he is also very angry."

"Livid," said Henrietta, last night's row popping back into her head. She shivered at the morbid memory, so cold. Sebastian had never treated her so icily in all their years together. It was a terrible feeling, being cast aside like that. "I tried to apologize. I tried to make him see I wasn't out to snag his title, his fortune."

"But he doesn't believe you?"

"No." Henrietta bowed her head. "He thinks I'm just another scheming flirt out to trap him into matrimony."

"I'm afraid he's going to stay angry with you for

a very long time, Miss Ashby. He feels duped—by a woman. Most men find that humiliating."

Not the comforting words Henrietta was hoping to hear. "So I've lost him?"

"I wouldn't say that."

"Then there's hope?"

"You're going to have to apologize again."

"Oh, I'll say anything!" cried Henrietta. "Just tell me the right words to say."

The courtesan shook her head. "You can't tell him in person. He will slam the door in your face, I'm afraid."

Henrietta slumped her shoulders forward. "So how will I tell him?"

"In a letter." Madam Jacqueline pointed to the desk. "Go to the vanity and collect a sheet of paper and quill."

Henrietta scrambled off the bed and hurried over to the cherrywood furniture. She plopped down on the quilted stool, snatched a quill from the inkwell, and readied her hand.

"You must feel guilty," said Madam Jacqueline.

"Oh, I do," Henrietta vowed.

The courtesan waved her hand in a dismissive gesture. "It does not matter if you *really* feel guilty, Miss Ashby. You just have to sound like you do. You must also sound remorseful."

Henrietta nodded sagely.

"And you must inspire Sebastian to want to return to you; remind him of the night the two of you shared."

Yes, that's exactly what Henrietta wanted to do!

"Now I want you to write down every word I say," said Madam Jacqueline. "You will then deliver the letter to Sebastian and let *him* come to you when the time is right."

Henrietta hurried through the house, looking for Sebastian. The letter clutched tight in her hand, a snippet of hope bloomed in her breast at the thought that all was not lost after all.

At the end of the passageway was a set of steps—at the top of the landing was Peter.

Henrietta darted up the stairs, while Peter bounded down to her. The two met in the middle.

"Henry, I've been looking for you."

"I can't talk now, Peter." She brushed him aside. "I must find Ravenswood."

He gripped her arm, preventing her flight. "Henry, he's gone."

Her heart shuddered. "Gone where?"

"Back to London, I think. He left this morning in great haste."

She groaned, "Oh no."

"What happened, Henry?"

There was no sense in keeping the secret from Peter. He was her ally, after all. She might as well confess the horrible happening to him.

"I made a terrible blunder last night," she said.

He offered her a handkerchief, his voice gentle. "What blunder?"

She sniffed and dabbed at her eyes with the napkin. "I tried to seduce him, Peter, but I failed."

He balked. "My dear, that was a rather bold move."

She sniffed again. "But I've been practicing for months."

This time he really looked ashen. "Good heavens, Henry, how?"

The story about Madam Jacqueline poured forth: about Henrietta's transformation from fumbling novice to skilled seductress—well, perhaps not *that* skilled.

"Really?" Peter furrowed his brow. "But I never noticed a change in you."

"That's because I wanted to charm Sebastian, not you. You weren't supposed to notice anything different about me."

Peter took in a deep breath. "Well, we must find a way to right this matter."

Henrietta had already found such a way: the letter. But now she had to find Sebastian so she could deliver it to him.

With newfound determination, Henrietta gripped her skirts and mounted the steps again. There was a heart to mend. No sense whimpering when there was work to be done.

Peter fell in step behind her. "Where are you going, Henry?"

"To London."

"Oh no." He followed her back to her room. "It's too dangerous."

But Henrietta dismissed his concern and set about gathering her things: a few toiletries to accommodate her on the short journey to London. She wasn't going to stay in Town for very long. She was going to deliver the letter, and then head back to the country. She wasn't even going to meet with Sebastian. That was a definite faux pas, according to Madam Jacqueline. Henrietta was to slip the letter under Sebastian's door or deliver it to him via a third party. And then wait. Wait for Sebastian to read the letter. Wait for his temper to cool. Wait for him to come to her. That was the plan.

"I'll take my maid with me," she said to reassure her alarmed brother-in-law.

"Your maid will not protect you from highwaymen, Henry."

Henrietta dropped a small trunk on the bed, and then dumped the toiletries inside. "Fine. I'll take you with me to London instead."

"No, Henry, *I'll* go to London," he said in a firm voice. "Alone. You stay here where it's safe."

She paused to glare at him. "I thought you wanted me to be with your brother?"

"I do."

"Then why are you trying to keep us apart?"

"I'm not, Henry." He moved to the other side of the bed. "It's dangerous on the road. It's better if I go and talk with Seb."

Henrietta mulled that over. Perhaps she should ask Peter to deliver the letter instead? After all, Sebastian was very angry with her. It might be better if she steered clear of the city altogether.

But what if Peter lost the letter on the road? Or what if he forgot to give it to Sebastian once he reached London?

No, it was better if she delivered the letter. At least then she wouldn't wonder about the missive, and if Sebastian ever got it.

Henrietta shook her head. "I have to go to London, Peter. I have to set things right."

"But you'll never find him once you reach London."

"Rot." She stuffed a fur-trimmed hat into the trunk. "I know where he lives."

"He won't be home, Henry. I'm sure of it."

"Oh?" A pair of boots next. "And where will he be?"

Peter raked a hand through his sooty black hair. "There's this place on the Thames near Marlow, an abbey."

Henrietta cringed. "Oh no, Sebastian's going to become a monk! I never thought my seducing him would upset him *that* much." She tossed a dress into the trunk without a thought to the potential wrinkles. "I have to hurry!"

Peter lifted his hands. "No, Henry, he's not going to become a monk."

A fluttery sigh of relief. "Then what's he doing at the abbey?"

"Seb sometimes visits the abbey. It's . . . Oh, never mind. The point is, the friars are very strict. They will *not* permit a lady inside."

Henrietta snorted. She would just slip inside then. She'd been doing that a lot of late, sneaking in and out of houses to visit Madam Jacqueline. An abbey would be no different. She could slip the letter under Sebastian's cell door, then quickly skirt away. That would work just as well.

"Henry, stop." Peter reach over the bed and took her by the wrist. "You cannot go after Sebastian. Let me deal with my brother."

Henrietta was about to argue, but the stubborn gleam in Peter's eye reminded her so much of Sebastian.

After a lengthy pause, she huffed, "Oh, all right."

"Promise me, Henry, you will *not* chase after Sebastian."

She crossed her fingers behind her back. "I promise."

Chapter 15

Henrietta squished closer to her maid for warmth. She was on her way to the abbey to look for Ravenswood. It was dark out. And cold. There was a brick beneath her feet to keep her warm; she had stuck it in the kitchen fire before setting out on the jaunt. That had been hours ago. Wrapped in a bearskin blanket, she was also spared from the lashing wind, boxed inside the sleigh.

"Where are we going, Miss Ashby?"

Henrietta sighed. Her maid had an unfortunate tendency to fret too much. "I already told you, Jenny, to the outskirts of London."

"Are we going to see that woman again?"

Jenny had always referred to Madam Jacqueline as "that woman."

"No, Jenny, we're not. We're going to an abbey."

The girl sniffed, her nose runny. "But why?"

Henrietta handed her a kerchief. "I have to deliver a letter."

"To whom, Miss Ashby?" Jenny blew her nose in the kerchief.

"To someone important," she said softly.

Henrietta peered out the window, daydreaming. Even though it was dark, it wasn't very late. About half past four, she reckoned. Still, her family would be worried about her. She had left behind a missive to ease their troubled hearts, indicating she was off to visit a "friend," but was it enough?

It would have to be. Henrietta had to deliver the letter she clutched in her hands. She couldn't trust the post or Peter to be messenger. This was too important. She couldn't risk another blunder. She had to do this one thing herself. And she had to do it right if she wanted Sebastian to forgive her.

Would he forgive her?

A bereft part of her was not so sure. She had never seen Sebastian so filled with fury. What if she couldn't get his temper to cool? What if he was still furious with her even after he read the letter? What would she do then?

Pestering doubts! And Henrietta had the whole of the journey to suffer with them.

A few hours later, the sleigh slid to a stop.

Henrietta peeked outside the window.

It was a large abbey, Gothic in architecture, with spiked towers and hideous gargoyles. A row of trees framed the path leading to the abbey door, and a tall iron gate bordered the wooded property.

The abbey appeared to be deserted. There was no light flickering through the stained glass windows. But perhaps the friars had retired early to bed? She hoped so. It would make things much easier for her. She could sneak inside the abbey without disturbing anyone and deliver the letter.

"Wait here, Jenny."

The maid grabbed her forearm. "Miss Ashby, no!"

Henrietta patted her hand in a reassuring gesture. "Don't fret, Jenny. I won't be gone long. I promise."

"But—"

"Please, do as I say, Jenny."

The girl sighed. "Yes, Miss Ashby."

Henrietta bobbed her head. She gathered her gloves and stepped out of the sleigh.

The snow was crunchy beneath her boots. She slipped on her gloves and lifted her hood, even though the wind had died. There was still a light snowfall dusting the earth.

After she bid the driver to wait, Henrietta scooped up the sides of her skirts and trudged through the snow.

It was quiet outside, the night still. Only her footfalls filled the silence, each step disturbing the frosty snow beneath.

The gate was open. A boon, for she had not the dexterity to scale the sturdy iron fence.

Henrietta peeled back the door, the icy hinges

creaking. She winced. In the eerie calm it echoed like a ghostly cry.

Quickly, though, she moved through the gate and followed the snowy path to the abbey door.

The looming trees hovered above her; their twisted branches sagged with snow, shielding the sky and the land from sight. It was like moving through a tunnel, she reflected, and she shivered at the chilling darkness.

She hastened her steps. Above the abbey door was a stone carving with the motif: *Do as thou wilt*.

Odd. Not the religious greeting she was expecting. But Henrietta had not come to contemplate dogma. She reached for the door latch and was surprised to find it unlocked. Another boon.

She opened the door and stepped inside the dark entranceway.

This is too easy, she thought, apprehensive. She'd expected more resistance. Peter had vowed the friars were strict; they did *not* permit women inside the abbey. So why was the door unbarred?

Perhaps the friars had never dreamed a woman would be so brash as to enter the holy dwelling in the first place, hence they did not lock the door? Or perhaps the friars just forgot to lock the entrance?

Oh well. She needn't fret too much. She was inside the abbey. That was all that mattered.

Henrietta skirted inside the great hall. The distant hum of male voices snagged her attention. The cloistered monks must be having dinner. And Sebastian was with them, surely. Now how was she going to find his room?

She could always peek inside each of the cells, she supposed. If the friars were gathered for a feast, their rooms should be empty. Henrietta could just sneak from cell to cell, looking for Sebastian's things. After all, the friars weren't likely to have fine woolen breeches and gold-threaded waistcoats. It should be easy enough to spot Sebastian's fine apparel among the plain monk garb.

Henrietta moved about the hall, looking for doors or a passage that might lead to the friars' private rooms, but it was too dim to see anything.

She squinted, waiting for her eyes to adjust to the blackness. And just as a corridor came into view, more voices murmured outside the abbey door.

Panicked, Henrietta blindly dashed into a corner—and collided with a stone statue.

A bit breathless, she gathered her scattered wits and ducked behind the carved edifice, just before the door burst open.

Light streamed into the murky abbey.

Lantern in hand, an inebriated gentleman stumbled inside. A dandy of the highest order. And on each arm was a . . . nun?

Long black habits draped the giggling girls.

Girls?

Giggling?

Henrietta pinched her brow. What the devil was going on?

Eager for a better look, Henrietta eased out of her hiding spot and rested her palm on the cold, sleek surface of the icon for support.

She quickly recoiled, though. And it took a great effort indeed to keep from shrieking.

To her horror it was the smooth expanse of a woman's bare bottom!

Henrietta eyed the blasphemous image in the dwindling light. The woman was perched on her hands and knees, legs spread wide, posterior thrust in the air.

Henrietta pressed her gloved hand to her lips, aghast. She had seen this kind of image before, in her naughty book of pictures. But *what* was it doing in an abbey hall?

The trio of peculiar characters moved through the passageway, taking the sole source of light with them.

Something was terribly amiss. And Henrietta was determined to find out what it was. She intended to be covert about her snooping. And she still intended to deliver the letter . . . but first she wanted to understand what was going on.

Stifling her distress and rampant heartbeats, Henrietta scurried after the party, keeping a good length behind them. She maintained her clandestine presence, while moving through the abbey walls in search of answers.

Heavens, was Sebastian in *here*? Henrietta had deemed the abbey a refuge: a place of contemplation. But it was a strange and frightening haven. She had never been inside an abbey before, but she was sure it wasn't supposed to have naked statues and giggling nuns scurrying about. So perhaps it wasn't an abbey?

But if it wasn't an abbey, then what was it?

And why would Sebastian be here?

Pulse tapping, she skirted to the end of the corridor. There stood an entrance to an underground passage.

Chortling, the foxed troop stumbled down the steps.

Henrietta raked her teeth over her bottom lip. She was taking a mighty risk, following the group. Sebastian might see her. Perhaps she should just turn around and go back to looking for his room? Forget about the dark abyss beckoning below?

But a boisterous cackle drifted up the spiral passageway, and Henrietta was firmly fixed on the idea of snooping some more.

Alone in the dark, she stared at the gaping chasm for a bit, listening to the din of unruly guffaws coming from the depths of the abbey.

After a moment of reflection, she stepped forward, and pressed her hand to the rough stone wall for support. Just a quick peek, she told herself. A brief glance to see what all the hoopla was about, and then she'd get back to her task—delivering the letter. After all, Sebastian was a noble man, if a bit of a rogue. He had resisted her for many frustrating years! So he must have a good reason for being in such a chilling place. And just as soon as she found out what that reason was, she'd get back to mending their tattered relationship.

Henrietta made her way down the abyss. Torch-light flickered from the landing, revealing a narrow enclosure.

She adjusted her bleary vision to the illumina-tion, and soon spotted a rack of habits dangling from hooks along the wall. Quickly she confiscated a black robe and slipped it over her mantle.

Camouflaged, she felt a bit better about making her way through the underground catacombs. Even if she stumbled upon Sebastian, he wasn't likely to recognize her in the black robe.

As she moved through the dark tunnel, she re-flected upon Peter's words. It appeared Peter had been mistaken; ladies *were* permitted inside the ab-bey. Nuns, at least. But that did not explain the na-ked statue in the great hall.

Sucking in a deep breath to ease the tight knot in her belly, Henrietta sallied forth.

More statues lined the tunnel—clothed, thank heavens—their stone faces veiled, their lips stuffed with gauze. No eyes? No mouth? What did it mean? One wasn't to see, to speak of the abbey? Of the goings-on inside?

Wending through the tunnel, Henrietta followed the echo of spirited laughter. At the end of the passage, the hilarity boomed.

On the threshold of a great round hall, torchlight blazing, Henrietta placed her gloved hand to her mouth, stifling a horrified gasp.

Strapped to a long wood table was a woman—a naked woman!—her arms stretched high above her head, her legs spread wide.

Henrietta clutched her queasy belly. A terrible fright gripped her. The shackled woman didn't seem alarmed, though, even with a horde of masked and heckling misfits surrounding her, groping her. In truth, she was cackling right along with her besotted admirers.

Henrietta grabbed the wall for support, vertigo brushing over her. She stared, stunned, as the men poured wine over the naked woman, squeezed fruit juice over her belly, then lapped up the sticky contents, using the woman as a plate.

It was a ghastly sight.

Henrietta pressed her back against the wall, hiding in the shadows. She slunk through the arena, desperate to see Ravenswood, to understand why he was here among such madness.

"Well, hello, luv."

She bristled. Breath trapped in her throat. She

looked up to find a masked stranger, blond curls mussed, breath tainted with spirits, blocking her path.

"You're a pretty little nun," he breathed, stroking her trembling chin with his knuckle.

Like a fox cornered by a hound, Henrietta's heart pattered. Sweat gathered at her back, under her arms.

Purple plumes covered his face, all except his eyes: dark green eyes, ever so cold. He said with a spurious smile, "Perhaps we should put you on the banquet table next?"

Appalled by the very thought, Henrietta stomped on his foot.

He yelped.

She skirted around him, dashing across the arena. She had to find Sebastian. She had to get out of this disgusting place!

Henrietta darted into another dark tunnel, tempted to scream Sebastian's name and be done with it. To hell with Madam Jacqueline's rule; Henrietta didn't care anymore if Sebastian spotted her. She just wanted to get out of the catacombs—and to take the viscount with her.

But how the devil was she going to find him in this dark hell?

Moving through the unfamiliar tunnel, Henrietta cringed upon hearing so many rowdy voices behind so many closed doors. After months of perusing Madam Jacqueline's naughty book of pictures, it didn't take much to imagine what was going on behind the barriers.

Henrietta stilled.

She recognized that male voice!

Taking a few steps, she pressed her ear to one of the doors. Drat! Her pulse was thumping so loud in her head, she could scarcely hear the goings-on.

But she had to be sure.

Henrietta reached for the latch and opened the barrier just a tad.

Her belly lurched. An overwhelming nausea gripped her.

Sebastian stood in the room, eyes closed, head tossed back. He was fully clothed, but for his parted trouser flaps. At his feet was a woman—a nun!—taking him into her mouth.

Henrietta cried out.

Sebastian's head snapped up. *"Henry!"* he roared.

Henrietta staggered back, bumping into the damp wall. Sickness roiled in her belly. She quickly hiked up her skirts and dashed back through the tunnel, into the noisy arena.

"Henry, stop!" a voice boomed behind her.

Masked fiends grabbed at her as she struggled to make her way out of the arena, but they were too overcome with drink to stop her frantic flight.

Blinded by tears, Henrietta ripped the habit away. She stumbled back up the winding steps, desperate to get out of the gruesome catacombs, to be in the cool night air again.

But each footstep was weighed by the burden of her broken heart. She wanted to scream and pound the floor. To lash out in grief.

Henrietta found her way to the abbey door. She burst through it, into the winter night. She took one step, then two before the nausea overwhelmed her and she retched into the pure white snow.

Whimpering and bleary-eyed from fresh, hot tears, she staggered down the path, looking for the gate, her coach. She opened her mouth to call for Jenny, but a sob came out instead.

"Henry!"

She shuddered to hear him say her name. "Get away from me!"

Sebastian grabbed her, hugged her in his arms.

It was a miserable moment, to be in his hold. She had longed for him for so many years, yearned for his touch. Now she just wanted to get far away from him.

"What the devil are you doing here, Henry?"

"Me!" She squirmed in his embrace. "What are *you* doing here?"

"Don't evade the question." He gave her a shake. "Answer me."

"I came to give you this." She pushed the letter into his chest. He let her go and grabbed the missive. "I wanted to set things right between us, but I'm such a fool!"

"You shouldn't have come, Henry."

Icy breath escaped his lips, his nose.

He was angry.

She didn't care.

"What is this place?" she hissed, wiping the tears from her eyes.

"My club."

"Your club?" she sneered. "This is where you gather with your friends?" She pointed to the abbey. "What the hell kind of a place is this?"

"Just that, Henry, the Hellfire Club."

A vile name indeed. "You meet in an abbey?"

"Our founder had the abbey restored more than seventy years ago."

"This has been going on for *decades*?"

Years of debauchery. Years of fiendish pursuits. And Sebastian was a part of it all. He wallowed in the decadence, the depravity. He *liked* it!

The ache tore at her heart.

"Is this what you do for pleasure, Sebastian? Celebrate vice?"

He was silent.

"*Why?*" she cried.

He took a step toward her, shoved the letter in his pocket, then grabbed her by the arms again. "Some of us are born good, Henry, and some of us are born damned. I wasn't born good, and I'm not going to fight fate."

She gasped. "Rot!" She twisted her arm to break free of his hold. "You have a choice, Sebastian. You *don't* have to come here."

He let her loose; combed a shaky hand through his thick and wavy locks. "Henry—"

"Who are the men inside?" she demanded, tears burning her cheeks.

He was breathing hard. "Men like me, Henry."

"The *ton* you mean?" Throat sore from crying, she croaked, "And you bed *nuns*?"

"Not nuns, Henry. Doxies dressed like nuns."

So that was it. No *ladies* allowed, but doxies . . .

No wonder Peter had tried to stop her from coming. He'd wanted to spare her from the hideous sight of his ignoble brother.

"But where are the friars?" she said. "Peter told me there were friars."

"Peter?"

Henrietta sensed she had rankled him even more with the confession about his brother, but she was too grieved to care. She just wanted answers, hurtful as they might be. Her world was shattering before her eyes, but she still wanted more from Sebastian. She wanted more truth.

Sebastian took a moment of repose before admitting, "We are the friars."

"Oh, I see." She sniffed. "The 'friars' bed the 'nuns' in the abbey." It was enough to make her retch again, admitting the words aloud. "You're a fiend."

"I know, Henry."

But she didn't know. That was the wretched truth. For eight years she'd loved, even worshipped, a dream. Sebastian wasn't a gallant knight. He was a villain, just as her sisters had said. And *she* had adored him. Seduced him. Wanted to *marry* him!

Oh God, it hurt, the candor. It hurt so much she wanted to scream. He looked so formidable in the shadows. So wicked. So *un*like her Sebastian. The hero she had dreamed up in her head.

"I want you to stay away from me," she sobbed. "Don't ever come near me again!"

"I won't," he said quietly. "I promise."

Chapter 16

Sebastian made his way back down into the banquet hall. He grabbed a bottle of spirits. He didn't care what brand it was, so long as it was hard. Hard enough to numb the crushing pain throbbing in his chest. He popped the cork and guzzled the liquid fire.

It was over, Henrietta's infatuation with him. After eight long years, he had ground her girlhood fancy to dust. It was ironic, really. To shatter her whimsical dream, all he'd had to do was tell her the truth. Tell her he was a loathsome villain.

Sebastian settled in a chair and took another swig of brandy, trying to blot out the memory of Henrietta's briny tears from his mind. He had devastated the girl. A deuced shame. But what other choice had he had? He was a fiend. And Henrietta was an innocent and foolish girl.

True, she had tried to seduce him. But under the misguided belief that they were soul mates. What rot! It was better for the chit to learn the truth about his vile nature. She was still young. Only twenty. She had plenty of time to find herself another mate. A more suitable husband.

Sebastian quaffed the rest of the drink, let it burn his throat and fill his belly. Henrietta was going to be all right. She was a charming, pretty little chit. She'd have a plethora of beaux by next Season's end. She would forget all about him, he was sure.

Bloody spirits! Not working fast enough. A cutting pain speared his heart, pinched his lungs, making it hard to breathe.

Sebastian gripped his brow and rubbed his aching temples. There would be no more adoring looks, he mused. No more fanciful gestures or spirited laughter or passionate kisses. Soon Henrietta would belong to another man. Soon she'd shower her husband with devotion. And Sebastian would be dismissed from her thoughts like a bad dream.

Good riddance, really. At least he didn't need to pretend anymore. Pretend that he was some gallant knight to shield the chit from the truth about his wicked ways. He was free. Free to be the man he was always destined to be: a villain.

A disgusting villain who'd just squashed Henrietta's heart.

Blast it! What the devil had possessed the girl to come down here in the first place?

The letter.

Sebastian fumbled in his pocket, looking for the cursed piece of paper she had come to deliver. He found it in the silk lining of his coat, all crumpled up.

He unfurled the missive:

Dear Sebastian,

It grieves me terribly, the hurt that I have caused you. When I think of last night, the warmth of your breath on my lips, the rampant beats of both our hearts, I am filled with remorse at the thought of losing all that is good between us. Forgive me.

Yours,
Henry

Sebastian stared at the letter, the words sinking into his woozy brain. Memory of last night's passionate tussle in bed with Henrietta pounded in his head.

All that was good between them? Yes, it had been good. Achingly good. But the girl didn't want his forgiveness anymore. She didn't want anything to do with him, in truth. She was gone from his life. Forever.

Sebastian's vision started to fuzz. Thank God! He let the bright torchlight, the besotted friars, the moans of wenches all mix together in his head.

The movement and noise swirled before his bleary eyes, in his drowsy ears. He dropped his head back, beckoned the darkness to come, to stomp asunder the misery in his gut. But instead, the buzzing antics of a fustian pest bothered his senses.

"She was mine, Ravenswood." The chap slurred his words as he took a seat opposite Sebastian. "You'd no right to take her from me."

Sebastian lifted his head, trained his wavering eyes on the grating mooncalf. But all he could see was purple feathers.

"Who the devil are you?" snarled the viscount.

The mooncalf fumbled with the laces of his mask.

"Emerson," Sebastian gritted.

A young upstart, Emerson was the son of an earl. He had joined the Hellfire Club to obtain a notorious reputation—and thus ruffle his officious father's feathers. Perhaps he even wanted to send the earl into an early grave with the shock of his wicked ways?

Whatever the matter might be, it was all rot. Emerson infamous? He was a peevish misfit with an iniquitous cruel streak. He enjoyed the brutality of life. Seeing others suffer, that was, for Emerson was a coward himself, too timid to show his face more than half the time. Like the other friars in the club, he preferred to wear a mask to conceal his identity.

It was all bloody absurd in Sebastian's estimation. If one did not *really* enjoy ignominy, one should not join a society like the Hellfire Club. Wearing a mask was a timorous pretense.

"What the deuces are you talking about, Emerson? What woman?"

"The spirited little wench you just chased after."

Sebastian hardened.

"She was mine, Ravenswood." Emerson pointed to his chest. Missed. And poked himself in the throat. "I'd picked her."

"Picked her for what?" Sebastian growled.

Emerson garbled his words. "To be our next banquet, o'course. Mmm." He licked his lips. "She'd have made a tasty dish, strapped to the table—"

Gripped by a pounding fury, Sebastian shot out of his chair, fists swinging. But vertigo nearly plunked him back into his seat.

Emerson, meanwhile, toppled out of his chair, and scurried on hands and knees to get away from the ominous viscount.

Sebastian gathered his composure and set off after the little rabble-rouser, knocking chairs and tables out of the way.

The friars erupted in guffaws, clamoring, "Go get 'im, Ravenswood!"

Regaled by the spectacle, the friars didn't care about the root of the fight.

Emerson scrambled under the banquet table. It was a sturdy structure, too heavy for Sebastian to tip. Instead, the viscount stomped to the other side of and grabbed the crawling wastrel by the ankles.

Emerson let out another holler and kicked.

Sebastian, thoroughly foxed, lost his hold on the scalawag, who disappeared into one of the tunnels.

Beneath burning torchlight and a hail of guffaws,

Sebastian could feel the darkness clawing at his eyes. And why the devil was he chasing after Emerson again? He didn't remember anymore.

Staggering into a nearby tunnel, Sebastian stumbled into an empty cell and collapsed on the bed. The blood pounded in his ears. Darkness pounded on his head. And Sebastian welcomed the blackness with a blissful sigh.

Meanwhile, on the other side of the catacombs, a distraught Emerson had curled into a quiet corner, the stinging tears of humiliation burning his cheeks. He didn't have a contusion on his body, but the bruise to his ego was sore indeed.

The ring of laughter still echoed in his ears. The friars' sporting taunts. He was disgraced. He could never return to the Hellfire Club. And all because of that savage brute Ravenswood. Emerson didn't know what had set off the viscount, but he was determined to make the man suffer.

Dearly.

But how?

A scrap of paper caught the besotted Emerson's eye. The same scrap of paper Ravenswood had been reading before he'd stomped after him like an ogre. The viscount must have lost the letter in the fury of the chase. It was now wedged under a chair leg, fluttering in the cold catacomb breeze.

Too busy drinking and heckling, the friars didn't pay much mind to Emerson as he crawled discreetly back into the banquet hall and snatched the letter from its precarious spot.

Quickly Emerson skulked back into the tunnel, away from the bacchanal, and read the letter.

The words danced on the page. He was foxed. He had to concentrate hard to get the inscription to stay still and make some sort of sense.

After a few deep breaths and a hard stare, he deciphered the content.

A love note!

He scrolled further down the missive.

From a *man*!

Emerson had never suspected Ravenswood to be the type to consort with a man. Henry, was it? What a fabulous piece of *on-dit*! It would surely ruin the knave once word leaked out.

Emerson cast his wavering gaze over the crowd of inebriated friars. He tried to remember their names. Was there a Henry among the rowdy lot?

But wait . . . Ravenswood had chased after a chit earlier in the night. The very chit Emerson had wanted to strap to the banquet table. And hadn't Ravenswood called her . . . Henry?

Could Henry be a woman?

But who the devil would name a woman Henry?

Blast it! Emerson rubbed his throbbing temples. He'd had too much drink. He couldn't think straight.

But soon the name dawned on him. Henry . . . as in Henrietta Ashby, the eccentric daughter of Baron

Ashby. Society talk about the flamboyant family was abundant. Could she be the woman in the letter?

Emerson was going to find out. And then he would have his revenge. The daft chit was in love with the viscount—and Ravenswood wanted nothing to do with her. What a perfect form of punishment for the viscount, that he should be made to marry the very woman he loathed. Cleary the viscount was angry with the wench. Clearly he'd hate to be leg-shackled to her for the rest of his days. But what choice would he have once the scandal broke? She was the daughter of a baron; Ravenswood would have to save her reputation. And spend the rest of his life in misery.

Perfect.

Chapter 17

Wretched tears! Henrietta stumbled on the first step, her vision fuzzy. It was almost dawn. She had dismissed her maid to bed. Henrietta didn't want to bother with a bedtime ritual: brushing her hair, washing her face, divesting her clothes. She just wanted to get to her own room and bury herself under the bedcovers. She wanted to forget all about Sebastian; to lose herself to dream and stifle the smarting pain in her breast.

She gathered her skirts and mounted the stairs again.

"Henry!"

Henrietta ignored her brother-in-law. She was too distraught to chitchat now—especially with him. He had tried to *help* her woo Sebastian, knowing who his brother really was: a scoundrel.

"Leave me alone, Peter."

Peter bounded up the steps after her and grabbed her by the arm, curtailing her retreat. "Henry, I've been waiting for you to come home. You went after Seb, didn't you? Please tell me what happened. Did Seb hurt you?"

A sardonic chortle. "He only devastated my very belief in goodness."

Peter looked devastated himself. "Henry, I'm so sorry."

She jerked her arm away. "Why didn't you tell me, Peter?"

"Henry, I warned you not to go after him."

"No, I mean *why* didn't you tell me he was a fiend?"

He raked a hand through his dark curls and sighed. "I thought you could save him, Henry."

Tears blurred her vision. "He's a monster, Peter. And you didn't even warn me. You wanted me to *marry* him!"

"He's not all bad, Henry. Really, he's not. He just needs someone to care for; someone to care about him."

She pointed to her chest. "Well, it's not going to be me."

Henrietta scurried to the top of the stairs. She bumped into her eldest sister. Having heard the commotion, Penelope must have come out to investigate.

"What's going on?" Penelope glanced from her husband to Henrietta. "Henry, where have you been?"

Henrietta brushed past her sister and rushed into

her room. She flopped onto the bed and cuddled her pillow. But the heady musk of Ravenswood filled her nostrils, triggering a memory.

Last night she had snuggled with Sebastian in this very bed. She could still feel the warmth of his breath on her skin, feel the soft touch of his lips, see the smoldering look in his eyes. He had been so tender, yet passionate. So much like the hero she had dreamed about for *eight* long years.

Henrietta tossed the pillow across the room. For eight years she had loved an illusion. For eight years she had worshipped a devil. The ache in her belly infested her lungs, making it hard to breathe. What a miserable waste of time, of devotion. So much effort squandered on seducing a scoundrel!

She grabbed the bedcovers, buried her face in the fabric, and bumped her head against Madam Jacqueline's naughty book of pictures. In a fit of pique, she tossed that, too—under the bed. There it wouldn't cause anymore trouble.

Henrietta nestled against the bedspread again. But still the smell of Sebastian haunted her.

She let out a sob, tears burning her eyes. She was such a fool!

"Henry?"

Penelope stood in the doorway. In her wrapper, she looked drowsy, but there was still worry in her eyes—and sympathy.

Henrietta's bottom lip started to tremble. "You were right, Penelope. Ravenswood is nothing but a wicked rogue."

Penelope quickly crossed the threshold and clambered up onto the bed. "Come here, sweet."

Henrietta surrendered to her grief and slumped against her sister. Slender arms went around her in a tight hold, and Henrietta wailed into Penelope's breast until her throat ached. She didn't even notice the other hands that stroked her hair and caressed her back. Or the dip in the bed as three more sisters gathered around her for support. All Henrietta could feel was the throbbing ache in her chest: an ache she feared would never go away.

Henrietta stared at her reflection in the vanity mirror. She looked different. Older? She certainly felt different. Even the world around her had changed. Less bright. Less hopeful.

"Leave my hair down today, Jenny."

The chambermaid nodded. "Yes, Miss Ashby."

Jenny picked up the hairbrush and started to comb it through her mistress's hair. She tugged at the locks to unravel the knots.

Henrietta tried to unravel some knots, too. Knots in her heart. All sorts of distressing thoughts came to mind, consumed her concentration.

Thoughts of Sebastian.

He haunted her dreams, disturbed her waking

hours. She was determined to be rid of him; her heart was still clinging to him.

Foolish heart! When would it learn? The world wasn't filled with heroes and knights. It was peppered with villains and an assortment of worthy men. Henrietta had to sift through the lot of scoundrels to find one such worthy man. But whoever he might be, he was not Ravenswood.

Henrietta remembered the viscount in the catacombs—with a nun. A doxy, really, but still, the horror of it all filled her head, the painful recollection a smarting spasm on her heart.

She closed her eyes and took in a deep breath to quell the tears threatening to surge again. She wasn't going to waste a minute more pining over the villainous viscount. She had already lost her youth to the man. She would not lose a moment more of her future. She *was* going to find herself a more respectable husband, one worthy of her affection. She was not going to be lonely and cheerless for the rest of her days because of the ruthless Ravenswood. She was adamant about that!

The bedroom door opened.

Henrietta looked over her shoulder. "Good morning, Mama. I'll be ready for breakfast in just a minute."

Henrietta was late—as usual. But it was unlike the baroness to be so impatient about her tardiness. In fact, it was family tradition to start the meal without her. So why had Mama come to fetch her?

"Jenny, I would like to speak with my daughter—alone."

Jenny bobbed a curtsy. "Yes, my lady."

The maid set the hairbrush aside and quickly skirted from the room.

Henrietta watched the girl go, then returned her attention to her curious mother. "What's the matter, Mama? Why did you shoo Jenny from the room?"

The baroness entered the boudoir and closed the door softly behind her. "Because there are some things a servant should not hear."

Henrietta lifted a brow. "Such as?"

"Private things, Henry." The older woman moved deeper into the room. "Now, what sort of fabric would you like your wedding dress to be made from?"

Henrietta paled. "Wedding dress?"

"And lilies are your favorite bloom, are they not? I shall put in an order for a hundred lilies at the hot house. No, two hundred."

Henrietta started to feel dizzy. "Lilies?"

"Now let's talk about the wedding menu."

Alarmed, Henrietta grabbed her belly. "*What* wedding, Mama!"

With a very innocent air, the baroness quipped, "Why yours, Henry. Now don't dawdle. We have a lot to do before Twelfth Night."

"Twelfth Night!" Henrietta sailed out of her chair, her mind a whirl. "But the marriage license?"

"Being fetched as we speak."

The room was spinning. "Who am I marrying?"

"Your betrothed, of course . . . Viscount Ravenswood."

Henrietta grabbed the back of the chair for support. She had a very profound desire to sink to the floor and cry. "Mama, what's happening?"

"It's very simple, my dear. You've disgraced yourself and now you must pay the consequences."

Those blasted tears Henrietta was fighting to keep down bubbled to the tips of her lashes.

"Now don't blubber, Henry." The baroness sashayed over to the vanity and picked up a lacy kerchief. She shoved it under her daughter's nose. "We have to get back to the matter at hand. Shall we serve goose or duck at the wedding luncheon?"

"Mama, I . . ."

"Goose it is. Now how about the soup? Pheasant, perhaps?"

Henrietta twisted the kerchief around her finger. "I don't want to marry Ravenswood."

"You don't have a choice, Henry."

"But I—"

The baroness touched Henrietta's lips, silencing her. "Perhaps you did not hear me, Henry. You've made a spectacle of yourself. The whole Town is in a tizzy about the shameful letter you wrote to Ravenswood. You are ruined. Your father is ruined. I am ruined. Your sisters and their husbands and their children are ruined. And you are going to marry Ravenswood and make it right. Is that understood?"

A great welter of shame stormed Henrietta's breast. The letter! "You know about the letter?"

"Everybody knows about the letter."

Grief and rage swirled together in Henrietta's belly. That bastard, Ravenswood! He couldn't just devastate her foolish girlhood fancy, he had to devastate her very respectability, too, by showing the letter all over Town?

Bile filled her throat, constricted her airway. Henrietta rushed over to the window and pushed back the curtains.

Air! She needed air!

"Get ahold of yourself, Henry," the baroness chided. "We have to fix this blunder."

Henrietta pushed and pushed against the frozen pane of glass. She didn't care if she shattered the icy sheet. She needed air.

At last the casement parted. Cold winter air whooshed inside the room.

"Henry." The baroness hugged herself to ward off the chill. "Close that window at once!"

But Henrietta did no such thing. She stuck her head out the opening and inhaled the biting wind, wishing the cold could numb her heart and the fury in her belly.

"Henry, you'll catch your death!"

Henrietta didn't care. In truth, marriage to Sebastian would be a death of a sort. To be leg-shackled to that villain for the rest of her days? She would be forever miserable.

"Enough of the dramatics, Henry." The baroness marched over to the window, yanked her daughter back inside the room, and closed the glass. "You didn't think Ravenswood such a terrible match when you wrote him that letter."

"Mama, I—"

"I don't want to hear it, Henry. Oh, this is all your father's fault!" The baroness lifted her hands heavenward, as though in prayer, before she scooped up the side of her dress and flounced over to the hearth. "He reared you like a boy. But you are not a boy, Henry. You cannot act like one!"

"I know, Mama," she said quietly.

Lady Ashby made a noise of distress, rubbing her hands together before the snapping flames in the hearth. "Then *what* possessed you to write such an outrageous letter?"

"I thought . . ." Henrietta slowly dragged her feet over to the bed. She wrapped her arms around the bedpost and hugged the wood with all her might. "I thought he loved me, Mama. We had a fight. I thought if I wrote him the letter . . ."

"All would be well again?" The baroness huffed. "Well, you got your wish, Henry. You're going to be the next Viscountess Ravenswood."

Henrietta shivered at the title: a title she did

not want anymore. She remembered the promise Ravenswood had made to her the other night: the promise to stay away from her—forever. Hopeful, she said, "He won't marry me, Mama."

"He most certainly will," the baroness proclaimed in a very pompous voice, "or there's going to be a duel."

Henrietta gasped. The very thought of Ravenswood and Papa in an empty field in the wee hours of the morning had her heart fluttering in distress. "But Papa's a terrible shot!"

Lady Ashby pointed to her chest. "*I* would shoot him, Henry."

Henrietta supposed even a blackguard like Ravenswood would not duel with a woman, so there was no other way to settle the matter—she had to get married.

She sighed. "But Ravenswood doesn't care for me, Mama."

And Henrietta didn't care for him. He was a devil, through and through. Oh God, what had she done! She should never have written that letter. She should never have visited with Madam Jacqueline. She had made such a terrible mess of her life. And now she was going to pay for her foolery.

Rightly so, she supposed. Who else should suffer but her? It was all her doing, all her wretched fault. And now her family was tainted by the scandal, too. What choice did she have but to marry Ravenswood? She had to save the family name, the honor of her parents and sisters. And she could not marry another, more respectable gentleman. Who would want her now, after such a disgrace? She had to marry. And she had to marry Ravenswood.

"Whether Ravenswood cares for you or not is inconsequential. The deed is done, Henry. You'd best prepare yourself for the wedding."

Henrietta rested her brow against the bedpost, the horror of her dismal fate sinking into her brain. "Yes, Mama."

She was going to be Ravenswood's wife. A few days ago she would have been thrilled by the news, but today she was anything but. Just the thought of being the next Viscountess Ravenswood, sharing a home with the lecherous scoundrel, made her heart hurt. The rogue was going to spend his marital days at his fiendish club. He was not going to give up his wicked ways for her, she was sure.

And she would have to endure the humiliation of it all, the disgrace. Didn't the *ton* already whisper about his immoral pursuits? Her sisters had heard the ghastly rumors, so the gossip must be widespread. She was going to have to bear the snickers and the pity. And she was going to have to endure a daily reminder of her foolery. Each time she was with her husband, she would remember her childhood fancy: the noble hero she had invented in her head. And each time she would feel the shame of her silly girlhood dream.

The smarting pain in her chest made it hard to

breathe. She had hoped to forget all about Ravenswood, to banish the villain from her heart and soul. She had hoped to find a better, more respectable husband. But both hopes were now dashed to bits.

"I can't believe I'm getting married," said Henrietta.

"Yes, it was rather a shock to us all. Your poor father almost had an apoplexy when he heard the news."

"Oh no, Papa!" Henrietta dismissed her woe at once and rushed to the door, panic knocking on her breast. "Is he all right?"

"Hold it right there, Henry!"

Henrietta froze with her hand on the doorknob.

"Your father is napping and I don't want you to disturb him. It took me all morning to calm him down."

A wave of horrendous guilt washed over her. "Papa must loathe me."

"Loathe you?" The baroness snorted. "He adores you, Henry. He always will. He doesn't give a fig about the scandal."

Henrietta turned around to face her mother again. "Then why is he so upset?"

"Because you're getting married! Your papa believed you'd live the life of a spinster forever—with him. He's upset because he's losing you."

Henrietta simpered. "Then he doesn't hate me?"

"No, Henry. He doesn't hate you."

Relief filled Henrietta's heart. She had already

lost Ravenswood, the hero she had dreamed up in her heart. And if she had lost her papa's love, too, it would have been a blow she could not have withstood.

"Do you hate me, Mama?"

The baroness was quiet for a moment, then said, "No, Henry. I don't hate you. But I'm very angry with you."

Henrietta bowed her head in shame. "I understand, Mama."

Lady Ashby sighed and opened her arms. "Come here, child."

Henrietta rushed into her mother's embrace and sobbed.

"There now, Henry. It will be all right. You'll see."

But Henrietta knew those words could not be true. Ravenswood was a devil. He would make her miserable.

"Perhaps we should talk about the wedding night, Henry."

Her corset suddenly seemed too tight, and Henrietta took in a deep breath to settle her nerves. She didn't need any instruction about the wedding night. Madam Jacqueline had made sure of that. But an alarming thought just entered her head: she was going to be Ravenswood's wife—in every sense of the word. And the wicked scoundrel did have a delicious touch; she knew all about *that*, too.

Well, Henrietta would not tolerate it, his spicy touch. She would not let the rogue play with her heart—or her body. He might soon be her husband, but Sebastian could go to the devil. Their marriage would be in name only. Let the lascivious bounder rut about with the "nuns" at his club. He would *never* touch her again!

Chapter 18

~~~~~~~

Sebastian opened his eyes. The room was spinning. He shut his eyes with a groan, willing the nausea in his belly to go away.

It was a few minutes of steady breathing before he flicked open his lashes again. Squinting, he focused on the familiar red and gold drapes and embroidered coverlet.

He was home.

How the devil did he get here? Sebastian had no memory of the journey to his London town house.

Slowly he rolled to the edge of the bed and sat up. He cupped his brow in his hands, cradled his throbbing head. He was stiff and sore and dizzy.

But soon the murky fog in his brain started to lift. And he saw Henrietta. She was standing under the gnarled trees, her cheeks stained with tears.

"Shit," he hissed, the memory of last night storming his weary brain.

That fierce ache in his breast returned, too. A bottle of spirits had dulled the pain for a short time, but the heady charm of intoxication was starting to fade. Sober now, he was still haunted by the wretched grief in Henrietta's eyes.

Blast it! She was a conniving chit, remember? She had tried to seduce him; beguile him into matrimony. He should wring the woman's neck for pulling such a stunt, not wallow in stifling guilt.

Sebastian lifted his head to look around the dim room. It was morning. He could see the sunlight peeking through the part in the drapes. He could also sense another presence in the room.

Groggy, Sebastian scanned the shadows in the bedchamber.

Nothing moved.

He trained his fuzzy vision on the furniture once more. And then he saw it, the figure in the armchair, ensconced like a wraith.

Sebastian grunted. "I suppose I have you to thank for bringing me home?"

Peter didn't say anything. His face was covered by darkness.

Sebastian stared at his brother, fury clawing its way to the forefront of his thoughts. "And I suppose I have you to thank for telling Henrietta about the Hellfire Club?"

Sebastian could not hide the wrath from his voice. Had Peter not betrayed the location of the abbey, Henrietta would never have stumbled upon him in such a compromising position. She would never have learned the truth about him in such a vile manner. She was a scheming flirt, true. But she needn't have witnessed him with the doxy. It was an unnecessary hurt; it would forever haunt him—and he loathed feeling remorse. It was deuced uncomfortable. And he had his pestering younger brother to thank for everything.

"Say something, damn it!" Sebastian regretted his clipped tone. The pounding started in his head again, and he said with more temperance, "Don't just sit there."

Peter abandoned the armchair and crossed the room.

Before Sebastian could blink, Peter grabbed him by the front of his shirt, pushed him to the bed, and shoved his knee under Sebastian's chin. The viscount couldn't breathe or say a word.

"You miserable son of a bitch," Peter growled. "You just had to devastate Henry like that, didn't you? You're a black-hearted villain!"

Peter got off the bed and started to pace the room with quick, angry strides.

Wheezing, Sebastian shot up, ready to pound his impudent brother into the floorboards. But vertigo knocked him off balance, and he slumped to his knees instead.

"Look at you," Peter sneered. "You can't even stand. Is this how you want to spend the rest of your days? On your knees, in a drunken stupor?"

Crippled by a sharp pain in his head, Sebastian sucked in a deep breath, trying to stop the room from spinning before his eyes.

"And to think," said Peter, "I offered to help Henrietta win your heart."

"What?" Sebastian barked, winced at the cutting pain in his head, then whispered, "You bloody ass, you've been *helping* the chit seduce me?" He was going to kill his brother just as soon as he could stand. "Is that why you sent her to the abbey?"

"I didn't *send* her. I made the girl promise not to chase after you. She didn't listen, though."

Sebastian snorted. "Henry never listens."

"Yes, well, that might have been *my* mistake"—he pointed to his chest—"telling the girl about the abbey. But why did *you* have to ruin her?"

Sebastian sat on his heels, vertigo passing. "What the devil are you talking about?"

Peter threw up his arms. "The letter you so cruelly passed all over Town."

Sebastian must still be drunk, for he didn't think the words coming out of his brother's mouth were making any sense.

"What letter, damn it?"

Peter stopped pacing. "The love letter Henry wrote to you. You know, the one about your breath, your heart, and other such rot?"

A vague recollection filled Sebastian's murky brain. "You know about the letter?"

"The whole Town knows about the letter! How could you be so ruthless, Seb? How could you flaunt that letter all over the city?"

"That's horseshit, Peter! I would never flaunt such a letter. And you damn well know it!"

"Oh, really?" Peter quirked a brow. "So how does the *ton* know about the missive?"

"Damned if I know. But I have the blasted letter right here." Sebastian reached across the floor for his crumpled coat. He shoved his hand into the silky pocket and rummaged for the missive.

Empty.

"I did have it," Sebastian murmured.

"Well, now London's greatest gossips have it." Peter stalked across the room and flung open the heavy drapes.

Sebastian squinted at the blinding light.

Peter moved away from the window. "And Henrietta is ruined!"

Sebastian hardened. "What are you saying, Peter?"

He smiled, the daft man. "I'm offering to be the best man at your wedding, Seb."

Sebastian roared. "I will *not* marry the girl!" And right away the spasms started pounding in his head again.

Sebastian wanted to keel over and die.

"And why not?" demanded Peter.

"Because she tried to seduce me! Trick me into matrimony!"

Peter snorted. "Well, you didn't give her much choice in the matter, now did you?"

Sebastian blinked. He had not expected his brother to say that.

"You're stubborn, Seb. The girl was in love with you. You were acting the pigheaded fool, so what other choice did she have but to seduce you?"

Sebastian murmured, "I can't believe I'm hearing this."

"She risked everything, Seb, to be with you. She went to see a courtesan, for heaven's sake! She put her reputation in jeopardy, her very heart and soul. And all because she believed you were worth the risk."

"That was her foolish mistake."

"Do you really believe that, Seb? Or are you just being a stubborn ass?"

Sebastian growled. "Get out, Peter, before I wring your neck."

He scoffed. "Don't play bully with me, Seb. I'll match you growl for growl."

Devil take it, what was the matter with Peter? Always the more docile, accommodating brother, he rarely encouraged a confrontation. He certainly never started one!

Sebastian rubbed his aching brow. "What the deuce do you want from me, Peter?"

"Sober and hitched to Henrietta."

"That does it." Sebastian sprang to his feet, wavered, and hit the floor again, clutching his throbbing head. "Bloody hell."

Peter tsked. "Pull yourself together, Seb. The wedding will be on Twelfth Night."

"Like hell!"

"I'm off to fetch the marriage license myself."

Sebastian growled, "You treacherous son of a—"

"What are you afraid of, Seb?"

Sebastian glared at his pestering kin, moving around in circles. "Stand still, damn it!"

"I am," Peter said dryly.

Sebastian humphed.

"Well, Seb?"

Peter folded his arms across his chest. He looked so much like Father when he did that, all officious and stern. It sent a shiver down Sebastian's spine.

What the devil were they talking about again? "Well what, Peter?"

"*Why* are you afraid to be with Henrietta?"

"Rot!" He snorted. "She's a wily flirt and I *don't* want her for my wife. How do I know *she* didn't show that letter all over Town, just to trap me into marriage? She could have come back to the catacombs, after I'd passed out, and stolen the letter from my pocket."

Peter snorted. "I think I can assure you she did no such thing."

"I wouldn't put it past the devious chit . . . And why are *you* so sure she's innocent?"

Sebastian gripped the bed for support, struggling to stand. But he failed and dropped onto the mattress.

"Because the girl hates you." Peter walked over to the armchair and collected his gloves. "No one is happy about the approaching wedding, Seb. Least of all Henry. She did *not* orchestrate this scandal, I assure you."

Sebastian wasn't prepared for the stroke of pain that lashed across his chest at Peter's words.

Peter slipped on his gloves. "You made quite an impression on the girl at the abbey, I understand. She doesn't give a fig whether you live or die anymore. Bravo, brother! "

Despite the pang in his breast, Sebastian gritted, "Good."

"I'm glad you think so." Peter moved to collect his greatcoat. "Now about the wedding . . ."

"Blast it, I haven't agreed—"

"Are you really going to leave Henry in disgrace? Her whole family?"

Sebastian was sorely tempted to let the conniving chit stew in her own foolery, but deep down he knew he would never really leave her in ignominy. Angry as he was at the girl, he could not abandon her in shambles. He had known Henrietta for far too long to just desert her at such a grim point.

"She should never have written that silly letter," Sebastian grumbled.

"No, she shouldn't have, but the deed is done. I'll summon the tailor to get started on the wedding clothes."

Sebastian growled in defeat. "Blast it all to hell!"

"It's your life, Seb. If you're determined to be miserable, so be it."

"And what other choice do I have but to be miserable? I'm being forced to marry!"

"Yes, that's true." Peter slipped into his greatcoat. "The wedding is going to take place whether you like it or not, so that's why I suggest you make the best of it."

"And how do I do that?"

Peter picked up his top hat. "Well, perish the thought you try to get along with the girl—your betrothed."

"What a ghastly word."

"Well, here's another ghastly word for you, your soon-to-be mother-in-law is hosting an engagement party on New Year's Eve. You have four days to sober up and pull yourself together."

"Damn you all!"

"I love you, too, Seb. And I suggest you be on your best behavior. The Ashby family is very upset with you. You have a lot of kin to appease."

"Shit."

"Especially the sisters."

"Why especially?" Sebastian snapped.

"Well, the Ashby sisters were always dead set against you marrying Henrietta. Once they suspected you might be smitten with the girl, they were determined to tear the two of you apart."

Sebastian hissed, "Is that why her sisters were always fussing about?"

Peter nodded. "They wanted to make sure you never had a moment alone with Henry; that you never had a chance to disgrace the girl. Well, so much for that." Peter adjusted his top hat. "And then there's the baron."

"What about the baron?"

"He's quite miffed, Seb. You are stealing his 'darling boy' away, remember?"

Sebastian rubbed his tired brow.

"And then you have Lady Ashby to confront."

"Surely *she's* happy about the wedding. She's been hosting masquerade balls for years hoping to marry Henry off. Isn't she getting her wish?"

"Yes, but she could have done without the scandal."

Sebastian gnashed his teeth. "I'm *not* the one who caused the scandal."

"A trifling detail." Peter headed for the door. "The engagement party is in four days, remember. Clean yourself up and be prepared to pacify a lot of angry Ashbys."

Angry Ashbys? *He* should be the angry one. *He* was the one being carted down the aisle in bloody chains.

"Buck up, Seb." Peter opened the door. "Think of it this way: it's a new start to a new year."

Sebastian growled.

Peter left the room and closed the door behind him.

Sebastian, feeling dizzy again, stretched out on

the bed. He closed his eyes, willing the thrumming pain into submission.

Marriage.

To Henrietta.

The thick fog in his head was making it hard for the words to sink into his brain. And how the devil had the letter made its way around Town anyway?

He tried to think back, but his memories were awash in shadows and sounds and fuzzy faces. He remembered reading the letter, but then . . .

"Shit."

Sebastian stuffed his head under the pillow, for he had not the strength to get up and draw the drapes. He wanted to sleep, to disappear into the darkness of dream. He couldn't remember what had happened to the blasted letter after he'd read it. He didn't want to think about the cursed piece of paper anymore. He didn't want to think about the approaching wedding, either. Or his intended bride. He just wanted to sleep and forget about the nightmare his life had just become.

But something pinched his pinky finger.

Sebastian stuck his head out from under the pillow and squinted. The ring on his finger felt tight, his knuckles swollen. He must have gotten into some sort of row the other night; he couldn't remember. But it was the design on the ring that really captivated him. The interwoven rope, the knot.

He thought back to Christmas Eve, the night Henrietta had given him the ring as a gift. He remembered the enchanting look in her eyes, the spirited sound of her laughter. He remembered the scent of jasmine in her hair . . . and the sultry kiss under the mistletoe.

Something twitched in his belly at the lusty memory. And now the vixen was going to become his wife.

The door opened.

The housekeeper, Mrs. Molony, shuffled inside. Without so much as a "good morning," the stout woman set right to work on making the bed—around his sluggish body. So accustomed to his frequent binges, she did her domestic duty without complaint or hesitation.

Humming an Irish jig as she fluffed the pillows around his head, she suddenly paused.

"When did you start believing in Irish folklore, m'lord?"

Baffled, Sebastian lifted his groggy head. "What the deuce are you talking about, Mrs. Molony?"

"The ring." She pointed to the bauble on his finger. "It's got a Celtic love knot."

Sebastian eyed the ring again. "It does?"

"Aye." Mrs. Molony moved about the room. She gathered the vest, the coat crumpled on the floor. "According to Irish lore, he who wears the charm will attract his one true love." The housekeeper lifted a curious gray brow. "And who might you be trying to attract, m'lord?"

But she didn't really want an answer. Having had

the pleasure of ruffling his surly feathers, she gathered the laundry and was out the door.

Sebastian glared at the shiny ring on his finger. Henrietta, the devious chit! She had given him a Celtic love knot.

He should not be surprised by her trickery. She was a skilled seductress. And she was going to be his wife. He was going to have to live with her feminine wiles for the rest of his days. He should be outraged. A part of him was. But another part of him was not so incensed. Marriage did afford him *one* pleasure, he mused.

Buck up? Oh, Sebastian intended to do that very thing. He intended to enjoy Henrietta very much—in his bed.

Chapter 19

⟨ ─────⟩⟨ ────⟩

The room was stuffy, filled with about a hundred guests or so. Not a grand gathering, but still a considerable number. The crowd was crammed together in a large parlor. An anteroom in the back served as a small dancing nook, but most of the gathered company was busy chortling and making merry.

Henrietta wasn't in the mood to celebrate, though. Her fast approaching wedding was a blight, not a boon. But she *was* in the mood to wring her betrothed's wretched neck.

A glance at the grandfather clock indicated the hour of twelve was almost upon them—and Ravenswood had yet to arrive.

The villain! He was probably at his vile club, too busy fornicating with a "nun" to come to his own engagement party.

Her heart cramped as she imagined him in the catacombs, wallowing in debauchery, touching another woman . . . the way he had touched her that night in the library.

Henrietta quickly dismissed the disturbing vision from her mind. She didn't care if Ravenswood touched another woman. Good riddance! He would never touch her again, that was for certain.

But did the man have to humiliate her, desert her in front of the *ton*? Was he really so angry about getting married he'd wrest from her even the semblance of a happy union? It wasn't as if *she* was delighted about the wedding, didn't he know? She was just as miffed as he was, more so, for she now had a scandalous reputation, whereas the bounder had already possessed one. He didn't need to make the evening more intolerable for her . . . unless he enjoyed making her suffer.

Her heart fluttered at the riley thought. To think she had ever cared for the devil. That she had once believed he cared for her. Secretly *loved* her, even!

She bit her bottom lip to keep it from trembling. Rotten tears! How could she still cry for the dastardly man? Better yet, how could she have been such a dunce in the first place? For years she'd thought Sebastian was a hero. Where had the foolish fancy come from?

"Henry, my boy, you look flushed."

Henrietta glanced sidelong to find the baron approaching, and smiled. It was a rather shaky smile, but still, she was glad to see her papa.

Depressed at the loss of his "son," Baron Ashby

had spent the last few days in seclusion, barricaded in his study. It had taken quite a bit of coaxing to get him out of the doldrums: she'd had to promise to visit him often after she was wed. And there was no reason that she couldn't keep the vow. Ravenswood clearly didn't want anything to do with her; he didn't give a fig about the engagement bash. So Henrietta might just be free of the rogue once she married him. Perhaps Ravenswood wouldn't care if she spent all her time at home with Papa? She could always hope.

"I'm fine, Papa. It's a little too warm in here, I think."

"Quite. Quite. Too warm." The baron locked his hands behind his back. "You and I shall play a game of billiards, Henry. How does that sound? We'll get away from all this ruckus?"

"Thank you, Papa, but I think we must stay and host the celebration."

However wretched it might be, she thought. An engagement party without the groom? The society papers would be awash with speculation. But Henrietta wasn't going to cower and dash off to play billiards. She was going to stand there with a fixed smile, and brave the curious looks and whispered words. She wasn't going to dishonor her family even more by disappearing in a scandalous fashion.

The baron made a sour face. "It's a curious night, Henry. Indeed it is. Ravenswood isn't here to enjoy the festivities. You don't want to play billiards." He sighed. "It's all so peculiar."

"Not so peculiar," she murmured.

Ravenswood was a scoundrel. It was just like the man to be so ruthless, to dishonor his duty by deserting her. But Papa wasn't privy to the viscount's true character. The baron disliked idle gossip, so rumor of Sebastian's immoral ways had never reached his ears. He thought the viscount a gentleman—one who happened to be "stealing" her away—but still a gentleman.

If only Papa knew the truth . . . but perhaps it was better if he didn't. Why trouble the aging baron with thoughts about Sebastian's wicked pursuits? It would only grieve him, unnecessarily so. She had to marry the viscount; there was no way to cry off and still salvage the Ashby name. So let the baron think the groom a noble man. What harm would it do?

"Nicholas, get away from the girl!"

The baroness was approaching, her deportment stern.

"Nicholas, shoo!" Lady Ashby flicked her wrist. "You look cross. Don't scold the girl in public."

"What rubbish!" The baron snorted. "Why, I was just having a friendly chat with the boy."

"Well, the guests are beginning to think you are unhappy about the forthcoming wedding."

"I *am* unhappy, Lara," the baron huffed. "The boy's too young to be leg-shackled. Nasty business, I say. Nasty."

"Yes, nasty business." Lady Ashby offered her

youngest offspring a pointed look. "But the girl's made her choice, Nicholas."

Henrietta winced. Her mother was referring to the letter she had written to Sebastian. A sultry letter of apology that the *ton* believed was part of a lover's quarrel. But since Ravenswood wasn't at the party, the blasted man, the *ton* was beginning to suspect it all a matter of unrequited love, that she had dreamed up the affair in her head. And since Henrietta *had* dreamed up the affair in her head, it was all the more embarrassing.

"Come along, Nicholas." The baroness tugged at his arm. "We have guests to greet." As the couple moved away, Lady Ashby whispered to Henrietta, "And you, my dear, had best get back to smiling."

The baron looked over his shoulder. "Billiards, Henry. Billiards!"

Henrietta watched her parents disappear amid a throng of guests. Alone again, she took in a deep breath to soothe the tumult in her head.

"Have you forgiven me yet, Henry?"

Henrietta pressed her lips together.

"I didn't think so." Peter was holding two glasses of chilled champagne. He offered her one, which she accepted. "Please understand, Henry, I wanted what was best for both of you. You cared so much for Sebastian, and I was so sure that he cared for you . . ."

Henrietta's heart throbbed at the words. She, too,

had believed that very thing, that Sebastian had cared for her. Heavens, she had believed the rogue *loved* her!

"I made a mistake, Henry. I should have told you about Sebastian's 'habits' from the start. Will you forgive me?"

She sniffed. "Yes, Peter, I will."

There was no sense in being mad at Peter anyway. It was her own wretched fault for being such a ninny. A stubborn ninny at that. Her sisters had warned her about Ravenswood's wicked ways. She should have listened.

"A toast." Peter lifted the flute. "To new beginnings."

They clinked glasses.

"And it's getting off to a charming start, that new beginning," she said dryly. "It's almost midnight, Peter, and he still isn't here."

Peter glanced at the grandfather clock. "So it is." He looked back at her. "But he *will* be here, Henry. Trust me."

"And how can you be so sure of that?"

"Because I have to believe there is a little good inside my brother."

Henrietta could admire that, familial devotion. But she didn't have to believe in it herself. "You have more faith in your brother than I do."

"Yes, I suppose that is my failing." He smiled. "Would you care to dance?"

"Thank you, Peter, but no. Why don't you dance with your wife instead? Penelope looks like she needs a respite from all the pestering guests."

They both looked across the room to see Penelope fending off a gaggle of matrons, all looking for a juicy tidbit of gossip about the viscount's absence. Loyal Penelope, however, was deft at deflecting the nosy inquiries. She simply retorted the viscount was delayed by a pressing matter of business; he would be there as soon as time allowed. It was the story they had all agreed to tell until the viscount made his fashionably late appearance. *If* the scalawag ever bothered to show up, that was.

Peter offered her a tender smile. "Will you be all right, Henry?"

Henrietta gathered her valor. "Yes, I will. Now off with you, Peter. Go and rescue your wife."

Peter nodded and set off.

Alone yet again, Henrietta sipped the chilled champagne, perusing the guests, letting her mind wander.

It was a deuced wonder, really. Peter and Sebastian. Both brothers. Both so alike in looks. Yet both so different in temperament.

She watched as Peter and Penelope waltzed in the anteroom. How odd to see one brother so content, so at ease with his wife, so happy, even. And to know that the other brother was so dark in spirit? It was all so peculiar, as Papa would say. How had Sebastian drifted so far into the shadows of life?

"Good evening, Miss Ashby."

Henrietta looked up at the handsome young man, and returned his smile. "Good evening, sir."

He bowed. "Lord Emerson. I'm delighted to make your acquaintance."

He was a tall man, slender in frame. A cap of blond curls covered his head. He had an air about him. An aristocratic air. Not haughty, per say, but bold, perhaps impudent at times. Still, he was gracious. He spoke well. He was dressed immaculately, that was for sure, in his embroidered dress coat and matching green silk breeches. And he had a genuine smile; that was a welcomed respite, indeed.

"I have come in place of my father," he said, "the Earl of Ormsby."

Henrietta had heard the name before, but she had never met the earl or his son. Was Mama inviting strangers to the party? It wouldn't surprise her. The woman was determined to make a good show of the engagement bash; make *it* the talk of the *ton* and not the scandalous letter Henrietta had penned.

"Is the earl unwell, Lord Emerson?"

"One might say so. The dear old man loathes the cold. He insisted I take his place at this gathering." Lord Emerson gestured to the guests before he returned his attention to her. "Might I congratulate you on behalf of my father and myself on your approaching nuptials?"

"Yes, of course. Thank you, my lord."

Henrietta tried to sound like a cheery bride, but

it was a deuced bother, the façade. Yet she had to go along with the charade. It was her responsibility, after all, to make right the mess she had made.

"It is a splendid match, Miss Ashby." The young lord's smile quivered. "If I might be so bold, Ravenswood is a very fortunate gentleman."

There was something familiar about Lord Emerson. Henrietta wondered if perhaps she had met him somewhere before. There was something in his manner, his smile that triggered a sense of déjà vu. A chilling memory.

For all his charm, there was a quality about Lord Emerson she suddenly did not like. His eyes?

What rubbish! She was a dreadful judge of character. She'd deemed Ravenswood a noble hero. Clearly her intuition was flawed. Emerson was every bit a gentleman, she was sure. And yet . . .

At length, Henrietta scrunched her brow, and said, "Lord Emerson, have we met before?"

"It is possible, Miss Ashby. We move in very similar circles."

"Well, I distinctly remember you from somewhere."

"Perhaps I remind you of someone?"

Henrietta was not satisfied with that explanation. "There is something familiar about you."

"Such as?"

"Your eyes."

He lifted a brow. "My eyes, Miss Ashby?"

"Something about the color . . . purple feathers!"

Emerson started. "Pardon, Miss Ashby?"

"Purple feathers. I remember now. You had a mask of purple feathers. We must have met at Papa's masquerade ball. Last summer, I believe."

"You are right, Miss Ashby." He smiled. "The masquerade ball. I do remember, now that you mention it."

There, she had solved that mystery. And now she could get on with her assessment of Emerson. He had good family connections. He was easy to talk to. He was a handsome fellow, albeit dull. But he was pleasant. He was the sort of man she *should* have set her cap for all those years ago. Not the dashing rogue Ravenswood.

Oh, why hadn't she had the good sense back then to partner herself with a more dependable dandy? A trustworthy and respectable husband who could not break her heart? She would not be in this muddle, then. But she had learned her lesson far too late.

"When is the happy union, Miss Ashby?"

"On Twelfth Night." One long and dreadful week away. "We will be married at the chapel in town."

"I can not wait to attend, Miss Ashby."

How distressing that the guests were more eager about the wedding than the bride!

"Yes, I'm looking forward to it myself."

Lud, she sounded so insipid!

"Well, Miss Ashby, until the joyous day, I bid you good evening."

Emerson bowed and wended through the crowd.

Just then the grandfather clock struck the hour of twelve.

Midnight! And the rogue Ravenswood was *still* absent.

Henrietta downed the rest of her champagne. She'd had enough. She was going to bed.

Three. Four. Five chimes.

She skirted across the room. She had made a good show of it. But her betrothed was still detained by "business." There was no sense in her standing there anymore, under the scrutiny of the guests. She was utterly fagged.

Ten. Eleven. Twelve chimes.

It was after midnight.

The assembly room door opened.

Henrietta gasped.

"Ravenswood!"

He looked like a fallen angel, dark, yet still sinfully beautiful. And those eyes! The deepest shade of blue—and so full of intent.

Sebastian headed straight for her.

Henrietta clutched her belly, for it was in a whirl. He had come, the blackguard. And dressed in the most striking attire. Dark breeches and boots. Form-fitting coat, tailed. A sharp blue waistcoat, so snug against his strapping chest.

The incredible flutters of her heart quickened even more. For four days she had cried and cursed his black heart, so determined to loathe him. And now here he was, a formidable devil. And she could not utter a word of resentment. Oh, it was there in her gut, the fury. But she was having a deuced hard time voicing her dander aloud.

"Happy New Year, Henry."

He whispered the words.

Her toes curled.

And then he kissed her soundly.

Chapter 20

❧ ❦❧ ❧

The sweet taste of champagne on Henrietta's warm lips had a besotting effect on Sebastian. Not the buzz from the guests, nor the music in the anteroom distracted him from her balmy kiss—only the sharp cut of her teeth was rather jarring.

He let her go and licked his lips, tasting blood. The wily chit. She had snatched away his bachelorhood by writing that scandalous letter, and now she had the brass to bite him—her betrothed. "Is that any way to greet your fiancé?"

"Why did you kiss me?" she hissed, breathless.

"It's New Year's Eve. Isn't it the way I'm supposed to greet you?"

Henrietta lifted her darling chin, took in a deep breath, and said quietly, "Go to the devil."

Sebastian quirked a mordant grin.

The feisty little hoyden. He was going to thoroughly enjoy bedding her. Already, looking into her rebellious eyes, absorbing the energy of her defiant spirit . . . aroused him.

"You look bewitching tonight," he whispered, eyes dropping to the sweeping cut of her fashionable frock. "Red suits your passionate nature."

"And black suits your dark and twisted heart."

"Touché, Henry."

"My name is Miss Ashby."

How very formal, the appellation. Cold and haughty, too. She had pestered him for years to call her by her nickname, and now she preferred their former, proper rapport? Very well, he would play along—at least until he got the fiery chit into his bed.

"I apologize, Miss Ashby."

"Rot!' she snapped. "You're late."

"Am I?" He glanced at the clock. "So I am. How dreadful. I hope I didn't cause too much of a stir."

The deep swell of her lush breasts was hard to miss. She was trying to keep a cap on her temper. Had he ruffled the chit's feathers with his tardiness? Capital. He was determined to wrest back some control of his miserable life. And since he could not choose his bride, he was damn well going to choose what time he showed up for the engagement party.

"Where have you been?" she gritted. "That vile club of yours?"

The chatter around them had dwindled. Many meddlesome guests circled the couple, eavesdropping. But there was still the lively music in the anteroom—and the duo's hushed voices—to keep the curious onlookers at bay.

He lifted a brow. "Jealous, Miss Ashby?"

"What rot!"

He had never liked her possessive tendencies before. But now . . . now he was not quite so averse to them. She had to care for him—even a little—to be jealous. And he liked the thought of that, as well.

"I rather think you're jealous," Sebastian murmured with a wolfish smile.

"I rather think you're a scoundrel."

"I am, Miss Ashby." He lifted his hand to brush the smooth texture of her rosy cheek. "And you are jealous."

"I loathe you."

She shivered under his touch, indicating otherwise, warming his blood. He had prepared himself for the chit's contempt. But now to feel the quiver of her arousal did his roguish heart much good.

"I'm flattered, Miss Ashby."

"I'm tired." Henrietta turned her cheek away. "I'm going to bed."

"Would you like me to join you?"

She gasped. "Why, you rotten—"

"Something the matter, Miss Ashby?" He slipped his arm around her waist and caressed the low curve of her back, insensible to the spectacle he was making in front of the guests. "You and I are about to be married. And since you've welcomed me into your bed before . . ."

"I will *never* welcome you into my bed again."

"Is that so?" he drawled, unconvinced.

"Our marriage will be in name only. I will never let you touch me, Ravenswood—ever!"

Sebastian frowned. He delved deep into her bay brown eyes, searching for truth. And he realized the chit was serious!

Now he was *really* livid.

"What about an heir, Miss Ashby?"

"Peter's will do just fine." She bumped his hand off her midriff. "You've always said so yourself."

The muscles in his jaw and neck stiffened. "And if Peter doesn't have an heir?"

She looked perplexed, as if she hadn't thought about that possibility. But she quickly gathered her features to say, "Why don't we wait and see what happens in the next . . . oh, five years? If there is no heir by then, we'll discuss the matter again."

Five *years*! Did she think to keep him from her room—her bed—for that long? Even the whole of their marriage?

Like hell! It was already insufferable, being forced to wed. But he damn well wasn't going to marry a cold fish!

He'd had a carnal taste of Henrietta once before. She was a feisty little wanton in bed. It was the only perk to the whole blasted affair. And if she thought to deny him her charming curves, her plump breasts . . . well, Sebastian wasn't going to stand for it.

"Good evening, Ravenswood."

Rankled, Sebastian smoothed his features into a bland smile. "Good evening, Baron Ashby."

The baron stretched out his hand in greeting. "How fare your business affairs, Ravenswood?"

Sebastian accepted the offered hand and wrinkled his brow. "My business affairs?"

"The reason you were detained, my lord," said Henrietta.

"Ah, yes, my business affairs." Was that what the devious chit had told everyone about his tardiness? Very clever of her. "All in good order, Baron Ashby."

"Glad to hear it, Ravenswood. Glad to hear it."

The baron was stiff and formal and so unlike his usual cheerful self. Well, Peter had warned him the baron was cantankerous. After all, Sebastian was stealing away the man's "darling boy."

But Sebastian didn't have time to comfort a malcontent Baron Ashby. His betrothed had just uttered a ghastly vow, and he was determined to set her right on the matter. A marriage in name only? Not if he had anything to say about it!

First, though, Sebastian had to pacify the baron and send him on his way.

"Baron Ashby, I understand you have leather-tip cue sticks?"

Henrietta offered him a quizzical look.

"Why, yes, Ravenswood," said the baron. "Yes, I do."

"We must play a game of billiards, my lord."

The baron's eyes brightened. "What a capital idea, Ravenswood!"

"Splendid!" Sebastian smiled. "How about a game tonight?"

The baron beamed. "A game? Tonight? Why, yes, Ravenswood. I would be delighted."

Henrietta pinched her lips and crossed her arms under her breasts. The baron was an easy man to cajole. She might not appreciate that, but Sebastian did. He had other, more pressing matters to attend to, and the sooner he appeased every angry Ashby at the party, the sooner he could upbraid his betrothed for even suggesting he steer clear of her bed.

And speaking of every angry Ashby . . .

"Good evening, my lord."

The baroness came to stand beside her husband. There was something cold about the woman. Her stiff deportment, her cutting glance. Sebastian intended to mollify her, too.

"Good evening, Lady Ashby." He bowed. "You look lovely tonight."

"Thank you, my lord," she said crisply.

To win over the icy baroness, Sebastian gathered all the flirtatious charm he had mastered over the years, and smiled. "My lady, I have a favor to ask of you."

The baroness opened her fan with a snap. "Yes, Ravenswood?"

"You must take my place at the Royal Pavilion in Brighton."

Lady Ashby's fan flickered fast. "The Royal Pavilion, my lord?"

"It's in a month's time. I've been invited to an assembly by the King himself. And you are family, Lady Ashby, so I insist you take my place. I shall be engaged elsewhere, I'm afraid." *Bedding my wife.* "So I must beg you to go in my stead."

Eyes glistening, lips twisting into a smile, the baroness—so besotted with pomp and presentation— quickly said, "Why, I'd be honored, Ravenswood."

"Splendid!"

Sebastian knew for a fact the baroness had never been invited to one of the royal assemblies. She had lamented the slight for years. Surely she would never be cross with him again for orchestrating the invitation.

The baroness beamed at her husband and took him by the arm. "Come, Nicholas. We have guests to entertain." She nodded to Sebastian. "Lord Ravenswood."

Sebastian bowed again. "Lady Ashby."

The baroness dragged her husband away.

The baron whispered in flight, "Billiards later, Ravenswood!"

Sebastian watched the quirky couple wend through the crowd and disappear. That was two Ashbys thoroughly stroked, flattered, and appeased. Now he need only placate the sisters . . .

Aha! He'd have the finest lace and ribbon and fringe in all of France delivered to their door. That should exonerate him nicely.

Now to throttle his betrothed.

Sebastian slipped a firm arm around Henrietta's waist and steered her to a more private nook. "We have a matter of business to discuss, Miss Ashby."

She smacked his hand away. "We have nothing to discuss, my lord. I will not be so easily mollified. You cannot offer to play billiards with me or drag me off to Brighton to dance with the King, and expect me to forgive you."

"Forgive *me*?" he choked. "For what?"

"You bandied that letter all over London and ruined me!"

He growled, "I did *not* bandy that letter. And might I remind you, *I*, too, was ruined by the scandal. I never intended to wed, Miss Ashby. It's done my reputation a terrible blow, the news of my pending nuptials."

"How dreadful for you." She smirked, then said, "But if you didn't show the letter all over Town, then who did?"

"I have no idea, but I can assure you, Miss Ashby, I will throttle the culprit as soon as I find him."

"Or her, my lord. You do have so many lovely 'nuns' in your life. Why, one might have thought she was doing you a favor, spreading the letter all over Town. Or better yet, maybe a 'nun' was jealous and decided to thwart you. Women can be so devious, my lord."

Devious indeed. Imagine trapping a man into marriage, then denying him the marriage bed. It was a bloody sin!

"Let's not forget who wrote that blasted letter in the first place," he gritted.

"Oh, I won't forget. And I will pay for my folly all the rest of my days—with my marriage to you!"

She flounced off. A bit shaky in her step, but still, she had made her feelings perfectly clear—she hated him!

"Evening, Seb."

"Go to hell, Peter."

Peter looked positively tickled.

Sebastian looked beyond his brother's annoying head to see a gaggle of protective sisters surround Henrietta. Devil take it, how was he supposed to get close to his betrothed with all those harridans buzzing about?

He sighed. "I've come to marry her, Peter."

Peter rocked on his heels, gleeful. "'Course you have."

"But it looks like she loathes me."

"'Course she does."

"So you, brother, are going to help me win her back."

"'Course I will."

"You'll take care of the sisters?"

"Already on it."

Peter strutted off, a light spring to his step.

Sebastian glared at the sexy little hoyden from across the room, waiting for the ideal opportunity to be alone with her.

The nerve of the chit to deny him—her soon-to-be husband—that deliciously tempting body of hers. Well, there was only one thing left to do. He was going to have to seduce the willful Miss Ashby.

The night was still. Henrietta stood by the terrace edge, gazing at the starry sky. It was cold, too, but she did not have a wrap. Too eager to get away from the festivities—and Ravenswood's smoldering kisses—she did not think to fetch one.

Alone, for her sisters had been summoned to the nursery—the children were in an uproar of some sort—Henrietta let the chill of winter nip at her nose. Maybe it would nip at her heart, too. Something had to cap the bubble of emotions roiling in her breast.

The dastardly knave! Ravenswood had strolled into the parlor at the stroke of midnight, tried to charm his way into *her* bed, and then had the gall to look stricken at the thought of being denied his marital right.

She humphed. Was she supposed to ignore his foul behavior, pretend he wasn't a degenerate? He had smashed her heart to bits that night at the abbey; he had exposed his true and wicked self to her. She didn't trust the man, she didn't even *like* the man anymore. And she would not let him near her heart or her body again. She'd pelt him with rocks first.

However, there was one misfortune she had not anticipated: the lack of an heir. In her steely determination to be rid of Ravenswood's touch, she'd forgotten about a babe. If she barred the viscount from her bed, she would never be a mother.

There was a sharp pang in her breast at the thought of being childless. She knew firsthand the grief it caused her sister Penelope. But Henrietta quickly dismissed the ache. It was better for her to remain fruitless. Peter and Penelope might still have an heir to secure the estate. Henrietta need not bring an innocent babe into Ravenswood's sinful world. The viscount would make a terrible father, teach their child to indulge in vice. And she could not bear to witness the degeneration of her own son, the corruption of her own daughter.

Henrietta bristled. A warm coat slipped over her shoulders, the scent of rosemary and lemon stirring her senses.

Drat! She didn't have any rocks.

"You'll catch a chill, Miss Ashby."

Oh, that gruff male voice! Did it have to make her quiver so?

She didn't dare turn around. "I'm not cold."

"You're shivering, Miss Ashby."

Sebastian rubbed her shoulders in slow and sensual caresses, making her heart tap and the sweat gather between her breasts. Did he think to beguile her with his gallantry? Henrietta had more fight in her than that.

"What are you doing here, Ravenswood?" she snapped.

"Can't I visit with my fiancée?"

Oh, now he wanted to spend time with her? It had suited him just fine, deserting her for most of the engagement bash, but now he was ready to cavort with her? Did he want more kisses?

That did it. Henrietta whirled around.

Big mistake. One look at the sinfully striking viscount, and her breath hitched. Her heart pattered, too. And that all too familiar sensation—desire—started to warm her belly. She might not like the rogue, but she still found him tempting to look at.

Henrietta had to keep her voice from squeaking. A dratted effort it was, too. "Won't it ruin your roguish reputation, visiting with your intended bride?"

"It will ruin my roguish reputation even more if my own bride despises me." Then in a gruff voice: "Come, Miss Ashby, let us forget about the past."

She was strapped for words. The gall of the man to suggest she overlook his wrongdoing. It wasn't as if he was remiss and had neglected to pull out her chair at dinner. The bounder had broken her heart! How was she supposed to forget *that*?

"You and I are to be married, Miss Ashby. Let us begin anew." He stuck out his hand. "Friends?"

She gawked at the offered truce. Was the cold seeping into the man's brain, freezing all his good sense? "You and I are not friends, Ravenswood."

"Why, Miss Ashby? Because we had a tiff?"

Tiff?

"Friends do quarrel, you know?" he said. "And a good friend will always forgive another's transgression."

"Then I must not be a very good friend," she said tightly.

He tsked. "Don't say that, Miss Ashby. You are a very dear friend . . . and a soon-to-be wife."

Her heart throbbed. Something was ringing in her ears: a shrill voice telling her to sweep up her skirts and run. She didn't, though.

"I asked you a question back inside the house, Ravenswood, but you never answered me."

"And what question would that be?"

"Why are you so late?"

"Ah, so you're still jealous," he said with aplomb, then softly, "I rather like it when you're jealous, Miss Ashby."

"I am *not* jealous," she hissed. "I just want to know the reason for your tardiness."

"Well, it is winter, Miss Ashby. The roads are terrible."

She humphed. "I don't believe you. Every other guest arrived on time."

"Bravo for every other guest."

Oh, the maddening man! "You left me alone on purpose, admit it."

"And why would I do that, Miss Ashby?"

"To humiliate me, you blackguard!"

He tsked again. "Such language, Miss Ashby. How unseemly."

He dared to lecture her on polite behavior? A lecher of the highest order? She was desperate for a rock.

"You were at the Hellfire Club, weren't you?" she charged. "Dallying with a *nun*!"

He lifted his deep blue eyes to stare at her with scrutiny. "And what if I was?"

She gasped. "So you admit it?"

"I admit nothing, Miss Ashby. I only ask: what *if* I was there? Would you be jealous?"

"Rot! I don't care if you romp around with a skirt."

"Is that so?" he drawled.

She gathered her shaky breath. All right, perhaps she cared a little. But not in the way he was suggesting. Jealousy, her foot! She was thinking about her respectability, that was all. The respectability of her family. She didn't want the Ashby name disgraced by Ravenswood's wild behavior.

She huffed, "I expect you to be discreet about your affairs."

"Well, I wasn't planning to have any affairs, but if you insist . . ."

She gnashed her teeth. "If you have even a dash of honor in your soul, you will not disgrace me—a *friend*—in public."

"Miss Ashby, I would never do anything so shameful." He brushed his thumb across the ridge of her brow in a feathery stroke. "Would it please you to hear I was not at the abbey?" He traced the pad of his thumb across her frosty cheek, down the rigid length of her jaw. "Would it please you to hear I haven't been back to the abbey since the night we quarreled?"

She shivered under his oh-so-ginger touch. Breathless, she said, "I don't believe you."

"Oh, believe me, Miss Ashby. For the past four days I've been shut up in my room, thinking about you—and our pending nuptials."

It took her lips a few moments to catch up with her bewildering thoughts. Was the daft man talking about the wedding night? As if she would ever consider letting him near her in *that* way again.

"A pity you squandered away your nights daydreaming," she quipped.

"Do not pity me, Miss Ashby. My time was pleasantly engaged with thoughts of you."

Oh, drat her treacherous heart for pulsing so! "I'm privy to your charms, Ravenswood. You will not win your way back into my bed with a few whispered words and an artful touch."

He reared his head—and hand—back, aghast. "Why, Miss Ashby, is *that* what you think of me? I'm hurt, truly I am. I was only thinking about our marital life together." He lifted his eyes heavenward, as though deep in thought. "I suppose I will have to buy a home in the more fashionable part of London, give up my bachelor residence for good. And you shall want to decorate the abode, I'm sure, so I'll summon an interior designer posthaste." His smoldering eyes met hers once more. "But I've no intention of bedding you, I assure you."

"Oh."

Why the devil did her heart hurt so? She had no desire to carouse with the viscount, even if he should woo her. He was a villain, remember? A fiend. Good riddance!

"You've made your feelings perfectly clear, Miss Ashby. Our marriage is to be in name only. I respect your decision."

Henrietta eyed him shrewdly. "You do?"

A curt nod. "Of course I do. I'm not a devil through and through, you know? I do have a 'dash' of honor." A dark fire sparked in his eyes. "And I shall prove it to you. We will settle this matter once and for all."

She shivered. A good sort of shiver. The kind that made her feel all warm and tingly. "Settle what?"

"Our strife, of course."

"And how do you propose we do that?"

"We shall have a contest."

"Gamble, you mean?"

He nodded. "It is the only reasonable way for two members of the peerage to settle a dispute. If I win, we start anew. Wipe the slate clean, if you will. And as forfeit . . . I can ask anything of you I wish."

Henrietta took in a sharp breath. *He* would request another kiss, she was sure. Or some other sexual favor, scoundrel that he was.

"And if I win?" she said.

"Then I suppose we don't begin anew, and as for-feit you can ask anything of me in return."

"A house, for instance?"

"Yes, I already mentioned—"

"No, I mean a house of my own, where *you* can-not visit." She smiled at the perky thought. "And you can keep your bachelor residence to boot."

Now *that* was the perfect way to spend the rest of her married days with Ravenswood—apart.

There was a dark gleam in the viscount's eyes. He was quiet for a moment. She doubted he would ac-cept her terms. But at length, he nodded slowly.

"Very well, Miss Ashby. A house it is."

She scrunched her face in misgiving. He was much too cavalier for her liking. What was the man scheming?

"I think I'd rather face you on the dueling field, Ravenswood."

"Miss Ashby, you are a woman . . . whatever your father might say."

"Rot! I'm a good shot. It would be a fair fight."

He said gruffly, "You would shoot me?" The fire in his eyes burned bright. "You hate me that much?"

She stared at his mesmerizing eyes, forgot her words for a moment, then said, "Shoot you, yes. Kill you, no."

But she'd like to wound the blackguard, make him feel some of the pain he'd made her feel.

"Well, Miss Ashby, while you might be able to shoot me, I could never shoot you."

She huffed. He was playing the gallant knight again. But she'd indulge his peculiar request. Anything to be rid of the man's sultry touches and whispered words. She trusted even a knave like Ravenswood would honor a challenge loss. And if she won the wager, she intended to buy the biggest house she could find and bankrupt him furnishing it.

"A contest it is then," she said.

"Wise decision, Miss Ashby."

What decision? It's not like she had a choice in the matter.

"So what shall we wager?" she said. "Who can irk the other the most?"

"Touché, Miss Ashby." He even offered her a little smile that made her heart jump. "I was thinking more along the lines of a duel—with snow."

"Snow?"

Sebastian hunched down and gathered a lump of snow into his hands. "Do you see that tree?"

Henrietta cast her eyes over the land. "The gnarled one by the marble urn?"

"That's right." He squashed the snow into a hard ball. "Whoever hits the tree wins."

Henrietta eyed the tree. About forty paces, she reckoned. She could do it.

"Can I hit any part of the tree?" she wondered.

Sebastian aligned himself with the target. "The center is preferable, but any part will do."

Henrietta nodded. "Very well, then."

She tucked her arms into Sebastian's coat, to keep

the garment in place, then she, too, hunched down and collected the fresh fallen snow. Rolling it in her hands, she watched her opponent.

Sebastian was first. He took a step forward, brought his arm back, paused, then pitched the snowball across the green.

It hit a sagging branch.

Sebastian didn't look too happy about his flimsy shot.

Henrietta, on the other hand, was tickled.

"I think I can beat that," she said with a smug air, and flounced over to the spot opposite the tree.

Sebastian took a step back.

But she could feel his hot stare on her the entire time.

Well, he would not intimidate her. In just a second she was going to be rid of the man for good. No more smoldering looks or spicy scents or toe-curling smiles. Not that she yearned for any of that anymore. Certainly not.

Henrietta eyed the tree trunk. She was a skilled marksman with a gun or arrow. Papa had made sure to teach her—well, he had hired someone to teach her the skill. Papa didn't have very good aim himself. But Henrietta was a brilliant shot. Always had been. This should be as easy as pilfering pastries from the cook's pantry.

She swung her arm, let the snowball fly . . . and watched it miss the tree entirely.

Henrietta stared, dumbfounded.

She had lost.

How the devil had she lost?

A triumphant smile slowly curled the viscount's lips. "Well, Miss Ashby, it looks like you've lost."

She gnashed her teeth. "So it would seem."

"That means I am the winner."

The conceited blackguard! "Yes, Ravenswood, I know."

"And I can ask anything of you I wish."

She huffed. "So ask."

He took a step back and made a sweeping bow. "Will you do me the honor of a dance?"

"What, no kisses?"

Drat! She had *not* meant to say that aloud. Her cheeks quickly warmed.

Sebastian quirked a mischievous brow. "No kisses, Miss Ashby. I am a gentleman, after all."

It took all her strength to keep from snorting.

He held out his hand. "Shall we?"

Henrietta stared at the large, muscular hand. Tickles of warmth spread through her. She was being a deuced ninny about this. She had lost the wager. Fair was fair. She needn't be squeamish. She just had to dance with the bounder and be done with it. She would find some other way to oust the knave from her life. There was no sense idling. She would not let the viscount intimidate her. She had more valor than that.

Henrietta slipped her hand in his. She shivered. He had such a strong hand. It very nearly oozed virility.

The music from the anteroom seeped outside, soft waves of sound intruding on the quiet terrace.

"You and I have never danced before." He gathered her in his arms for a waltz. "Why is that?"

Henrietta gritted, "Because you've never asked me to."

"Ah, yes." He swept her across the terrace. "But we were not betrothed back then. We are now, though, and I think this is a splendid way to begin anew, don't you?"

She didn't say anything. She was too busy trying to keep her footsteps in sync, for the bounder was making her forget her thoughts, her very sense of self.

Curse him! He was arousing feelings inside her she would rather have stomped asunder. Feelings of warmth and security, even. Since girlhood she had known she would feel safe in the viscount's arms. That the rogue could still inspire her foolish childhood fancy was intolerable. Henrietta wanted to wrest free of his hold and dash back into the house; to barricade herself in her room, against the viscount's wicked charms.

"It's starting to snow," he said softly.

Henrietta lifted her eyes to the heavens. Powder puffs drifted from the night sky, a light flurry sprinkling the earth.

She whirled beneath the falling snow, a horrendous sorrow washing over her. It was so perfect, she thought. The romantic night, the viscount in her arms—and it was all an illusion. Four days ago, she would have laughed with joy to have been in such a moment. Now she only wanted to weep. The viscount in her arms was a fallen hero. The night was cold and dark, so like the sentiments in her heart.

She resented Sebastian asking her to dance. The playful waltz only reminded her of her childish foolery. And she wanted so much to forget.

"What's the matter, Miss Ashby?"

He whispered the words. Henrietta almost wished he'd said the name "Henry," instead.

"I'm feeling dizzy," she fibbed. She wanted out of the viscount's arms. She wanted out of the illusion he was only helping to sustain.

Sebastian stopped. But he did not let her go.

"Come," he said. "We'll go inside. You can sit down in there."

"No." She shrugged off his coat and handed him the garment. "I'll return to the house alone. I think I will retire to bed. You have a game of billiards to play with Papa."

She headed for the terrace doors.

"Good night, Miss Ashby," he said quietly after her.

Henrietta paused, then quickly skirted back inside the house.

* * *

A figure lurked in the shadows.

Emerson was in hiding from Ravenswood. He did not want an encore of their last row, so humiliating for him. He had come to tonight's festivity to rejoice in his machinations, to see the viscount wallow in agony . . . but something had gone awry.

It was obvious the little slut didn't want the viscount anymore. But the viscount so earnestly wanted her.

Peculiar.

His diabolical mind whirling, Emerson started to think it might work out even better this way. If the hussy Miss Ashby resented the viscount, it would make the lovelorn Ravenswood miserable. All Emerson had to do was keep the girl at odds with the viscount, make sure she crushed the ogre's heart to bits. Disgraced him, even.

Now *that* was an even better form of revenge.

Chapter 21

⟨~~~⟩

The little bell chimed as Sebastian opened the door. He stepped inside the shop and perused the shelves of knickknacks: porcelain dolls, ceramic vases, china figurines. He just might find a treasure of some sort in here, he mused. He had already been to three other establishments, but had failed to find the right gift for Henrietta.

He grumbled. Last night's seduction had not gone as well as he had hoped. For a man accustomed to getting what he wanted from a woman, that was very discouraging. At one point during last night's waltz, Henrietta had looked positively green!

It was time to amend his approach to courting. The chit was smitten with him. She wanted his kisses, he thought with a wicked grin. But she was fighting her attraction to him. He needed something with which to soften her ornery disposition. And a gift should redeem him nicely, get her to surrender to his charms. It had always worked for him in the past. After a row with a mistress, he'd flash a pricey trinket, and all her tears would magically disappear.

Behind the ornate wood counter was an elderly gentleman. "Good morning, my lord." He smiled. "How may I help you?"

Sebastian eyed the trinkets along the wall. "I'm looking for something special."

"For your wife, my lord?"

A tight knot formed in the viscount's belly at the word. Yes, Henrietta was going to be his wife. But it was a brutal business, getting used to the word.

"My soon-to-be wife," said Sebastian.

With a sage nod, the elderly shopkeeper moved away from the counter and headed for a nearby cluttered shelf. He picked up a shiny box with opal inlays.

"How about this, my lord?"

The shopkeeper opened the box and turned the tiny key.

A quaint tune escaped. Charming . . . but not charming enough. He was looking for a unique present, one with veiled implications mayhap. The chit had given him such a gift on Christmas Eve: a ring with a Celtic love knot. Now he had to find something equally significant with which to woo his stubborn Henrietta.

"What else do you have?" said Sebastian.

Beside the window was a table filled with trinkets. The elderly shopkeeper lifted a small clock with hand-painted daisies.

Sebastian eyed the piece. Pretty. But Henrietta was never on time for anything. She might think such a gift an ill-mannered gesture on his part.

The viscount shook his head. "Anything else?"

As the shopkeeper shuffled about, a reflection skimmed Sebastian's eye. "What is that?"

"My lord?"

"Over there." He pointed across the crowded room. "Inside the glass display."

The shopkeeper pushed aside a gold birdcage to reach the display. He opened the case and removed the trinket. "This, my lord?"

"Yes, that's it." A slow smile spread across the viscount's face. "It's perfect."

A soft touch . . . a sinful smile . . . sensuous lips. "Ouch!"

Henrietta's sultry reflection was dashed to bits by the sharp pain in her arse.

"Forgive me, miss," said the seamstress.

"Stand still, Henry," the baroness reproached. "There's just a few more pins."

Henrietta sighed. One more fitting and then she wouldn't have to think about the wedding dress anymore . . . not that she was thinking much about the wedding dress at all. Rather, a certain rogue was keeping her thoughts engaged, filling her head with erotic memories.

"Ouch!"

"Forgive me, miss," burbled the seamstress, pins trapped between her teeth.

"Stop squirming, Henry," from the baroness. "Whatever is the matter with you?"

How about a rush of wicked thoughts storming her weary brain?

Oh, Henrietta had to get off the stool. She had to get out of the room. She had to get out of the house! All the wedding buzz was making her harebrained. It was a faithful reminder of her betrothed, Ravenswood. She needed a breath, a moment of repose from all the preparations . . . from the thought of her roguish fiancé and his sweet and kissable lips.

"Ouch! Drat!"

The seamstress plucked one last pin from between her teeth and jabbed it into the back of Henrietta's dress. "Finished, miss."

Well, thank heavens for that! Henrietta's poor rump was bruised, no doubt.

"Now be careful, Henry." The baroness offered her hand for support. "Don't tear the lace."

Henrietta took her mother's outstretched hand and stepped off the stool. The seamstress unfastened the buttons, and gingerly, Henrietta slipped out of the white glacé silk and fine lace garment.

In a few minutes, she was draped in a sage brown day dress and scurrying from the bedroom, leaving Mama and the seamstress to quibble over stitching details.

But the rest of the house was full of activity, too. There was so much to do before Twelfth Night. Flowers to arrange. Cakes to bake. Linens to iron. Silverware to polish. So much to think about. Thank heavens her sisters and Mama insisted on helping. Henrietta didn't think she could do it all alone—but the preparations could wait a few minutes, surely?

Henrietta moved through the house, searching for Papa. Perhaps he'd like to play a game of billiards now? She hoped so. She needed a respite.

Henrietta tiptoed through the passageways so as not to attract the viscount's attention, for he, too, was sheltered somewhere in the house, the dratted man. The family had insisted Ravenswood stay at the house until the day of the ceremony. Despite all his charm, it seemed no one trusted the rogue to show up for the wedding. The arrangement had put Henrietta in high dudgeon. But ironically, it had pleased the viscount.

Odd. The man was acting so peculiar, spouting fresh starts and clean slates, wanting to spend time at the house. It wasn't like Ravenswood at all. And it made her wonder all the more what the viscount was scheming. She certainly didn't believe he had changed into a gentleman, that he respected her decision to marry in name only. The wily devil was up to something, she was sure. But what?

"Sneaking about, Miss Ashby?"

Not quiet enough, her tiptoeing.

Henrietta squared her shoulders and turned

around to confront the viscount, a retort ready on her lips.

But one look at the sinfully handsome rogue, and all thoughts of a rejoinder deserted her.

He had a mischievous look in his eye. More of an imp than a fiend. He was smiling, too. And she didn't like the fact that his charming grin could still curl her toes. It made it deuced hard to hate the man.

"I'm not sneaking about," she said firmly, even though her belly was in a knot. "I'm looking for Papa."

"The baron is in his study."

With a curt bob of the head, Henrietta pivoted on her toes and headed for the study.

She had to get away from Ravenswood. One look at the dashing viscount, and it was hard to keep her anger in place. He had such a devastating smile . . . and a sensual glow in his eyes.

"But he is asleep, Miss Ashby."

Henrietta paused.

"I was just there myself," he said. "The baron is napping, I'm afraid."

Drat!

"Perhaps I can assist you, Miss Ashby?"

Now why the devil did that sound so . . . wanton?

Henrietta turned around once more. "I highly doubt that, my lord. I wanted to play a game of billiards with Papa."

"Well, I might not be as savvy as your Papa, but I daresay I'd make a fair opponent."

He was smiling. Not with his lips, but with his eyes.

She pinched her brow, fearing his proposal some sort of trick. Besides, she didn't want to spend more time with the dastardly viscount. She wanted him to leave her alone.

Wait! Perhaps a game of billiards *was* the ideal opportunity to get the viscount to stay away from her. She was a skilled billiardist. If she made another wager with the viscount—and won, this time—she could wrest from him another promise for a home of her own. Separate apartments would be grand, the best solution to this dreadful predicament.

After a thoughtful pause, she gave a brisk nod. "Very well, Ravenswood."

A few minutes later, Henrietta was hunched over the billiard table, eyeing the ivory cue ball. "Shall we make the game more interesting?"

Sebastian quirked a black brow. "What did you have in mind?"

"Winner gets to make another wish."

He perused her for a moment, his eyes smoky. "All right, Miss Ashby."

Henrietta dismissed the shiver tickling her spine, and returned her attention to the cue ball.

With a loud crack, the white ball struck the red ball. One point for her.

She moved around to the other side of the table. Again she positioned herself, struck the red ball and nicked Sebastian's cue ball. Two points for her.

She was very good at three-ball. In a short while, she'd have that fashionable apartment in Town.

"Magnificent," he breathed.

Henrietta felt a measure of satisfaction at his words. She was good, true. But magnificent?

"A rump to satisfy a man's hunger."

Henrietta balked. Heat invaded her belly, stormed her breast. She missed the red ball and the cushion, forfeiting a point. Drat!

She stood up and glared at Ravenswood, indignation roiling in her gut. "How dare you . . ."

But Sebastian wasn't staring at her. He was looking out the window. Apparently, hers was not the rump being admired.

Henrietta followed his gaze to the workers outside, bringing in a boar. Tonight's dinner, no doubt.

She quickly swallowed her outburst.

Sebastian glanced back at the table. "Is it my turn?"

Oh, the haughty knave! He'd done that on purpose, she was sure. To unnerve her, the wily bounder.

Sebastian arched his splendid form. Henrietta could not help but note the hard muscles in his calves as he stretched forward. Or the brawn surging through his arms as he positioned the cue. The black curl that dropped over his eye just then only made the man more irresistible. Blast it!

Sebastian struck the red ball, knocked her cue ball, and scored two points.

Henrietta twisted her lips.

The viscount moved around the table for another shot. "How did you sleep last night, Miss Ashby?"

"Terribly." *Thanks to you*, she thought.

He scored another point. "I figured as much."

The game at hand dismissed from her mind for a moment, she demanded, "And how did you figure that?"

Another loud crack as the red ball rolled across the table. "I was out for a walk late last night. I saw the candle burning in your window."

Henrietta took in a sharp breath. He was watching her through her bedroom window! Did he see her undress?

"Fret not, Miss Ashby. I was a perfect gentleman."

She wanted to snort, but instead composed her features. Her pursed lips and pinched brow clearly betrayed her ire. The man could read her thoughts.

What was happening to her? Days ago, she'd have made a ready quip *and* retained her cool deportment. To think the scoundrel could unravel her guard with a little banter and a dashing smile, after months of training with Madam Jacqueline, was very disquieting.

"Why were you so restless, Miss Ashby?"

"I could ask the same of you."

He moved to the other end of the table, his dark blue eyes on her. "I had a very distressing problem to solve."

"About what?"

"Shopping."

He was funning with her. No man thought about shopping, especially a rake like Ravenswood. He only thought about vice.

"And you, Miss Ashby?" He scored another point. "What kept you awake?"

The relentless attention of one dashing rogue, she mused, still piqued. But she wouldn't tell him that. Instead she decided to have a bit of fun herself.

"A mouse," she said.

"How dreadful."

"A rat, really. I tried to shoo the pest away, but he just kept coming back. Stubborn little bugger."

Sebastian missed his shot.

Henrietta lifted her brows. "Oh, is it my turn?"

She swished her hips and moved to the other end of the table.

She could feel Sebastian's hot gaze on her back the entire time. It seared her right through her clothes.

Concentrating hard, Henrietta struck the red ball. She missed Sebastian's cue ball, but still, one more point for her.

"A rat, eh?" he said. "I'm surprised you didn't scream."

She snorted. "I'm not afraid of a wee rodent."

"That's very unusual—for a woman."

"Rot!" Another score. "I would never make such ungodly racket."

"I've heard you make ungodly racket before, Miss Ashby."

She stiffened. The dark timbre of his voice sent shivers down her spine. He was alluding to the wicked night she'd spent in his arms; the cries and groans of sweet passion that he'd ripped from her throat.

Memory of those sinful encounters, so full of pleasure, stormed her weary mind. She tried to shoo the haunting sentiments aside and concentrate on the game, but alas, it was fruitless. She missed her shot. Drat!

He said in a soft voice, "I see it's my turn again."

Henrietta meshed her lips together. How could the rogue still affect her so? How could the sound of his watery voice still make her sweat and her body ache?

Sebastian made his shot. Two points for him.

She pinched her lips even more. He was trying to make her lose, the blackguard. She had to get ahold of her scattered wits. She had to win this wager if she wanted the bounder to keep away from her.

"Yes, my lord, you are very familiar with ungodly ways, aren't you?"

Sebastian made his shot. He nicked her cue ball. Another two points for him. But he did not return to the game right away. Instead he propped the end of his cue stick against the ground and rested his hands over the tip.

Henrietta could feel the caress of his eyes. Her flesh warmed; her bones trembled. She tried to still the rampant beats of her heart, but the long stare he gave her only made her even more jittery.

"You and I are about to be married, Miss Ashby . . . Perhaps I intend to reform my ungodly ways and start anew."

"A rogue cannot reform his ways," she countered, her breath a bit uneven. "Those were your words, my lord."

"And you believed me?"

She huffed. Was he funning with her again? It was deuced hard to tell when he set his smoldering eyes on her like that. She had the profound impulse to pick up the hem of her skirt and start fanning herself.

"I believe you are a scoundrel, Ravenswood."

"I was, true . . . but I think it's time for a change."

At last he broke away from her eyes.

Henrietta let out a little sigh, for another moment more, and she'd be reduced to a pile of cinder.

"And why change now?"

Sebastian made another shot. One more point for him. Drat!

"Well, we are about to wed, Miss Ashby. A change seems fitting. A fresh start for both you and me."

She didn't believe him, but wondered anyway, "And how do you intend to change?"

"Ah, that is the difficult part, so I will need your help, I'm afraid."

Henrietta widened her eyes. "Why do you need my help?"

"Well, I cannot go it alone, Miss Ashby. I need someone to be my moral guide."

"Rot! If you want to change your wicked habits, you can do so by yourself."

He lifted a brow. "You mean the way you seduced me without any instruction?"

Her breath hitched. "I never . . ."

His head cocked. "You tried."

Henrietta gathered her garbled words. "That was different."

"How so?"

"It was a foolish mistake. I should never have gone to see Madam Jacqueline."

"You're right, you shouldn't have. It was a terrible blunder, very imprudent."

Was he berating *her* about inappropriate conduct? The hypocritical knave! "How dare you!"

"Is something the matter, Miss Ashby? I was only agreeing with you."

Henrietta clamped her lips shut. She squeezed the cue stick hard.

After a moment of repose, she gritted, "And what will you do once you've reformed your ways?"

Sebastian took another shot. "Oh, I don't know. Take on the role of straitlaced husband. Have a brat or two . . . Oh, never mind about the brats. I'm not to touch you—ever. But I'd like to give the ordinary, respectable life a try."

The urge to slam her cue stick over the billiard table was hard to tamp. The miserable wretch! He was spouting everything she'd wanted to hear from him in the past. But it was all a lie. He was a devious sort. For some nefarious reason, he wanted her to believe him, to lower her guard.

Well, she'd do no such thing. She refused to believe a man like Ravenswood could change. It was impossible. He was too much of a scoundrel to ever reform. And even if he ever changed, the transformation would be short-lived. In a few weeks or months he'd tire of the "ordinary, respectable" life. He'd go back to his vile club and surrender to his old degenerate ways. And she was not going to be the wife left behind in tears. Never! If the rogue wanted to dabble with respectability, he'd have to find some other poor woman to play house with.

"Well, Miss Ashby, it looks like I've won."

Too engrossed with her distressing thoughts, Henrietta had lost track of the game. But it appeared the bounder was right. He'd scored the most points.

Why did she keep losing every wager?

Sebastian set his cue stick across the billiard table. "And for your challenge loss, I request your presence . . . in my bedchamber."

Chapter 22

⤛⟋⟍⤜

Henrietta stared at Sebastian's closed bedroom door.

He'd retired from the billiard room ahead of her, she needing a moment to gather her scattered wits. She just *knew* he was a villain, no matter the gallant pretense. He was going to woo her, she was sure. Try and coax from her a sexual favor of some sort. That's probably why he'd agreed to stay at the house in the first place; to have his way with her. He was privy to the months she'd spent under Madam Jacqueline's tutelage. He likely wanted to see for himself just how much she had learned from the courtesan. Surely he believed he had a "husbandly" right to do so.

A reformed rogue, indeed.

She took in a deep breath, a jumble of jitters in her belly. The bounder might have bid her to join him in his bedchamber, but she'd no intention of submitting to his wicked charms. Certainly not. She was going to honor her challenge loss by coming to his room. But that was all she was going to do.

Fingers trembling, Henrietta rapped on the door.

"Enter."

He had such a booming voice.

She quelled a shiver and pushed open the heavy barrier. She stepped inside the room.

The scent of cologne greeted her. Henrietta inhaled the spicy fragrance and tried to ignore the heady effect it had on her.

"How good of you to join me, Miss Ashby."

She snapped her attention to the viscount.

He stood by the bed, shoulder propped against the ornate bedpost in a very suggestive pose. To make matters worse, he wasn't wearing his coat; it was flung over a chair in a careless manner. Only the crisp white of his shirt was stretched across the taut muscles of his strapping chest. It was open, too. Just a tad. The white fabric parted at the neck, a tuft of dark curls evident.

Henrietta was in deep trouble.

She licked her lips. "Of course I came. Are you suggesting I would dishonor my word?"

The smoldering look in his eyes made it hard to sound petulant. It made it hard to breathe, too. She had an absurd urge to wriggle free of her warm and confining corset. The man really was a rogue. One smoky look and he had her wanting to shed her clothes. Blast it!

"I have the utmost faith in you, Miss Ashby." The deep rumble of his voice tickled her spine. "You would never break your vow."

Henrietta ignored the patter of her heart to affirm, "That's right. I'm not a coward, you know?"

Sebastian moved away from the bedpost. He sauntered toward her, each deliberate step provocative, mesmerizing.

Henrietta could feel the nerves coil in her belly. She didn't budge, though. The door was open behind her. She was safe. Really.

"I know, Miss Ashby. You are very brave."

The husky drawl of his voice made her toes curl. He paused in front of her, the rich musk of him swirling around her, making her a bit dizzy with giddy euphoria.

Her words trembled, "Why have you summoned me here?"

Eyes dark and intent, he pressed his thumb to the swell of her cheek. "I have something for you."

Her breath hitched at his tender touch; her pulse tapped hard and fast. "You do?"

He stroked her cheek in an oh-so-gentle caress. "Something I think you'll like very much."

He was going to kiss her. She could sense it. Every nerve inside her was fluttering. Well, he was going to get a sound smack for his impudence. Maybe even a bite on the lips, the bounder.

"Close your eyes," he whispered.

Hypnotized, Henrietta's lashes fluttered closed. She was woozy on her feet. Her lips pouted . . . and something nestled in her hands.

"Open your eyes, Miss Ashby."

She blinked. A black velvet purse with golden cords rested between her palms. "What, no kisses?"

Drat! Had she said that aloud *again*?

"No kisses, Miss Ashby." Mirth sparkled in his delft blue eyes. "I am a gentleman, remember? I will honor your sincere wish. I will never touch you in that way again."

She twisted her lips. "What is this?"

"A Christmas present."

"Christmas was last week."

"And I apologize for my belated gift," he said, voice contrite.

She wrinkled her brow. "But why are you giving me a present?"

"Can't a man give his betrothed a gift?"

She made a moue.

"Go on," he said. "Open it."

With a sigh, fearing this some sort of trick, Henrietta slowly opened the little velvet purse and reached inside the blackness.

Her fingers struck something cold. Glass?

Carefully she removed a small glass globe, perched on a wooden stand. Inside the globe were two figurines, intertwined . . . dancing. She shook the globe; the water inside swished and little bits of white resin swirled together like snow.

It reminded her of the engagement party, dancing with Sebastian under a tender snowfall.

Her heart pinched.

"Do you like it?" he said, eyes intent upon her.

"It's beautiful," she whispered, tears filling her eyes. And if anyone but Sebastian had given her the present, she would have been touched.

But knowing it came from him, knowing it came from the one who'd crushed all her girlhood dreams, made it bittersweet.

Why was he doing this to her? she wondered. He wasn't acting like a rogue. He was acting like the hero she had always wanted him to be. But she knew it was a lie, a façade. And she didn't understand why he was being so cruel.

A muffle of female voices filled the house just then, her sisters. Shouts about "flowers" and "water" echoed throughout. The blooms from the hothouse must have arrived.

"You should go, Miss Ashby, before your sisters discover us together. We don't want to cause another scandal, do we?"

It was growing dark. Sebastian journeyed across the snowy land, looking for Henrietta.

She'd disappeared from the house a short while ago. He wasn't alarmed, though; he suspected her whereabouts. But he was confused.

Earlier that day, he'd made the chit tear up with his gift. That was a good thing, right? A lass often wept with joy, so she must have liked the present . . . Then why was she still avoiding him?

The viscount grimaced. Henrietta was so *un*like an ordinary lass. It was deuced hard, reading the whimsical chit sometimes: a quandary he had never faced before. It had always been so easy for him to see a woman's thoughts in her eyes. Not so with Henrietta. He sensed many conflicting sentiments whenever he looked at her. She clearly wanted his kisses, he thought with a grin, but sometimes it also seemed as if she wanted to jab her cue stick into his eye.

Sebastian's smile faded. Evidently the girl was still miffed with him. The gift had somehow failed to impress her. So what was he going to do now?

Sebastian could hear the steel blades cutting the ice. Soon the pond came into view . . . and a lone shadow skating over the icy surface.

He stood back for a minute, watching Henrietta, thinking about the time he had skated in *her* arms. She was so determined to be different. So stubborn, too. And she was a feisty sprite. Bedding her would be bliss. Now if only he could convince the chit life under the covers with him wouldn't be so abysmal.

Sebastian ambled over to the pond's edge. "It's late."

Henrietta skated to a stop. In the twilight, it was hard to see her eyes, but he could *feel* her fierce stare.

"What are you doing here, Ravenswood?"

"I've come to escort you back to the house," he said. "It's almost dinner."

"I'm not hungry."

She skated off, the willful chit.

Sebastian glared after her. He couldn't follow her onto the ice; he had no skates. He had to find some other way to coax her off the frozen pond.

"Miss Ashby, I cannot leave you alone on the ice."

He had to raise his voice; she'd skated to the pond's *other* edge.

"And why not?" came the indignant retort.

"Because I am a gentleman, Miss Ashby, and I cannot abandon you in the wilderness."

She had beguiled him once with just such a rejoinder. Now he had used her own words against her. Apparently she didn't appreciate that, for he heard her snort across the pond.

He said, "Your father would have my head if I let you get eaten by a bear."

Was that a "good riddance" he'd heard?

Sebastian sighed. She was going to be *very* obstinate, wasn't she?

"It's getting dark," he tried next. "You won't be able to find your way back home."

"I can see the lights in the house just fine from here."

True. Blast it! It appeared he didn't have any other choice but to go after the mulish girl.

Sebastian tested the ice with the tip of his boot.

He didn't fare too well with skating blades. Perhaps he might fare better without them.

He would soon find out.

With a tentative step, he rested one boot on the ice.

Still standing.

He took another step.

Again, he was still standing.

Encouraged, he slid one boot in front of the other.

Big mistake.

Sebastian landed on his rump with a wicked thump.

A bit dazed, he took a moment to hear the lyrical laughter.

So the little vixen took pleasure in his foolery? Funny, but he didn't mind. Making her laugh, that was. Hearing the musical chortle was rather infectious, and he found himself grinning, too. Good thing it was too dark for her to see. He didn't want her to think he enjoyed making an ass of himself.

But as long as she wasn't crying or cursing him, he was content to let her have her fun.

"I'm glad you are amused, Miss Ashby."

"Encore!" She giggled.

Staggering, Sebastian tried to regain his balance. "Didn't you once promise to catch me if I fell?"

"And you believed me?" she quipped, using *his* words against him this time.

In the end, Sebastian surrendered to the ice and sat down, the cold, wet surface chilling his arse.

"It looks like I need your help, Miss Ashby."

"Rot!"

"I need you for balance, I'm afraid."

She humphed.

"Really, Miss Ashby, I'm stranded without you."

She was quiet for a moment, then said, "Just crawl back to shore."

"The devil I will! A man of my station on his hands and knees? Outrageous."

She skated to the center of the ice, but no farther. "You would rather a mere chit assist you?"

"I would rather my betrothed assist me."

She was silent again.

"You have a way of getting into trouble, Ravenswood," she said after a brief pause.

As do you, he reflected, but thought it prudent to keep the sentiment to himself.

"Does this mean you'll help me, Miss Ashby?"

She huffed. "I suppose so."

A loud crack.

Sebastian scrambled to his knees. "Henry, don't move!"

Henrietta froze.

But it happened again, the splinter of ice.

"Sebastian!"

"Henry, be still!" he cried. "I'm coming!"

With care, Sebastian started to crawl across the ice. His heart throbbing, the most vile hurt hacked at his breast, taking his breath away, his very wits.

"I'm almost there, Henry."

Another deafening fracture.

She let out a sob. "Sebastian, hurry!"

The fright in her voice twisted his innards, made his pulse pound. He scrambled across the ice as fast as he could. But he didn't want to put too much pressure on the thinning sheet. It might rupture before he reached Henrietta.

It was too late, though.

Another loud snap.

Henrietta looked up at him, her eyes glossy wet with tears, before the ice gave way, and she plummeted into the dark depths with a shrill scream.

"Henry!"

Wild with fear, Sebastian dropped to his belly and carefully slid across the frozen pond.

Henrietta thrashed in the frigid waters, but her winter garb was like an anchor, dragging her back beneath the chilling surface.

The shrieking stopped.

She disappeared beneath the water.

"Henry!"

Sebastian reached the frosty rupture and plunged his arm into the freezing pond. He searched for her, frantic. And then he felt it. The soggy velvet. And he grabbed her by the scruff of the neck, hoisting her to the surface.

Henrietta gasped for air. It was the sweetest sound he had ever heard.

"Oh God, Henry!"

Sebastian yanked her through the gap in the ice.

Her teeth were chattering, cracking like fireworks. She was cold to the touch, her skin pale, her lips blue. He had to get her into the house. Fast.

"Hang on, Henry," he whispered, cradling her in his arms.

It was too risky to stand. Too much pressure. The ice might split even more. He had to drag her across the fragile surface, keep the weight on the ice even.

Sebastian reached the pond's edge at last. He shrugged the greatcoat off his shoulders and wrapped it around Henrietta. She was shaking so hard, her sweet eyes shut tight.

Sebastian scooped her in his arms. "Don't you dare leave me, Henry."

He kissed her chilled brow and started to run toward the house.

Chapter 23

Henrietta was feeling much better. Ensconced in a soft chair, wrapped in a blanket, she perused the winter landscape from the parlor window, content with the respite.

It'd been two days since the mishap on the ice. Two days of constant fuss. Family and servants alike bombarded her with attention. The solitude in the parlor offered her a chance to reflect.

Sebastian had saved her life. The memory was clear; he had pulled her from the frigid water. She was grateful. Truly, she was. The dark dampness had filled her lungs, touched her bones, swallowed her alive. She had gasped for breath, for life . . . and Sebastian had wrested her from death's cold grip. She was beholden to him, eternally. But she still mistrusted him.

Henrietta sighed. The viscount was a hero. The whole household was in accord. Even her sisters believed him more of a saint than a sinner. And while

Henrietta didn't disapprove of the accolades, she was confused. Had the man really changed? Could such a renowned scoundrel reform his wicked ways?

The parlor door opened.

"You have a visitor, Miss Ashby."

Henrietta eyed the butler. "Who is it, Wilkes?"

"Lord Emerson."

Ah yes, the young gentleman from the engagement bash. "Show him in, Wilkes."

A short while later, comfortably seated, Emerson was holding a cup of tea and smiling. "You look well, Miss Ashby. I can't tell you how relieved I am to see you recovered."

"Thank you, my lord." She smiled in return. "I appreciate the well wishes."

"It's been the talk of the countryside, you know? Your little mishap."

Little?

"You must promise to never go out on the ice again," he said.

"Well, perhaps not never."

"Really, Miss Ashby. If I were your betrothed, I would forbid you from ice skating."

Henrietta frowned. "My lord—"

"You are too precious to lose, Miss Ashby."

She sighed. He was not the most debonair of men, so curt and authoritative. But she supposed his intention to protect her was honorable, albeit misplaced. "Thank you, my lord."

Emerson was staring at her. There was something

aloof, even frosty about his eyes. Pleasant manner notwithstanding, she sensed a chill from him.

Oh, she was just being a ninny. Perhaps she was still recovering from her accident. Her brain was a bit foggy at times, her concentration blurred. But whatever the reason for her peculiar unease, she was sure Emerson was an agreeable gentleman.

"How is your father, my lord?"

"The earl?" Emerson sipped his tea. "Bedridden, I'm afraid."

"I'm sorry to hear that."

"Don't be, Miss Ashby. The earl is strong-willed. He's too stubborn to die."

Emerson laughed. Not a hearty laugh. A cold chortle, really.

What rubbish! The man had spoken very fondly of his papa the night of the engagement bash.

Henrietta gathered her wayward thoughts, and with an airy inflection said, "So tell me, Emerson, are you looking forward to the London Season?"

He set his teacup aside. "I am indeed, Miss Ashby. I think I will settle down this year."

She quirked a brow. "But you are so young, my lord."

"At four-and-twenty? Perhaps. But I much prefer the domesticity of marital life. My own parents had a very happy marriage. And I wish to have a family, Miss Ashby. I'm not like the other young bucks of the *ton*. The sins of bachelorhood do not tempt me."

Unlike her betrothed, she thought bitterly.

Emerson crossed his legs. "I must say, I am impressed, Miss Ashby. You've managed to tame London's most renowned bachelor."

Henrietta wasn't so sure about that. Ravenswood tamed? Not with a whip and a ring of fire . . . but then again, the viscount was acting rather odd. Like a gentleman. Had the thought of marriage *truly* altered him?

Oh, Henrietta didn't know what to think anymore!

"Ravenswood riveted?" he said. "I'm astonished, really I am. I believed him un-catchable . . . but, if I might be so bold, you are very tempting bait, Miss Ashby."

Tempting indeed. She was a dunce. But for the silly letter she had penned to Ravenswood, she would not be in this bind.

Yet Henrietta did not care for Emerson's false flattery. Rather, she was curious to know more about the man's association with her betrothed. "Do you know the viscount well, my lord?"

"Not at all." He flicked his fingers. "But one does read the papers."

She pinched her brow. "The papers?"

"The society pages. Rumor has it . . . Oh, listen to me prattle away about idle gossip. It's most inappropriate. Do forgive me, Miss Ashby."

"Yes, of course, my lord," she murmured.

Society pages? Rumors? A tight knot formed in her belly, making her ill. A reformed rogue, indeed! What sort of scandal was her scoundrel of a betrothed embroiled in now? And to think she had considered the idea of his transformation!

"I don't know how these rumors ever get started," said Emerson. "But it's good to know the tittle-tattle is all nonsense. You are a miracle worker, Miss Ashby. The whole *ton* agrees."

Oh good, she was a veritable spectacle. A sideshow amusement. She could hear the showman now: come and see the miracle worker tame the beast Ravenswood.

Rot! If she had any sway over the rebellious viscount, the man would *not* be in the society papers!

"Well, Miss Ashby, I've taken up enough of your time." Emerson stood. "I just dropped by to offer my good wishes for your health. We wouldn't want you to miss your own wedding, would we?" He winked. "Good day, Miss Ashby."

"Good day, my lord."

He gave a curt bow, then quit the room.

Henrietta twisted her lips; blood throbbed in her head. She was too miffed to even notice Emerson had winked at her. All she could think about was her ignoble fiancé, causing so great a stir it was splashed all over the society papers.

Henrietta picked up the little porcelain bell on the table beside her and shook it for all she was worth.

The butler appeared. "You rang, Miss Ashby?"

"Wilkes, do we have a copy of the paper?"

"I believe so."

"Will you fetch it for me?"

"Right away, Miss Ashby."

The butler left the room—and Henrietta stewed.

The wily bounder! How could Ravenswood do this to her? Expose her to gossip and ridicule? She had asked him to keep his immoral behavior a secret, to hide his lecherous conduct from polite society. But it seemed he was too much a devil to grant her even that simple wish.

Henrietta took in a shaky breath, her heart fluttering. She was right to mistrust the viscount. She was right to think him a knave. The man was a gentleman in name only. He had not a scrap of respect for her.

The butler soon returned with the paper. "Here you are, Miss Ashby."

"Thank you, Wilkes."

"Will there be anything else?"

"No, that will be all, Wilkes."

The butler bowed and once more deserted the room.

Fingers trembling, Henrietta peeled back the pages of the paper. She scanned the society section, looking for any mention of Ravenswood.

At length she saw it, the snippet of gossip:

. . . and now for a festive bit of news. A confirmed bachelor is prepared to take wedding vows on Twelfth Night. How romantic! One has to applaud the bride for her charm and beauty . . . and her clever wiles. A friend near and dear to the groom purports the gentleman vowed never to marry, but the lady in question enchanted him until he proposed . . . although I hear the groom might be disenchanted after the wedding. Oh, the trials of matrimony!

Henrietta saw red. Why, the lecherous, scheming bounder! How could he besmirch her like that? Imply she had "enchanted" him into proposing, and now intended to neglect his husbandly needs. Did he think to humiliate her into wifely submission?

Near and dear friend, indeed. It was the viscount who had spread the vile tale. She had told no one but him of her intention to marry in name only, so *he* had to have spread the rumor somehow.

Henrietta slapped the paper against the tabletop. "Bloody hell!"

"Good morning, Miss Ashby."

She gasped. So rankled by the slanderous gossip, she'd failed to spot the viscount in the room. He was dressed in dark breeches, crisp linen shirt, and form-fitting waistcoat: a devilishly handsome sight. And she wanted to scratch out his eyes.

"Good morning, Ravenswood," she gritted.

He swaggered into the parlor, seemingly unperturbed by her display of pique, and settled into Emerson's former chair. "You look well, Miss Ashby."

Well, she felt like a dunce. He looked so much like

the hero she had always wanted him to be. But he was only playing the part of a hero; she understood that now. Ravenswood was a scoundrel through and through. He would never change. He would charm and flirt and spin yarns of treachery to get what he wanted, but he would never be true . . . or good . . . or trustworthy.

"I have something for you, Miss Ashby."

He slipped out of the chair and knelt.

Alarmed, Henrietta said, "What are you doing?"

"Well, it occurred to me we haven't had a proper courtship." He rummaged in his vest pocket and removed a . . . ring. "And since we are starting anew, Miss Ashby, I think this might be appropriate."

Henrietta blinked. The shimmering emerald was square cut, set in white gold. It was stunning . . . breathtaking . . . "Beautiful."

He slipped the ring over her finger. "I'm glad you think so. It belonged to my mother, and I'd like you to have it. Think of it as an engagement ring."

Henrietta eyed the dazzling bauble . . . and quickly realized the viscount was up to his old wicked ways: charming and flirting and spinning yarns.

She slipped the ring off her finger. "I can't accept this."

The blue pools of his eyes dark and stormy, he said, "And why not?"

"Because we don't have a real marriage. Our union will be in name only."

The flinch in his cheek, the square of his shoulders indicated he was upset by the news. It seemed he'd not expected a return to their former formality. Rather he had assumed a more intimate acquaintance after his daring rescue. But Henrietta was not going to let the rogue think that he'd earned a place in her bed just because he'd saved her life. Gratitude was one thing, enslaving her heart was another.

"You should keep the ring, Ravenswood."

"And give it to whom? You are going to be my wife, Miss Ashby. You are the only wife I will ever have."

Henrietta gathered her valor and returned the jewelry. "I'm sorry, but I can't take the ring."

"I see." He pressed his lips together.

She wanted to sink under the blanket, his stare was so smoldering. Instead she gathered the coverlet close to her breast.

He pocketed the ring. "I am sorry, too, Miss Ashby. I thought the ring would be appreciated. Forgive my impudence."

Sebastian took in a slow, deep breath. He looked more furious than repentant, though, and Henrietta loathed to rankle his temper even more. He had saved her life, after all. But she would not let the viscount's heady charm beguile her into a wretched circumstance—like that of a brokenhearted wife. He would not woo her—or humiliate her in the papers—to get her to surrender to his will. She was defiant . . . but she would give the man the gratitude he deserved. That much she would do.

"Since you are here, Ravenswood, I must thank you."

He lifted off his haunches and growled, "For what?"

"For saving my life, of course."

"Oh? So you've noticed?"

"What rubbish! Of course I've noticed. The entire household has noticed."

"Well, you're welcome," he said crisply. "I hope you are feeling better, Miss Ashby?"

"I am," she said, trying to sound aloof, but feeling dreadfully guilty on the inside for being so uncouth. "Thank you for asking, my lord."

Yet why was *she* feeling guilty? She had every right to keep Ravenswood at bay. His charm only increased with each passing day. And Henrietta had to guard her heart. He was an irredeemable rogue. The vicious gossip he had spread in the paper was proof of that.

"Good day, Ravenswood."

"Good day, Miss Ashby."

Quietly he walked out of the room.

Sebastian was alone in the library, the newspaper spread out across his lap. It was dark out; he didn't know the time. The room was dim, too, but for the snapping flames in the hearth.

"There you are, Seb." Peter sauntered into the room and went straight over to the table of spirits. "Brandy?"

"No."

Peter quirked a brow. "No brandy?" He set the decanter aside. "Are you feeling all right, Seb?"

Sebastian tossed the paper across the room. "Read that, Peter."

Peter placed his drink on the table, picked up the newsprint, and held it close to the firelight. "Read what?"

"The snippet near the bottom."

After a silent moment, Peter whistled. "Tough luck, old boy." He picked up the glass again, and sat down next to his brother on the settee. "How did that get into the paper?"

"Devil if I know."

Sebastian was mesmerized by the dance of fire. The hypnotic crackle soothed his temper. He had suspected something was amiss when he'd first walked into the parlor and observed Henrietta cursing and smacking the furniture with the newspaper. Her subsequent cold deportment had told him something was definitely wrong, and as soon as he'd recovered the paper, he'd realized what that something was. No wonder the chit was still miffed with him. The gossip might not mention him or her by name, but the "wedding vows on Twelfth Night" gave away their identities. And knowing Henrietta's wary nature, she probably thought *he* had voiced the vicious sentiments.

Bloody hell.

"Well, is the story true?" said Peter.

"That Henrietta doesn't want me to share the marriage bed? I'm afraid so."

"Now that's *really* tough luck, old boy." Peter shook his head in commiseration. "By and by, who is this 'near and dear' friend?"

"Probably the same scoundrel who bandied Henrietta's letter all over Town. Someone's been eavesdropping on my private conversations with the chit."

"Ah, you have an enemy . . . but then again you must have so many enemies, Seb."

Sebastian glared at his brother. "Are you trying to be helpful, Peter? If you are, stuff it!"

Peter chuckled. "All right, I'll be helpful. How shall we discover the identity of this scoundrel?"

"Forget the scoundrel, Peter. I'll deal with him later, whoever he is. First I have to mollify my betrothed."

"Why don't you offer the girl a present?"

"I've already tried that, Peter. I gave her Mother's emerald ring. A fat lot of good it did me, though. She threw the bauble back in my face."

Peter sighed. "I wish I could be more obliging, Seb, but deuced if I know the working of a woman's heart. I misjudge my own wife more'n half the time." He took a swig of brandy. "You know who we need right now?"

"Who?"

"Father."

Sebastian creased his brow. "Why Father?"

"Because Father was a philosopher," said Peter.

"Don't you remember, Seb? He was always spouting psalms or poetry or some other sage canon."

Sebastian remembered all right. He remembered being a boy, interned within the schoolroom on a glorious summer day, reciting from the texts of historians and philosophers and scientists alike.

A disciplinarian, Father had served as both parent and teacher, determined to fill the young minds of his sons with clever doctrines. He'd espoused truths and mores with frightening fervor. And he'd expected his offspring to obey the teachings, to live by them. Not a violent man, the viscount was nonetheless capable of instilling fear. And to two impressionable boys, the imposing image of the former viscount had made a lasting impression. To this day, Sebastian could still flinch at the memory of his father's glower.

Peter said, "I bet Father would have a ready verse to debunk the mystery of a woman's heart."

"Well, if Father had such a poetic verse, it didn't do him much good."

"What do you mean?"

"He and Mother didn't have the best rapport, Peter."

"Rubbish! Mother was very happy."

"Mother was rich."

Peter pinched his brow. "So?"

"So of course she was happy. She spent her days shopping—far away from Father."

Peter scrunched his brow. "Father wasn't that bad, Seb."

"Oh no? Don't you remember our time in the schoolroom, dissecting the *History of Rome*, while every other young scamp was out and about, looking up ladies' skirts?"

Peter scoffed. "You make childhood sound so miserable, Seb. Father used to take us on outings in the country, don't you remember?"

"To instruct us on flora and fauna."

"What about the trip to Italy? It was a very pleasant sojourn."

"We spent the entire time in a monestary learning Latin. Hardly pleasant."

Peter made a moue. "You have a selective memory, Seb."

"You have a defective one, brother."

"Do you really think so?" Peter frowned. "Do you think I've buried the unpleasant memories?"

"I do," said Sebastian. "Now if only I could do the same."

Peter glanced at him askance. "What do you mean, Seb?"

A dark thought coming to mind, Sebastian said, "Do you remember what Father used to say about good and evil?"

Peter scrunched his brow. "No."

"He used to say that some of us were born good and destined to return to heaven, while others were born damned. That there was nothing one could do about his fate. If you were born damned, all the good deeds in creation couldn't save you."

Peter nodded. "Ah, yes, the idea of predestination. I remember now."

"Do you think Father was right?"

Peter shrugged. "He was spouting church dogma centuries old."

"Does being old make the theory untrue?"

"Well, no, but it doesn't make it true, either."

"I was just wondering."

Peter glanced at his brother again. "Did you take that theory to heart, Seb?"

Sebastian looked at the hearth and inhaled the scent of burning wood. He wanted to deny it, but could not. In truth, he *had* taken the theory to heart. Considering his wicked disposition, he'd reasoned he was one of the damned, and redemption was impossible, good works fruitless. Long ago, he'd resigned himself to his fate.

But now . . . now he didn't want to be doomed anymore. Now he wanted a warm and willing wife in his bed, not a cold fish. His parents had suffered a lonely sham of a marriage. He didn't want the same cursed destiny. But how to get the chit to trust him?

Change his dastardly ways?

Sebastian snorted.

Even if he tried to be a true gentleman, could a scoundrel really change his ways? He wasn't so sure. After everything he had done for Henrietta, she still loathed him, considered him a fiend. Maybe he was one. Maybe that's why she didn't want anything to do with him anymore. Perhaps she could see him for what he really was and always would be: a villain. And maybe all the good deeds in creation couldn't change that.

"Listen, Seb." Peter elbowed his brother in the ribs. "I know Father was an important figure in our lives, and all, but don't let what he said so many years ago shape your life today."

Sebastian mulled that over. Even if his brother was right, it did not negate the fact that he was still a rogue. It was what he was good at . . .

Well, then, perhaps it was time Sebastian put the rogue inside him to good use. He had saved Henrietta's life, offered her gifts, acted the gentleman, and she still rebuffed him. Clearly good deeds did not impress her. Perhaps she wanted something a little more scandalous . . .

Well, if the chit still desired his kisses, he was going to give them to her.

Chapter 24

Henrietta set the candle down. Feeling a pinch of remorse, she opened the black velvet purse and removed the glass globe. Carefully she placed it on the mantelpiece.

Sebastian was not going to like finding it there when he returned to his room. He was going to be downright furious, she was sure.

But Henrietta had to give back the present. She should never have accepted it in the first place. It was inappropriate. She didn't care for the viscount. To keep such a gift suggested their engagement was meaningful, that their marriage would be, too. But that was not the case, and she didn't want Sebastian to think otherwise.

Henrietta sighed. She didn't like to be so ill-mannered. After all, Sebastian had saved her life. But she'd expressed her gratitude. She was not, however, prepared to trust the rogue with her heart and soul.

Henrietta picked up the candle, about to tiptoe

from the room. She shrieked instead, and dropped the flame.

Sebastian stomped on the candle, dousing the flickering light. But it'd already scorched the rug, the scent of burned thread filling the air.

"Good evening, Miss Ashby."

Oh, that husky male voice! It made her shiver right down to her very toes.

"Forgive the intrusion, Ravenswood. I was just . . ."

Sebastian took the poker by the hearth and stabbed at the dwindling flames, the fire sparking anew with life.

"You were just what?" he said.

The room brightened, the glass globe aglow.

Henrietta chewed on her bottom lip, dreading the inevitable quarrel. But Sebastian did not notice the globe. Oh no. He noticed her instead.

Smoldering eyes drifted up her frame in a slow and sensual stare, stirring goose pimples to tease her flesh.

"Have you come to bed, Miss Ashby?"

She gasped. "No, I have not!"

"Pity," was all that he said.

The rogue! "How dare you assume—"

Lips so low she could feel his warm breath on her cheeks, he said in a dark timbre, "Miss Ashby, when I find a beautiful woman in my room, so scantily attired, I must assume she has come to bed."

Confused, Henrietta peeked at her ensemble and stifled another gasp. Drat! She was dressed in her night rail and wrapper! It'd wholly slipped her mind.

Quickly she gripped the woolly wrapper by the collar, hiding her breasts.

He tsked. "It's not like you, Miss Ashby, to be so bashful."

"And it's wholly like you to be such a scoundrel," she quipped.

He grinned. The audacious man actually grinned.

Henrietta pursed her lips. "What happened to the gentleman inside you?"

"He went away."

"Oh, did he now?"

Slowly he nodded. "You chased him away, I'm afraid."

"And how did I do that?"

"By coming to my room so late at night."

She stiffened at his whispered words, so carnal in tone. He was doing it again, making her quiver—and ache. Oh, how she ached! Deep inside her belly. All the feelings she'd tried to repress bubbled in her breast. Feelings of longing. Of need. For him . . . for his touch . . . for his wicked kiss.

To quell the loud beatings of her heart, she took in a deep breath. "I said I was sorry. Now if you will excuse me."

"Do you really want to go?"

Her breath hitched. Softly he traced the line of her brow with his thumb, rounded her eye, then stroked the top of her cheek in a sensual caress.

"I think you'd rather stay," he murmured.

Henrietta's heart clamored in her breast when he bussed her brow. She was rooted to the spot. Blood throbbed through her veins.

"I think you want to be with me, Henry."

Her lashes fluttered closed as he kissed the ridge of her nose. Her nickname had never sounded so sinfully delicious. She was mesmerized by his charm: the deep rumble of his voice, the deft stroke of his finger, the heady taste of his hot lips.

"I think you want me to make love to you," he said.

Wanton lips brushed hers, stirring a flutter of desire in her belly. It shouldn't feel so good to be with him, she thought. He was a scoundrel. He had devastated her heart.

But it did feel good.

So achingly good.

"Do you, Henry? Do you want me to make love to you?"

Arched on her toes, she was a hair's breadth away from his sinfully sensuous lips. But she would not admit to her need outright. It would only give him clout over her. She did want his kisses, though. So much so, it hurt deep inside.

"Sebastian," she breathed instead.

A warm mouth meshed hard over hers.

It appeared to be enough of a surrender, his whispered name. He would not make her confess her wanton hunger. She was grateful for that.

Henrietta pressed her limbs against him, eager to feel the dips and grooves of his hard body, to mold her frame to his. And what sweet pleasure it was, to have such gnarled muscles rubbing her tender flesh. Even in her woolly wrapper, she could feel the brawn, the sculpted curves of his magnificent figure.

So full of passion, she kissed him with wild abandon, and he, rogue that he was, smiled against her lips with smug satisfaction. She wanted to bite the wicked grin off his face, but alas, she was blissfully distracted by the hot thrust of his bold tongue into her mouth, taking her breath and her wits away.

"I know you, Henry," he breathed between kisses, suckling on her bottom lip. Nipping at it, too.

She trembled under his deft ministrations, her knees weak.

"I know what you like." The moist tip of his tongue skimmed over her swollen lips. "You like to watch, Henry, don't you? You like to look at pictures in books."

He broke away from the kiss.

Henrietta was about to have a snit in protest.

But Sebastian pushed her back, pressed her up against the bedpost, intent on keeping her aroused, it seemed, for he unfastened his trousers just then.

Henrietta gasped to see the turgid flesh exposed. It was so swollen. So big. And after looking at all those luscious men in Madam Jacqueline's naughty book of pictures, she was most giddy to see Sebastian in such a carnal way, too.

"Look at me, Henry." He kissed her between words. "I want you to see what you do to me."

He took her by the hand.

Henrietta took in a deep breath at the feel of hot flesh between her fingers. Eyes brimming with wonder, she stared at the hard length of him in her sweaty palm.

Sebastian nuzzled her temple and said in a throaty whisper, "Do you see what you do to me, Henry?"

He thickened in her hand.

Henrietta bit her bottom lip to keep from groaning. She was dizzy with giddy passion, moist with sweat.

He nipped her earlobe. "Do you see how you make me feel?"

Henrietta shuddered in his embrace. She squirmed against the bedpost, wanting out of her woolly robe. She wanted to feel his flesh against hers.

But first she wanted more kisses.

She pinched his hair and tugged, searching for his sinfully heady lips, all the while stroking the long, stiff shaft of muscle between his legs.

"What do I make you feel?" He flicked his tongue over her mouth. "Tell me, Henry."

But Henrietta didn't want to admit the truth. She didn't want to open her heart to him, only her body. Just for one night.

She arched on her toes, reaching for his lips.

But he did not kiss her.

"Tell me, Henry. Tell me what I make you feel."

Her belly a knot of need, Henrietta huffed with unquenched lust, still too stubborn to say a word.

Sebastian pushed her hand away from his throbbing erection. He pressed up against her instead and started to rock his hips.

Oh, sweet heaven! Henrietta bumped her head against the bedpost in passionate bliss. She let out a groan of pure lust, grabbed Sebastian by the waist to keep from collapsing onto the floor.

"I'll make the ache inside you go away, Henry."

He was hoarse. And so hard, thrusting against her belly in tantalizing torment. The scoundrel!

"Tell me what you feel, Henry."

Hips swirling, he undulated against her midriff. She closed her eyes, fighting the rush of heady desire building in her loins. She was wet deep down. So wet. And she could feel her resolve cracking under the pressure of her need.

Henrietta cried out, "Hungry."

He kissed her: a reward for her compliance. "What else do I make you feel?"

She gasped, "Wet."

He thrust against her again. "What else?"

Weakly, she said, "Frightened."

Sebastian took her lips in his for a thorough kiss. "I promise, Henry, you won't be frightened of me after tonight—ever again."

She wanted to believe him. Her heart ached for those words to be true.

With deft strokes, Sebastian slipped the woolly wrapper off her shoulders.

Henrietta didn't feel the chill of the room. Her body was on fire. She held Sebastian tight, not wanting to let him go, not wanting him to leave her in such a desperate state.

"Henry, you vixen."

He scooped her in his arms and set her down on the bed. Her night rail rucked up to her waist, he nestled between her splayed thighs.

Henrietta moaned at the exquisite pressure pushing against her pulsing core. He teased her for a moment, dipping the cusp of his swollen arousal inside her dewy flesh. She wanted to curse him, the dratted man! If he made her beg, she'd never forgive him.

The tip of his erection nudging the moist folds of her tender flesh, he said in a ragged whisper, "Do you like this, Henry?"

Henrietta gasped for breath. "Truthfully . . . I don't."

Sebastian stiffened. Slowly he eased his erection away from her.

"But I thought . . ." He looked dumbfounded. "Henry, I thought you wanted me to . . ."

"No," she said, then nipped at his bottom lip. She held his lip in her mouth for a moment before she slowly let it slip between her teeth. "I'd much rather be on top."

His nostrils flared. With a violent shudder, Sebastian yanked her to her feet and dragged her over to the cushy armchair by the crackling fire. He kicked the ottoman away and settled in the seat.

"Come here," he bade.

Before Henrietta could shriek with giddy pleasure, she was in Sebastian's lap, straddling him.

"Is this better?" he growled.

She couldn't resist a smug grin. "Much."

He humphed, not amused by the little trick she'd played a moment ago. But he deserved as much, the rogue, for teasing her senses in such a cruel fashion.

But now that Henrietta had the advantage of being on top, she was positively rife with mirth . . . and adoration . . . and curiosity.

Hands trembling, she fiddled with the buttons of Sebastian's linen shirt, eager to feel his hot flesh and blood beneath her fingertips. He didn't touch her in return. Instead he gripped the armrests, giving her autonomy to do to him as she willed.

Henrietta was tickled. She was also a bit nervous, hence her fumbling fingers. But at last, she spread the soft fabric of his shirt apart.

Impressed, she perused the wide expanse of knotted muscle. Dark curls, rough to the touch, covered his strapping chest. Her fingers raked through the matted hair, stroked firm pecs, and teased the sensitive nubs of his nipples.

"You're beautiful," she whispered, awed.

At her words, he took in a deep and shuddering breath.

Henrietta scooted down the length of his firm legs, and lowered her head, flicking her tongue over one jutting nipple.

He flinched.

She grinned.

With sinful pleasure, she parted her lips and sucked.

Sebastian hardened beneath her even more. She didn't think the man could get any harder. For some wicked reason, she was pleased to know that he could.

She nipped his nipple. "How do I make you feel?"

Sebastian growled. She could hear the rumble in his breast.

She nipped him again. "Tell me."

"Hungry," he gritted.

She sucked on the tight nub. "What else?"

"Hard."

With a lanky stroke, she licked his nipple. "What else?"

He whispered, "Frightened."

Henrietta lifted her eyes to meet his torrid gaze. She was mesmerized by the fiery gleam in the dark blue pools.

"Touch me," she beseeched.

Quickly he crushed her in his embrace, tangled his fingers in her long tresses, and kissed her hard.

Henrietta could feel the breeze on her backside, the cool caress of winter air. Apprehensive, she didn't want Sebastian to remove her night rail. She didn't want him to see her bare, so vulnerable.

"I want you, Henry," he growled in wanton hunger. "I want to see and feel all of you."

The mulish man! He was determined to break down all her defenses, wasn't he? And he was doing an admirable job of it, too, for Henrietta was soon stripped of her flimsy night rail and cushioned against Sebastian's hot flesh in stark intimacy.

"That's it, Henry." He kissed her roughly. "Don't hide from me."

So she didn't.

Henrietta lifted off her haunches, kneeling, her breasts at Sebastian's mouth. It was only fair, she reckoned. She'd had the pleasure of him in her mouth.

Sebastian groaned, and quickly parted his lips.

Henrietta cooed at the profound pleasure rippling through her limbs. His lips moved over her breast in fluid strokes, suckling her, stoking the flames of lust in her belly.

"Oh, Sebastian!"

She twisted her fingers in his hair. The pinch at her breast as he sucked on her nipple was divine. And with his strong hands rubbing her backside, she was being licked and kissed and stroked into a dizzying frenzy.

Snug against him, Henrietta started to rock her hips, simulating the same torturous thrusts he had tormented her with before.

Sebastian bucked beneath her.

"You little witch," he groaned, and cupped her hips, guiding her down to his pulsing erection.

Henrietta stiffened.

"Don't, Henry," he said, breathless. "It'll hurt more if you're tight."

Well, *that* didn't make her feel better.

"It's all right, Henry." He kissed her neck, and slipped his fingers between her legs.

It was Henrietta's turn to buck.

Sebastian chuckled. "Did you like that?"

Henrietta could only lick her lips. Words deserted her. A deep and thrumming need in her belly ballooned. Sebastian's fingers only made the ache inside her stronger. She was wet and trembling and she wanted release.

Henrietta gasped at the hot feel of Sebastian's flesh thrust inside her. She stiffened, a bit stunned to find herself impaled over the thick length of him.

But soon the pinch in her loins eased. The pounding need returned. And Henrietta started to rock against the throbbing flesh inside her, looking for relief.

She gazed into Sebastian's eyes, so full of warmth. Lost in the zeal of his fiery gaze, she undulated in quick, piercing strokes.

He was breathing hard. She was, too. The sweat on his brow glistened under the glow of firelight.

It was pure rapture, being one with Sebastian. The

knot in her belly twisted even more. She opened her mouth to cry out. Sebastian silenced her with a firm kiss.

She groaned against his lips, gripped him tight. It was so intense, the relief. A burst of energy washing through her, sating her.

Sebastian thrust hard into her, so deep. He shuddered, pouring his seed into her with a feral moan.

It was over. For a few minutes, Henrietta couldn't move. She was slumped over Sebastian's body, gasping for air, trying to ease the thundering beats of her heart.

"Henry," he whispered, stroking the damp ridges of her spine. "It'll be like this forever."

Henrietta took in an uneven breath. Forever? With Sebastian? No. There was no such thing as forever. Not with a man like Sebastian.

Good heavens, what had she done?

Chapter 25

~~~

Sebastian let out a deep, sated sigh. He had not felt so fulfilled in . . . well, ever. And to think, he was going to spend the rest of his days bedding Henrietta. A wolfish smile touched his lips.

Sebastian opened his sleepy eyes to find the room dark—and the bed empty.

Lips falling, he groped along the bedcovers, searching for another warm body, but he didn't find one.

He shot to his feet.

Candlestick in hand, he stalked over to the low-burning fire and ignited the wick.

Soft light filled the dim room. He lifted the candle high, searching the space for Henrietta, but she was gone.

It burned in his gut, the fury. How could she leave him after the intimate night they had shared?

Wait! She was in his room, remember? Of course the chit had dashed away. Come morning, she had to be in her own bed or the house would be in an uproar. Not that it mattered to Sebastian if the house was in a tizzy; the chit was going to be his wife—funny how that word didn't seem so ghastly anymore. Still, Henrietta clearly didn't want to upset her parents. She must have tiptoed from the room after he'd fallen asleep. Smart woman. If he'd been awake, he would not have let her leave. To have her in his arms was a peace unlike any he had ever known. And Sebastian wasn't keen on giving up such bliss—ever.

Less livid, Sebastian let the tension ease from his corded muscles. But then the glimmer of glass caught his eye.

He took in a sharp breath. Perched on the mantel was the glass globe he had given Henrietta as a gift.

So that's why she'd been inside his room. She'd come to give back the present.

The fury in his belly made a hasty return. He moved about the room, snatching his clothes. He shrugged into his trousers and put on his shirt.

Dressed, he quit the room and headed for the ground floor. Instinct pressed him to pound on Henrietta's bedroom door, but he refrained from the impulse, heading for the billiard room instead. He was too riled up to confront the chit just now. He needed to soothe his temper.

Inside the billiard room, Sebastian used his candle to light a few more wicks, brightening the space even more.

He grabbed a cue stick from the mount on the wall, and with a hard crack, sent the cue ball shooting across the green felt tabletop.

The stubborn chit. Did she mean to torment him? Bed him and then leave him? Did she think to deny him such exquisite pleasure all the rest of his days? Deny herself the same delight? She had enjoyed their mating as much as he had. How was *she* going to live without his touch?

He growled at the thought.

Peter had been right; it was a deuced mystery deciphering a woman's heart.

Sebastian paused, the creaking door interrupting his sour musings.

Henrietta stood in the door frame, candle in hand.

She was stunning, all bedraggled from their heated coupling. Auburn hair mussed in a whimsical fashion, rosy lips still swollen, her woolly wrapper an untidy mess. She was a lascivious sight. And he wanted her again so much it hurt.

Sebastian smacked the cue stick against the billiard table. "Why did you give back the gift?"

"I can't accept the present," she said. "You and I can never truly be husband and wife."

"Why?"

She stepped deeper into the room. "Because you don't want a wife. You just want a warm body in your bed."

His nostrils flared. "Is that so?"

"Do you deny it?"

He thought about it for a moment, then said, "No, I don't deny it. And why shouldn't I want my wife's warm body in my bed?"

"You've been lying to me this whole time, haven't you?"

"Damn it, Henry!"

"You've only been acting the part of the gentleman to get me to submit to your will. You even spread that ghastly gossip in the paper to try and get your way."

"Now *that* I did not do," he vowed.

"Then who did?"

"I don't know."

But she didn't believe him; he could tell by the skeptical tone of her voice. "Probably the same scoundrel who flaunted my letter all over Town."

"That's right! Believe me, Henry!"

"I don't believe you," she said softly. "And it was a mistake being with you tonight."

It made the blood pound in his veins to hear those words. A mistake? He had given the woman his body, even opened his heart to her. And she called it a mistake?

He gnashed his teeth. "So why are you here?"

"I just wanted to tell you."

That's it? She'd traipsed into the room looking like a wanton temptress just to tell him to go to the devil—again?

Horseshit!

Slowly he moved around the billiard table. "You're lying, Henry."

"No, I'm not."

But the flux in her voice told him otherwise.

He took the candle from her hand and set it aside, growling, "The hell you're not."

Her eyes were glossy under the firelight, her cheeks flushed. He could hear her quick, uneven gasps of breath.

The mulish chit might think she didn't want him, but the scoundrel in him could sense her arousal. She had come looking for more kisses. And he was too much of a rogue not to give them to her.

Sebastian crushed his mouth over hers, determined to prove to the willful Henrietta she desired his touch as much as he desired hers.

And what a sweet victory it was, for the heady taste of her in his mouth sparked a fire in his belly too feral to tame.

"You want me, Henry," he said roughly between kisses. "I know you do."

She whimpered.

He thrust his tongue into her mouth, drinking in the balmy taste of her.

The blood pounding in his head started to pound in his cock, too, and he pressed the turgid flesh against her belly, gripping her rump to keep her flush against him.

She groaned, stirring the lust in his throbbing erection even more.

In one deft movement, he scooped her in his arms and carried her over to the billiard table.

He propped her darling rump on the table's edge, and wedged her legs apart with his thigh.

"Tell me again this is a mistake," he said in a ragged whisper. "Tell me you don't want my touch."

Fingers groping along her moist thighs, he fondled the wet folds of feminine flesh between her legs.

She whimpered again, much louder.

He raked his lips over hers in savage thrusts. His finger did a little thrusting, too.

It was hard for him to plunge inside her; her tense muscles clamped tight around his finger. But it also made the encounter all the more pleasurable for her.

And when he added a second finger to her heat, pounding into her, those stiff muscles jerked and throbbed, bringing her to orgasm.

"Do you want more?" he said in a dark timbre. "Do you want to feel me inside you?"

She squirmed on the table, an evident yes. But it was not enough. He wanted her to say it.

Henrietta didn't have on her night rail, only her woolly wrapper. And he was quick to divest her of that.

She shivered in the nippy night air.

Sebastian cupped a plump breast in his sweaty palm, kneading, stroking the hard nub of her nipple with his thumb.

"I can't hear you, Henry."

He dropped his head to the full swell of her breast and started to suck.

Fingers knit tightly in his hair, pinching and pulling.

"Do you want more?" he breathed, and licked the rosy bud in a determined stroke. "Tell me."

She only thrust her breast deeper into his mouth, making wanton, unintelligible sounds to boot.

With a ragged breath, Sebastian pushed away from her.

She teetered on the table's edge, dazed, and grabbed the billiard cushions for support. She looked ready to murder him. But despite the twisting pain in his groin, he would not slake her lust before she asked him to. He wanted her to admit the truth. He wanted her to say it aloud, damn it! She *needed* him as he *needed* her.

"If you don't want it, Henry, I won't give it to you."

She gnashed her teeth.

God, she was beautiful in the candlelight. A glorious and naked display of pique. It was going to be pure torment, walking away from her. He prayed the chit was not so mulish as to bite her tongue.

She was breathing roughly, her swollen breasts heaving, the dark and rosy nubs of her nipples jutting forward in aching points.

But she did not say a word.

Blast it!

"Have it your way, Henry."

His cock stiff with desire, he moved slowly toward the door.

"Wait!" She sounded strangled.

Sebastian paused. He glanced over his shoulder, taking in the glorious curves of her flesh, burning inside with a pounding need to ravish her.

"Yes, Henry?"

She whispered, "I want you."

He took in a deep breath of satisfaction.

Slowly he sauntered back over to the billiard table.

Trembling, Henrietta watched him with a rapacious look in her eye. It stirred his blood to have her stare at him with such unabashed longing.

He kissed her softly.

"I'll give you anything that you want, Henry."

She opened her legs wider. Evidently she wanted *him*.

Sebastian nestled between her splayed thighs. He stroked her rump, the small of her back. He kissed her over and over again with heady passion.

Sebastian pushed the cue ball away, let it roll across the table.

"Lie down," he bade.

She did. She settled onto the billiard table, her legs still coiled around his hips.

"You're so beautiful," he breathed, moving his eyes over every dip and curve of her womanly form. And with her russet red locks spilling across the table like the glorious streaks of a setting sun, she looked every bit a divine temptress.

Sebastian unfastened his trousers.

He stood at the table's edge, propped his hands beneath her delectable arse to hoist her hips, and slowly sank into her warm, wet sheath.

Henrietta arched her head back and gasped.

Gentle at first, he rocked against her throbbing flesh, mesmerized by the expression of joy and sweet surrender etched on her darling lips.

"Henry, you feel so good."

She lifted her rump to meet each thrust, giving him room to plunge deeper inside her.

Sebastian gritted his teeth, holding his orgasm at bay. He was buried inside her to the hilt. So deep. So good.

He undulated with more vigor.

Henrietta's soft cries and murmurs intensified.

She closed her eyes tight.

"Look at me," he said with a desperate edge to his voice.

Dark red lashes fluttered open, lids heavy with heady arousal.

His muscles flexed. He pumped harder into her.

"Oh, Sebastian!" she gasped.

He thrust into her over and over again. Deeper. Rougher. Riding her like a ship in a stormy sea. Clinging to her like a lifeline.

Henrietta let out a strangled cry. He could feel the spasms of her sheath grip his throbbing rod.

With a few more piercing strokes, he let his own orgasm spill forth, pouring his seed into her with a growled oath of satisfaction.

He felt weak. All the life drained from him and pumped into Henrietta. And it felt so bloody good.

Sebastian lifted her off the table and gathered her in his arms.

She sighed in his embrace, wrapped her arms around him in a weak hold.

"My sweet Henry."

He combed her mussed curls away from her eyes, kissed the top of her head in a tender gesture.

She was slick with sweat.

"Here." He took the wrapper off the billiard table and helped her wriggle back into the woolly garment. "I don't want you to catch a chill."

She was back in his arms, hugging him, still sitting on the edge of the billiard table.

Sebastian gripped her in a protective hold. Surely this was going to make every last thing right between them.

Chapter 26

Henrietta slowly moved across the grounds, enjoying a morning stroll. She needed the cool winter air to help clear her befuddled senses.

Her body still burned for Sebastian. She had been so sure that a night of coupling would slake the desire in her belly. But it did nothing of the sort. If anything, she longed for the viscount even more. Drat!

What the devil was she going to do now?

Oh, Henrietta was a mess inside! It'd felt so good to be with Sebastian. A part of her had no regrets about the other night. After years of longing, to be with the man was a welcome relief.

But another part of her was filled with remorse. She'd had a taste of sweet pleasure last night. And she wanted to feel those warm sentiments again and again. Yet she couldn't let a scoundrel like Ravenswood so close to her heart. The man had lied to her, spread a dreadful tale about her in the paper. He only wanted a tussle in bed. Maybe two or three. But after he had had his fill of her, he'd abandon her.

Retreat to his old, immoral haunts. Devastate her.

She had to be more diligent in her rebuff. She could not let her flighty emotions get in the way of reason. She did not care for the man. She lusted after him, true. But the one had nothing to do with the other. Madam Jacqueline had said so herself. It was wholly possible to desire a man and yet dislike him.

So all Henrietta had to do was stomp asunder her desire. But how? How to forget the balmy taste of his lips? The incredible thrust of him so deep inside her? How to dismiss his sultry voice from her mind or the spicy touch of his strong fingers from her skin?

"Henry!"

Henrietta hardened. "How did you find me?"

Sebastian ambled down the snowy hill, a vision in regal gray, his curly black hair scruffy from the tender breeze. "I followed your footsteps."

She glanced at the trail of impressions. "Oh."

She wasn't thinking with a clear head, was she? And it was all the viscount's fault. He always unsettled her with his dazzling presence. She simply had to shoo him away.

But it was hard to think about getting rid of Sebastian when he looked so dashing in his tight trousers and flowing greatcoat. Her heart pinched at the handsome sight of him.

"What are you doing here, Ravenswood?"

He kissed her.

Henrietta gasped. The blood warmed in her veins, goose bumps spread all over her flesh.

Did she have to enjoy the man's kisses so much? Did all her wits have to desert her when he kissed her so?

Henrietta sighed, blissfully content to keep her lips attached to his till time immemorial. As long as she was kissing him, she wasn't thinking about the rogue within him.

He let go of her lips—far too soon.

Reason intruded.

Breathless, she demanded, "What the devil did you do that for?"

His own breath ragged, he said, "Every time you call me 'Ravenswood' or 'my lord' or some other infernal title, I'm going to kiss you. I don't care if the whole of the *ton* is there to witness it. You *will* call me Sebastian."

Why, the surly devil. "You wouldn't dare!"

There was a dark glow in his blue eyes. A glow of passion. Of intent. "I most certainly would, Henry."

"Fine," she gritted. "What are you doing here, *Sebastian*?"

"Where would you like to go for our wedding tour?" he said in a matter-of-fact manner, his stormy deportment blithe once more.

Henrietta blinked. "What?"

"I'd like to make the arrangements, Henry. How does Paris sound?"

Henrietta couldn't hear him very well; her heart was pounding in her ears. "Paris?"

"That's right. You've always wanted to visit Paris, haven't you?"

She needed a moment to gather her wayward thoughts. A terrible ache throbbed in her breast. She had dreamed of touring Paris with Ravenswood for years . . . but not with this Ravenswood, the immoral scoundrel.

A knot formed in her throat. A wretched sob. She swallowed to keep the howl at bay. Sebastian was no hero. She had discovered that dreadful truth at the dark abbey. He might look like a hero in his dapper garb. He kissed like a hero, to be sure. But he was not a hero. Hard as it might be for her to let go of a girlhood dream, she had to. He would only make her miserable. Break her heart—again—with his unfaithfulness and wicked pursuits.

Henrietta took an unsteady step away from him. "I won't go to Paris with you, Sebastian."

He stiffened. "And why the devil not?"

"Because I don't care for you . . . and I don't want to pretend like I do."

His nostrils flared. "You cared for me last night. You *wanted* me last night."

Memory of the other night filled her head. It was a struggle to keep her words firm. "I wanted your body, not you."

That struck a sensitive chord. He looked positively livid.

"A woman can lust after a man, too," she said. "*You* should know how easy it is to feel a fire in your belly, but nothing in your heart."

A sharp pang gripped her breast at her own words. Apparently it wasn't easy for her to feel a fire in her belly and nothing in her heart.

The man looked haggard. "What do you want from me, Henry?"

She took in a shaky breath. "I want you to leave me alone."

He flinched at the word "alone."

"You didn't want me to leave you alone last night," he said. "You enjoyed rutting with me, admit it!"

She cringed at his vulgarity. He was angry, lashing out. Still, she didn't like to think about him "rutting" with her. She'd rather think about him . . .

What? Making love to her? That was almost as nasty a thought, for it implied an emotion. And Henrietta was trying so hard *not* to get emotional.

"I want to forget about last night," she said, tamping the hurt in her breast. "I want to live apart from you once we're wed."

"No."

He breathed the word quietly, but the intense conviction burning in his eyes was impossible to ignore.

"Sebastian, I don't want to pretend—"

"We're not going to pretend, damn it! You're going to be *my* wife. You will live under *my* roof. And you will sleep in *my* bed."

She met his steely stare. "Then I suppose you'll have to force me to your bed, for I won't go willing again."

Sebastian took in a hard breath. "So you want to live apart from me, do you? What about a child?"

"What child?"

"You might be enceinte, Henry."

She gasped. That was true. She might have a babe . . . but that did not change anything. "Then I will raise the child alone."

He thundered, "You would deny me my own child!"

She felt a pinch of regret, but quickly shooed the sentiment away. "You are not fit to be a father, Sebastian. What will you do with a son? Teach him to be a 'friar' at your club? What about a daughter? Will you raise her to be part of the demimonde? A 'nun,' perhaps?"

He looked genuinely appalled. "You think me such a fiend?"

"Yes!" Tears welled in her eyes. "I think you're wicked. And if I have a child, I won't let you hurt it."

"I don't want to hurt the babe!" He dug his fingers in his hair and let out a curse. "Blast it, is living with me really such a terrible fate?"

The tears burned her cheeks. "Yes!"

"Why?!"

"Because I . . ."

He took her by the shoulders. "Tell me, Henry. Tell me why?"

"I can't forget."

Brow pinched, he said, "Forget what?"

"You . . . in that abbey . . . with that woman."

Sebastian sighed. "Henry, listen. It won't be like that anymore. I won't go back to the club, I promise."

"No." She wrested free of his hold. He wanted to get under her skirts, to beguile her into believing he had honorable intentions. "I won't let you charm me into some sort of trap. I don't trust you, Sebastian. I will never trust you . . . not with my heart."

Henrietta lifted her skirts to dash through the snow, tears burning her eyes. But she didn't care. She had to get away from Sebastian. She had to get away from his promise to change. A promise he couldn't keep.

"The little slut," Emerson grumbled

He trudged through the snow, making his way back to the front of the house. He had come to see the wench, to gauge how the piece of *on-dit* he'd planted in the paper had affected her. But apparently it'd had no effect on her at all.

The harlot! It was bad enough he'd had to wade through the muck of winter looking for her, but to find her in that bastard's arms! She didn't even care about the foul gossip he'd spread, curse her.

Seething, Emerson kicked up the snow. Yesterday she had looked ready to skin the viscount alive. But today she was kissing him. It was just like a woman to be so fickle. And it burned in Emerson's gut to know that his plan to destroy the couple had failed. Once more, Emerson found himself humiliated at the hands of the viscount. It was more than he could bear.

Settling into the sleigh, Emerson ordered the driver back to Ormsby Manor. And during the hour-long journey, the bile in his belly churned.

Emerson would not let Ravenswood win again. Palms fisting, he vowed to destroy the viscount, make the man feel the misery of defeat. And he was going to use that hussy Miss Ashby to do it. If Ravenswood wanted the little strumpet, then Emerson was going to take her away from him—by any means necessary.

Back at Ormsby Manor, Emerson entered the house, rife with newfound resolve. But his curmudgeon of a father put a swift end to that.

"Is that you, you blundering numskull?"

Emerson hardened. The clip-clop of the earl's cane resounded throughout the hall.

"Yes, Father," he growled.

The old miser hobbled into the foyer, as cranky as ever. "Where the devil have you been?"

Emerson gritted, "I was tending to a personal affair."

"What was it? A gaming debt? I'll not give you more money!" The earl brandished his cane. "Mark my words. I'll let you rot in debtors' prison first!"

Teeth grinding, Emerson sidestepped the earl.

"Come back here, you varlet of a son."

But Emerson ignored the earl and mounted the steps instead.

"A pox on you!" the earl cried. "You're nothing but a disgrace. I'll not leave you my estate. I'll live forever! See if I don't."

And he was just spiteful enough to live forever, too, Emerson thought, infuriated.

It was intolerable, living under the earl's thumb. Emerson wanted the roost to himself. But the old penny-pincher wouldn't die.

Well, Emerson was going to get *his* way in one matter at least. He was going to destroy Ravenswood. He was going to take Henrietta away from the viscount, devastate the man. And he was going to do it in front of the entire *ton*.

Footsteps pounding, Emerson stormed into his bedroom.

The startled chambermaid shrieked.

Seething with ignominy, Emerson eyed the feeble maid. He needed to feel in control. It burned inside him, the desire for power.

He slammed the door closed and advanced on the whimpering wench. With a rough movement, he grabbed her and tossed her onto the bed.

Chapter 27

~⟨∘⟩~

Henrietta had a terrible habit of sneaking off without telling anybody, but she was at her wit's end. A visit with her dearest chum was the perfect respite. The duke and duchess had been invited to the wedding, but the couple weren't scheduled to arrive for another day or so. Henrietta couldn't wait that long to confide in her best friend, so she'd slipped out of the house with nary a thought for the turmoil she might cause. She had left behind a note, though. She wasn't alone, either. Her maid was with her, so there was no reason for anyone at the house to worry about her. Henrietta had every intention of returning home in time for the wedding. She wasn't going to disgrace her family by running away. She just wanted to be with a friend.

"There it is, Miss Ashby," said Jenny. "The castle!"

It was night. Henrietta peered at the castle through the frosty sleigh glass. It was a very dark structure, constructed of stone. Ancient, too. Spire rooftops capped the round towers flanking the castle gates.

But despite the look of an imposing edifice, there was a warm glow coming from the keep's windows. The fiery glow of candlelight. A welcoming glow. And Henrietta was suddenly anxious to be inside the keep. To be with her dearest chum. To shed the misery inside her soul. She wanted to shake the darkness that had come over her heart after yesterday's tiff with Sebastian. But she was having a deuced hard time of it. The viscount's words haunted her still:

I won't go back to the club, I promise.

Henrietta closed her eyes at the pang in her breast. A shame the offer was nothing but a falsehood. A capricious man like Sebastian could never change and commit to marriage. He'd be overwhelmed by ennui within months of the ceremony, perhaps even weeks. And Henrietta wasn't about to let him break her heart again.

And what the devil was the matter with the man anyway? she wondered. Why was he so insistent that they have a real marriage? He didn't need her to slake his lust. All he had to do was visit that vile club of his and fornicate with a "nun" if he needed to satisfy his carnal desire. Why couldn't he just let her be?

The sleigh came to a stop before the pompous main doors.

A footman appeared to assist Henrietta and her maid from the sleigh. He attended to the luggage, too, as Henrietta whisked inside the drafty main hall.

The butler appeared. "Good evening, miss."

Henrietta presented him with a calling card. "Miss Henrietta Ashby to see the Duchess of Wembury."

With a brisk nod, the butler disappeared again.

Henrietta tugged at her gloves, divesting herself of the soft leather. All the while she perused the mighty entranceway, noting some rather vile-looking gargoyles perched high above her head. But scaffolds filled the grand arena, indicative of a restoration.

As Henrietta took in the keep's gothic atmosphere, hasty footsteps pattered toward her.

She turned around and beamed. "Belle!"

Mirabelle rushed into her arms. "Henry!"

With a spirited laugh, the young ladies warmly embraced. Oh, it was such a joy to be with her chum again! Five months had passed since the masquerade ball. A dreadfully long time. There was so much to catch up on.

"You look well, Belle."

Henrietta spied her chum's regal attire. A faint butter yellow frock woven from the finest wool.

Mirabelle looked dashing in her accouterments, the dress matching the rich golden threads of her long and wavy hair. She looked happy, too. It burned in her amber eyes, the joy.

A joy Henrietta had lost.

"Henry, what are you doing here?"

Henrietta divested herself of her cape. "I'm sorry, Belle. It was very hasty of me, I know. Am I intruding?"

"*You*, my dear, are always welcome."

Henrietta smiled. "Thank you, Belle. I just had to see you."

Another tight squeeze of a hug. "Is something the matter, Henry? You're going to be married in two days! I'm all set to visit *you*. Why are you here?"

Henrietta bit back her sorrow. "I just had to see you, Belle."

"Come here, luv." She folded her arm around Henrietta's waist. "I'll show you to a room."

A few minutes later, Henrietta was snug and warm in a spacious guest bedroom. Her maid was sound asleep in the servants' quarters, and the Duchess of Wembury was pouring her unexpected visitor a hot cup of tea.

"Here you are, Henry."

"Thank you, Belle."

With a cup of warm tea in her hand, a sympathetic friend in the room, and a soft divan behind her, Henrietta was feeling very much at ease.

"So what's it like living in a castle, *Your Grace*?"

Mirabelle snorted. "There's so much to do here, Henry." She snuggled next to her chum on the divan. "For instance, I have to sit with the housekeeper every morning to go over the day's meals. I mean, right down to how many peas I want on each plate! It's all such a bloody bother."

Henrietta smiled. Her chum was exaggerating, but Henrietta could commiserate with the woman's newfound responsibility. Mirabelle had not been

reared to govern a household like other young ladies of the peerage. A merchant's daughter, she
had lived a simple life before she'd met the Duke of
Wembury.

And speaking of whom . . .

"How did you snag a *duke*, Belle?"

"With my womanly grace and charm."

Mirabelle's husky laughter was infectious. An orphan with *four* seafaring brothers looking after her,
she wasn't one for womanly grace and charm. In
truth, her boyish tendencies matched Henrietta's—
making them the best of friends.

"Really, Henry, I didn't know Damian was a duke
when I first met him. I thought he was a navigator."

"A navigator?"

She nodded. "He was serving aboard my brother's ship."

"And what were *you* doing aboard your brother's
ship?"

Mirabelle grinned. "I'd stowed away."

Henrietta balked. "But why, Belle?"

"I wanted to be a sailor."

Henrietta sipped her tea in bewilderment. "And
the duke? Did he want to be a tar, too?"

"No, Damian was stranded in America with no
credentials. He needed to disguise himself as a navigator to get back home to England."

"And you fell in love with the man?"

Another snort. "The bounder stole my heart."

At the thought of a certain bounder stealing and

then breaking *her* heart, Henrietta's breast smarted.

"Now, Henry, why are you here? Is something the matter?"

Henrietta tried to keep her composure, but Mirabelle's soothing voice and comforting company had her blurting out, "Oh, Belle, I've made a terrible blunder!"

Startled, Mirabelle set down the cup and saucer. "Tell me, Henry. What's wrong?"

Henrietta sniffed. "It's Ravenswood."

"Yes, I see you finally did something scandalous to get the viscount's attention. He's asked you to marry him. I'm so happy for you, Henry. I know you've loved Ravenswood for years."

Henrietta's teacup rattled in her hands. "That's just it, Belle. I don't love him, not anymore. I don't think I ever really did."

"What do you mean, Henry?"

"I was smitten with Ravenswood, but I never truly loved him. How could I? I didn't even know the man, not really."

Mirabelle took the china from Henrietta's shaky grip and put it aside. She clasped Henrietta by the hand. "What's happened, Henry?"

"Ravenswood's a rogue!"

A snort. "The duke was once a rogue, too. I think he still is at times. What has *that* to do with anything?"

But Henrietta didn't want to dampen her friend's spirit with the belief that once a rogue, always a rogue. And since Mirabelle had married the duke of all rogues, it just didn't seem appropriate.

"Ravenswood and I don't suit." Henrietta battled with tears. "I don't trust the man. I don't even like the man anymore. And now I have to marry him because I wrote this silly letter and . . ."

"Hush." Mirabelle stroked her hand. "It's all right, Henry."

Softly, she said, "It will never be all right, Belle. I'm doomed to marry a man I don't love."

Mirabelle bit her bottom lip. "Henry, I'm so sorry. Are you sure you cannot make a go of the marriage?"

"Very sure, Belle. Ravenswood, he's . . . he's not the man I thought he was. And I don't have the courage to trust him, to sacrifice my heart to him the way you sacrificed your dream of seafaring to live on land with the duke."

The duchess shrugged. "It wasn't really a sacrifice, Henry."

"What do you mean?"

"I love Damian more than the sea."

At another sharp twinge in her breast, Henrietta said, "How do you know when you're in love, Belle?"

The duchess sighed. "Well, I suppose it's all a matter of fear."

Henrietta wrinkled her brow. "Fear? What do you mean?"

"Well, I wasn't always so sure I'd be happy with

the duke. In truth, I was very sure I'd be *un*happy with him. But I was just afraid of getting my heart broken."

Henrietta could understand that. "What changed your mind?"

"I almost lost Damian," she said quietly.

"How?"

"He was injured in a fight. Very nearly died." The duchess smoothed her skirt. "I quickly realized I would rather risk my heart being broken than live without the duke."

"But he didn't break your heart, did he, Belle?"

"No, he didn't." She smiled. "And I'm very glad I took the risk."

There was a terrible ache in Henrietta's belly. She had risked it all, too, to be with Sebastian: her reputation, her heart. And it had turned out miserably. She just couldn't risk it all again.

"I'm very happy for you, Belle." And she was. She was just devastated *her* happy ending had turned out to be such a nightmare. "You're the best person I know, and you deserve all the contentment in the world."

Mirabelle's face fell.

"What's the matter, Belle?"

The duchess sat up and twisted her fingers in her lap. "Oh, Henry, I've lied to you!"

Henrietta blinked. "What?"

"I don't want us to have any secrets. I have to tell you the truth, even if you hate me forever."

Alarmed, Henrietta sat up, too. "What is it, Belle?"

"I'm not the best person you've ever known."

"Belle—"

"Really, Henry, I'm not." Restless, the duchess abandoned the divan and started to pace before the great hearth. "I'm not a merchant's daughter, either."

Henrietta quirked a brow. "You're not?"

She paused. "No, I'm a . . . pirate's daughter."

Henrietta eyed her chum with scrutiny. "Be serious, Belle."

Mirabelle wasn't smiling, though. "I am, Henry."

Henrietta swallowed. "Good heavens, Belle, you *are* telling the truth!"

Mirabelle nodded. "And I wanted to be a pirate, just like my father . . . and my brothers. That's why I stowed away, to prove to the stubborn brood I could be a good buccaneer." She bunched her fingers. "Do you hate me, Henry?"

Bowled over, Henrietta gawked at her comrade. "Hate you? No. I could never hate you."

"Really, Henry?" Mirabelle rushed back to the divan and took her by the hand. "You don't think ill of me?"

"I could never think ill of you, gel. You rescued me from a tree, remember? I'm forever in your debt. I'm just stunned, is all."

And she was. Good God, Mirabelle was a pirate! And here Henrietta had thought she'd lived the simple life of a merchant's daughter. What rot! Mirabelle had sailed the high seas and plundered for treasure. It was scandalous . . . It was something Henrietta would have done.

"So what's the best treasure you ever found, Belle?"

She grinned. "My husband."

A loud scuffle erupted somewhere in the castle just then.

Henrietta looked at the door. "What the devil?"

Mirabelle sighed. "Just ignore them."

"Them?"

"My brothers."

Henrietta perked up. "Oh, will I finally get to meet the Hawkins brood?"

"Are you sure you want the pleasure?" she said dryly.

Henrietta quirked a brow. "Do your brothers live here, too?"

Mirabelle snorted. "No. But they refuse to go home until they're *sure* I'm happy."

"But you are happy, Belle."

"Unfortunately, they don't think Damian is such a treasure."

Henrietta scrunched her brow. "Why, Belle?"

She waved a dismissive hand. "They're just being overprotective."

Henrietta didn't blame the brood. According to Sebastian, the Duke of Wembury was once dubbed the "Duke of Rogues." Not a very valiant title, that.

"They don't think the duke is worthy of you?" said Henrietta.

"They don't think *any*one is worthy of me. They're always up to something or other to make the duke's life difficult."

Henrietta lifted a brow. "You don't seem alarmed by their attempts at sabotage."

"Oh, this marriage will last forever," she said with confidence. "I'd shoot my brothers otherwise. They know it, too. They're just being stubborn. But they're going to have to get used to the duke being my husband." Mirabelle patted her belly. "Right quick at that."

Henrietta noticed the little bump then. "Why, Belle!"

But Henrietta wasn't all that giddy. Deep down, thoughts of motherhood beset her. Her own experience with motherhood, that was. She might be enceinte, too. And what hurt the most was the idea of denying Ravenswood his child.

You would deny me my own child! he had cried.

Henrietta hated to do such an unseemly thing. But what other choice did she have? If she was enceinte, she had to protect the babe from Ravenswood's villainy. She had to protect herself, too.

A knock at the door.

"Wait here a minute, Henry."

Mirabelle headed for the door and opened it.

In stepped a formidable figure, eyes steel blue and locks dark like a midnight sky.

The "Duke of Rogues."

And he looked . . . smitten.

"There you are, Belle," he said in a raspy voice.

He lifted his hand to her hair and cupped the back of her neck in a gentle caress. He kissed her then. A deep yet tender kiss.

Henrietta took in an uneven breath at the affectionate sight. Something pressed on her heart. A sense of loss. The loss of Ravenswood and *his* tender kisses.

Mirabelle nipped at the duke's bottom lip. "Where are my brothers?"

"Locked in the pantry."

She groaned. "Oh, Damian!"

He grinned. "I've given the butler the key with the order *not* to let them out until morning."

The duchess huffed. "You are not going to leave my brothers in the pantry, Damian."

"It's just for tonight, Belle." He whispered, "I want to be alone with you."

Oh, the husky words of passion! How Henrietta missed hearing those words from Sebastian. Well, she missed hearing them from the old Sebastian; the old Sebastian she had dreamed up in her head.

"We won't be alone tonight," said the duchess.

The duke gathered his dark brow. "Why the devil not, Belle?"

Mirabelle cocked her head. "Because we have company."

The duke turned his head—and smiled. "Miss Ashby, we meet again."

Henrietta scooted off the divan to greet the approaching duke. "Your Grace."

He took her by the hand and pressed a kiss to her knuckles, as he had on the night of Papa's masquerade ball.

"Damian, please," he said. "Miss Ashby, this is an unexpected pleasure. We were set to visit you in a day or two. Congratulations on your approaching—"

But an elbow to the ribs—and a sharp eye from his wife—stopped the duke from finishing the felicitation.

"Er, shall we have a late supper, then?" the duke suggested.

"Yes, of course," said Mirabelle. "You must be famished, Henry. Damian will escort you to the dining hall."

The duke quirked a brow. "You are not accompanying us, Your Grace?"

Mirabelle made a moue. "*I* have four brothers to rescue. I will join you in the dining hall in a few minutes."

"Very well," the duke acquiesced. He offered Henrietta his arm. "Shall we, Miss Ashby?"

With a smile, Henrietta slipped her hand into the duke's arm.

"We'll talk again later, Henry," the duchess whispered before they parted ways: Henrietta to the dining hall and Mirabelle to the pantry.

As Henrietta moved through the castle with her escort, she couldn't help but reflect upon the duke.

He seemed a good sort of man. Not the notorious "Duke of Rogues." And he and the duchess seemed to be *really* happy.

So if the duke could reform, could Sebastian, too? Could *she* be happy with Sebastian, after all?

The troubling thought stayed with her throughout dinner and well into the night.

Chapter 28

Sebastian was at his wit's end. He was getting married in two days and where was his bride? Off gallivanting about the countryside, visiting the Duchess of Wembury.

He rubbed his tired brow. He wasn't daft enough to think his betrothed's hasty departure had nothing to do with him. She was avoiding him, fighting him tooth and nail. And she was winning, the mulish chit. There had to be some way to convince the woman he wasn't going to hurt her, that she could trust him. But how?

He was dumbfounded. What did Henrietta want from him? Blood? His head on a pike?

Sebastian needed help—and he could think of only one woman in the world who could give it to him.

Across the room, a paneled door opened in the wall.

Sebastian quirked a brow.

Very theatrical.

Madam Jacqueline entered the room adorned with Oriental furnishings. She herself was bedecked in a fresh white turban and flowing wrapper. Jewels sparkled from her ears, her wrinkled throat, her slender fingers.

She moved with grace and confidence. Her steps dainty and refined, she impersonated womanly charm. But Sebastian didn't doubt she could be cruel—if she wanted to be. One didn't become the most notorious courtesan in England by being meek. One had to be shrewd and devious.

It bothered Sebastian to think that the innocent Miss Ashby had come to the ruthless woman for help—and all because she'd wanted to seduce him. He was only grateful the cunning courtesan had not destroyed the imprudent chit.

"Lord Ravenswood." She smiled. "I am surprised by your visit."

"Are you, Madam Jacqueline? I wonder if perhaps you've been expecting me for quite some time?"

There was a gleam of pleasure in the woman's eyes, a smirking glow that was hard to ignore. She had everything, Sebastian mused. But for all her wealth, her links to royalty, she had no blue blood in her veins. It infuriated her, he reckoned. To have so much power, but be denied one critical thing: lineage. She had to enjoy having the aristocracy come to her for help. To have the rich and lofty lords and ladies at her feet had to give her a sense of accomplishment and pride, vengeance even.

"Tea, my lord?"

"No, thank you."

Madman Jacqueline poured herself a steaming cup. She reclined on the divan and perused him with enchanting green eyes.

Sebastian could see why the woman commanded the attention of kings and gentlefolk alike. She had a mesmerizing quality about her.

"To what do I owe the honor of your visit, Lord Ravenswood?"

He took in a deep breath. "I presume you've heard about my wedding to Miss Ashby?"

She sipped her tea with feminine poise. "Yes, I read the announcement in the paper. Congratulations."

"Thank you," he said stiffly. It was deuced uncomfortable having to ask the woman for assistance. But pride be damned, he had to figure out some way to get Henrietta to be his *wife*. She didn't want to live with him; she didn't want to touch him. How was he supposed to put up with that for the rest of his days? "I believe you offered Miss Ashby some advice—on how to seduce me."

"I did indeed, my lord."

"Well, I need some advice in return."

The woman lifted a painted brow. "How can I be of help?"

He shifted in his seat. "How do I seduce Miss Ashby?"

It was a very subtle quirk of the lips. "I beg your pardon, my lord?"

"You heard me," he growled.

"But you are engaged to marry the girl."

"Yes, but the stubborn chit doesn't want anything to do with me anymore."

"Really?" The courtesan was filled with mirth. How she must take pleasure in his discomfiture! "And why is that, my lord?"

Disgruntled, he said, "She doesn't trust me."

"Why?"

"Because she discovered I'm a scoundrel."

"I see." Another sip of tea. "Have you offered her diamonds?"

Restless, Sebastian shot out of his chair and stalked about the room. "Madam Jacqueline, I think we both know I'm not some sort of innocent fawn. I've bedded the girl, offered her gifts, saved her from drowning, and *still* she wants nothing to do with me."

Again Madam Jacqueline raised a brow. "Impressive."

He growled, "What do I do now?"

The courtesan set her teacup aside and folded her hands in her lap. "It sounds like the girl does not love you anymore."

There was something very striking about that word: "anymore." It implied Henrietta had once loved him. To think she didn't care a whit any longer was . . . crushing.

Try as he might to convince himself the chit's esteem didn't mean anything to him, he knew that to be a lie. Whenever Henrietta looked at him, he *felt* noble, even heroic. He always had.

It was hard to admit, but over the years Henrietta's faith in him had been a soothing comfort, an inspiration even. When he was with her, he forgot about his immoral ways. He forgot about his loneliness. He felt only . . .

"What do you want, my lord?"

Sebastian looked at the courtesan, his reflection shattered. "I already told you."

"To seduce your fiancée? Why? Do you want Miss Ashby to worship you again? . . . Or do you want her to love you for who you really are?"

Love him for who he really was? A scoundrel? "She will never love me for who I really am."

"And who are you, my lord?"

He took in a deep breath. "A villain."

The courtesan cocked her head. "Perhaps you should change."

"I can't change."

"And why not?"

"Because once a rogue, always a rogue."

She tsked. "Miss Ashby was once naïve. She's not anymore. People do change, my lord."

"Yes, all thanks to you," he grumbled.

"You don't like the change in Miss Ashby? You would rather she blindly worship you?"

"No." He gripped the chair back tight. "I suppose . . . I suppose I'd rather she love me."

And he did. He didn't want Henrietta's blind adoration. He didn't want another warm body in his bed. He wanted the woman to be his wife. He wanted her to understand him, to comfort him, to care for him, blast it! And he wanted to do the same for her.

"Do you love her?" Madam Jacqueline asked.

Did he? Could he? Or was he afraid, as Peter had suggested? Afraid of failing Henrietta, of not being a man worthy of her affection?

His pulse was pounding. True, he'd never tried to be Henrietta's hero. But he was sure he would fail at the endeavor. He had not the heart of a hero. He had not the heart of a good man, even. He had the heart of a villain, as his father had once said.

"I don't know," he admitted.

Madam Jacqueline nodded sagely. "Then I suppose the question is: can the girl love you? Does she still love you?"

Sebastian was in turmoil. So much revelation, so much truth was pouring into his soul, he didn't know what to make of it all. "How do I find out?"

Voice steady, she said, "If the girl's as mulish as you say, I don't know that you can. Perhaps you should resign yourself to your fate?"

He gawked at her. "And this is your practical advice? Give up?"

"You have already tried everything. You said so yourself."

"But there must be *something* else I can do."

She lifted her eyes heavenward. "Well, there is one thing."

"What?"

She looked back at him. "You can die."

He glared at her. "You mock me."

"Not at all, my lord. You asked for my advice, and I have offered it."

"To die?"

"That's right."

Sebastian gnashed his teeth. "And just what would that accomplish—other than to put me out of my misery, of course?"

"Well, if the girl truly loves you, she will admit it once you are dead. You see, my lord, the will can be very strong to protect the heart. But dead, you do not threaten her heart anymore. She will let down her guard, and if she weeps over your corpse, she loves you."

Sebastian was beginning to think the woman's turban was wound too tight. "So I die, and Henrietta admits she loves me?"

"I'm afraid it's the only way to get the girl to confess her true feelings, my lord."

The old woman was daft. And Sebastian had wasted his time in coming.

"How enlightening, Madam Jacqueline," he said with a curt nod. "I thank you for your time."

She smiled. "Not at all, my lord."

Sebastian headed for the door with brisk strides.

"Lord Ravenswood?"

He paused. "Yes, Madam Jacqueline."

"When you see Miss Ashby again, please tell her I am very proud of her."

Sebastian quit the room.

Chapter 29

Henrietta stood in front of the mirror and eyed the fine lace of her wedding dress. Four emotional sisters gathered around her.

Penelope whispered, "You look so handsome, Henry."

"Like an angel," confirmed Tertia.

Cordelia sniffed. "I can't believe you're getting married."

"About time, too," from Roselyn.

Henrietta smiled at her sisters, but her spirit was heavy. All sorts of distressing thoughts marched through her head. Thoughts of her betrothed. Throughout her stay at the castle, Henrietta had observed the duke and duchess in loving interaction. A part of her had ached deep inside to have that same kind of rapport with Sebastian. Yet another part of her had warned her to be reasonable. Sebastian was not the duke. Even if the duke had reformed his roguish ways, it did not mean Ravenswood would, too. She had to remember that. She had to ask herself one simple question: was she willing to risk her heart to be with the viscount?

Oh, why couldn't she ever make up her mind?

The bedroom door opened.

Henrietta looked over her shoulder. "Hello, Mama."

The baroness stepped inside the room, her dress a regal bronze in hue. "You look lovely, Henry."

"Doesn't she, Mama?" Penelope pinched the bride's cheeks to add some color. "A veritable princess."

The baroness nodded. "Ladies, I'd like a moment alone with my daughter."

The sisters bobbed in obedience and cheerfully quit the room.

The baroness closed the door. "How do you feel, Henry?"

"Nervous," she admitted.

The older woman smiled. "I was nervous, too." She picked up the veil draped across the bed. "Here, let me help you with this."

Henrietta squatted, for Mama was a tad short.

The baroness artfully pinned the flowing white headdress to her hair, then picked up the crown of white roses. "And now for the finishing touch."

With a gentle stroke, Mama set the ring of flowers on her head.

Henrietta peered back into the glass, perusing her polished appearance. The nerves in her belly thrummed. It was almost time to make the wedding march. It was almost time to become the next Viscountess Ravenswood.

She felt terribly queasy.

"I'd like to give you something, Henry."

"What is it, Mama?"

The baroness held up a sparkling floral brooch, set with rose pearls and diamonds. "My mother gave it to me on the day I married your father. I thought I would never part with it . . . but I'd like you to have it, Henry."

Henrietta eyed the brilliant gem and sniffed. "Thank you, Mama."

The baroness pinned the brooch at Henrietta's throat, the soft rose a subtle brightness against the ivory lace and silk. "Your father is waiting for you below stairs. He will escort you to the chapel."

"I'll be down in a minute, Mama."

The baroness kissed her cheek. "You will be happy, Henry."

She whispered, "How do you know, Mama?"

"Because I'm your mother; I know everything."

Henrietta smiled. As soon as the baroness left the room, she searched for a kerchief. She rummaged through the paraphernalia scattered across the vanity and pried a lacy napkin apart from the rest of the clutter.

She dabbed at her eyes. There was such tenderness in the expressions around her, such warmth. What a chilling contrast to the rogue she was set to marry in a matter of minutes!

A knock at the door.

Henrietta wiped her nose. "Come in."

She gasped. Sebastian stepped into the room, an achingly handsome sight in dapper blue garb of linen and silk. With a white waistcoat and fresh white gloves, he looked every inch the gentleman.

"What are you doing here?" she said.

"I had to see you before the wedding." He dropped his sexy eyes to her toes and slowly lifted his gaze. "You look beautiful, Henry."

She shivered. "Thank you."

"Really, you look stunning."

"Yes, I heard you."

A dashing smile. "I just wanted to make sure you believed me."

She pursed her lips. "What do you want, Sebastian?"

"To promise you I will make you happy. I won't grieve you the way my father grieved my mother."

She looked at him, baffled. "What about your parents?"

Henrietta didn't know very much about the former viscount and viscountess. Sebastian had never mentioned the couple.

"They didn't have a very good rapport," he said. "Father wasn't the best sort of husband. He was very aloof, strict even. Not an easy man to love."

Her breath hitched. "What are you saying?"

"I know you've had a good upbringing, Henry: a mother and father who care for each other. I want you to have the same in our marriage. I want you to know that I will make you happy, if you give me the chance."

Henrietta's heart fluttered. She didn't know what to say, what to think. He'd offered to make her happy, but did he care for her?

"Once a rogue, always a rogue," she said. "You said that once."

"People change, Henry . . . you did." He moved toward the door. "I'll be at the church."

Quietly he left the room.

Henrietta's wedding dress swished and swooshed as she paced the room in fretful contemplation. He was asking her to give him a second chance, to trust him. Could she? Dare she?

The hour of ten chimed somewhere in the house. It was time!

Henrietta rushed to the bed and grabbed the snowy, fur-trimmed cape, scarf, and matching gloves. Her belly in a whirl, she quickly quit the room and bustled through the passageway, over to the steps.

But the whisper of voices from the landing below had her rooted to the spot.

"She's going to be late for her own wedding, Peter."

"Don't fuss, Penelope. We'll get her to the church on time."

"Oh, I still can't believe it, Peter! A prostitute?"

"Well, Seb was desperate, Penelope," her husband hissed. "You know how much trouble he's been having with Henry"

"But to visit a woman of ill repute two days before his wedding? It's most unsavory."

A woozy Henrietta grabbed the banister for support before she rolled down the stairs.

The ache in her belly throbbed. She gasped for breath. Quickly she skirted across the hall before Peter and Penelope saw her, and sprinted down the servant stairwell.

Tears filled her eyes. Sickness roiled in her gut. Two days! She was gone two days and Sebastian grew so "desperate" for a woman he went to see a prostitute!

Henrietta pounded down the steps, surprising the cook in the kitchen. She brushed past Mrs. Quigly and dashed through the scullery, abuzz with preparation for the wedding luncheon. Once she was in the main part of the house, she passed the dinner hall and the sounds of clattering silverware—the table was being set for the guests—making her way to the back of the dwelling.

That fiend! He just couldn't keep his hands off a doxy, could he? It was in his blood, the wicked inclination to rut about with anything in a skirt. And if she wasn't around to ease his lust, he'd find some other whore to bed . . . and that's all she was to him, wasn't she? A whore? All that rot about making her happy. The man wanted only one thing from her: carnal pleasure.

Henrietta wiped the blasted tears from her eyes. Oh, she was such a fool! She had considered giving the villain a second chance. She *knew* she couldn't trust him, that he was an unredeemable rogue.

A wretched sob in her throat, Henrietta ducked through the terrace doors, and took in a sharp breath to quell her sorrow.

She yanked on her gloves and sniffed. She deserved another broken heart. She always wavered over every decision. Even a sound one. She had marked Sebastian a rogue. And he was. A despicable rogue! So why had she mulled over the idea that he could reform?

It didn't matter anymore. This time she was *sure* Ravenswood was a rotten scoundrel. A black devil. And she would not falter in her belief again. She might have to marry the bounder, but she did not have to let him near her heart again.

Henrietta had to stay away from the house. It was stifling, the merriment inside. The festive din of wedding preparations was such a sharp contrast to her crushed spirit. She could not go to the church just yet, either. She needed to be alone.

"Miss Ashby."

Henrietta looked up, dazed. "Lord Emerson?"

Emerson had his hand tucked inside his breast pocket. "How delightful to see you."

She sniffed. "What are you doing here, my

lord? Why aren't you at the church with the other guests?"

"Oh, I won't be attending the wedding, Miss Ashby . . . and neither will you."

He pulled out a pistol.

Sebastian stood beside the altar, waiting. It was just like Henrietta to be late for her own wedding.

The preacher flipped through the Bible, the pages snapping. The chapel, brimming with society's most fashionable members, was quietly abuzz with idle chitchat.

Sebastian girded himself for a long wait.

He reflected upon his earlier talk with Henrietta. Would she accept his offer to make her happy? He hoped so. He didn't want to spend the rest of his marital days in strife. And he wasn't quite desperate enough to heed Madam Jacqueline's advice, and prostrate his corpse at Henrietta's feet to get her to forgive him.

But what if the chit rebuffed his offer?

It triggered a cramp in his chest, thinking about such a lonely existence. A ruthless irony, really. The girl had adored him for years; he could have snatched her at any time to make her his wife. But now that he was going to marry her, she didn't want a fig to do with him.

Perhaps he was a villain, as Henrietta had said? Unredeemable, as his father had suggested? It would certainly explain all the trouble he'd been having, if he was damned to live a life apart from his wife . . . in darkness.

Sebastian had to acknowledge the possibility. Maybe he just wasn't meant to be with Henrietta?

But then he remembered the fiery pulse of his heart whenever he was with the woman, and he had to wonder, if he wasn't destined to be with the chit, then why did he feel so at peace with her?

Sebastian wasn't going to give up on Henrietta just yet—or himself—he vowed. Madam Jacqueline had suggested one practical piece of advice: change. He was going to give it a try. He had frightened Henrietta with his boorish behavior at the Hellfire Club; now the chit didn't trust him. But he was determined to prove to her he was not the same man anymore; he would reform. It was better than croaking, as the courtesan had suggested.

The chapel door burst opened. A breathless Peter stumbled inside. He righted himself quickly, smiled at the loquacious guests, and with brisk, confident strides, marched down the aisle.

Sebastian growled, "Where the devil is the bride, Peter?"

Peter whispered, "Ah, there's a bit of a snag, Seb."

"What sort of snag?"

"Why don't you come with me?" The man's fixed smile cracked. "Now."

Sebastian glowered at his brother. After a few whispered words to the preacher and a courteous nod to the guests, Sebastian strutted down the aisle after his brother.

The Duke and Duchess of Wembury were seated in the pews. Sebastian recognized the couple from the night of the baron's masquerade ball. At the harried looks on their faces, though, he started to suspect something was dreadfully amiss. Had Henrietta confessed to the couple that she didn't trust him? . . . Had she confessed something more? That she didn't want to marry him?

As soon as he and his brother were clear of the chapel, Sebastian demanded, "What's happened, Peter?"

There were two horses waiting out front. Both men quickly mounted.

"It's Henry, Seb. She's missing."

Sebastian could feel the blood drain from his face. A cold darkness nestled in his belly, chilling his soul.

With a hard kick, he set the steed at a gallop.

Chapter 30

～∽◯◯∽～

The house was in an uproar.

Sebastian and Peter just stood in the door frame, observing the commotion. Fans fluttering, the Ashby sisters either cried or argued. Husbands comforted wives. Children ran rampant. The servants bustled this way and that, fetching drinks, blankets . . . smelling salts?

Had someone fainted?

Sebastian stepped into the tumult. Peter closed the door.

The viscount scanned the polished marble floor, looking for Lady Ashby. But the baroness dashed into the foyer just then, a small bottle in her hand.

So who had fainted?

It was then Sebastian noticed the unconscious baron slumped in a seat by the grandfather clock.

The baroness knelt beside her husband and stuck the small bottle under his nose.

Within moments, the baron stirred, coughing and

sputtering. "Gads, get that foul thing away from me!"

Restless, Sebastian snapped, "Where is Henry?"

"Oh God," the baron groaned. "Henry! Where's my Henry?"

Penelope stepped forward. "She's gone, Sebastian."

The viscount's breath hitched. "What do you mean, 'gone'? Gone where?"

"She's . . . she's . . ."

Penelope, too distraught to answer, looked at her husband for support.

"She's run away, Seb" said Peter. He paused, then: "With another man."

Blood throbbed in Sebastian's head, howled in his ears. Henrietta had left him? Disgraced him at the altar?

"Apparently the other man's been visiting quite a bit," said Peter. "The butler remembers seeing him at the engagement party. The young lord came to visit with Henrietta after the accident on the ice, too."

It was crushing, the pressure on his chest. Sebastian could hardly breathe. All this time he had thought to woo Henrietta, to share a life with her . . . and she was having an affair. No wonder she had rebuffed him at every turn. She had another lover!

He fisted his palms. The bile in his belly burned. Had she planned to humiliate him at the altar from the start of their engagement? Was this some sort of retaliation for breaking her girlhood dream?

A frantic Peter intruded upon Sebastian's morbid reflection.

"We have to go after her, Seb."

Sebastian blinked and swallowed the bitter taste in his mouth. "No, Peter."

Peter balked. "You're not serious, brother?"

"I am."

"But you love the girl, admit it!"

Sebastian snatched his brother by the cravat. "The devil I do! Besides, the girl's made her choice, and I won't force her to change her mind."

Sebastian let go of his brother before he strangled the man. He wasn't angry with Peter. He was angry with himself.

Curse her! The scheming chit had made him *want* to be a better man. She had fooled him into thinking he might have a chance at a warm future with her, that he wasn't damned after all.

What tripe! She and her lover must be roaring with laughter. And that was the greatest reprisal of all, getting the dim-witted viscount to think he'd had an opportunity at happiness. Had she and her paramour bandied that letter all over Town, too? Orchestrated the whole engagement just to devastate him?

The fury inside him billowed, hacked his insides to mush.

"Seb, I know you're angry, but we have to go after the girl," Peter implored. "If nothing else, think of the Ashby name!"

Listless, Sebastian said, "It's not the Ashby name that's ruined, it's mine."

"But she's run off with another man!"

"She's off to marry her lover, I'm sure. She'll be home in a few days, a beaming new bride from Gretna Green. The gossip will fizzle. It always does."

But the rancor in Sebastian's gut would never fizzle away; it would haunt him all the rest of his miserable days.

Peter huffed, "It isn't right, Seb."

The baron groaned. "Oh, my darling Henry! What will I ever do without the boy?"

Lady Ashby fluttered a frilly lace fan across her husband's flushed cheeks.

Peter nudged his brother. "Look at the baron, Seb. We have to do something for his sake."

Sebastian did not like to see the baron in such distress, but Henrietta had made her choice. What right did he have to go after her?

"No, Peter."

"But the baron doesn't want the girl to wed another man."

"The baron doesn't want Henrietta to wed *any* man," said Sebastian. "Even me. But we both know the girl has to get married now."

Especially now that she might be enceinte.

His heart pounding, a darkness smothered Sebastian. The chit might be pregnant with his child. She *needed* a husband. She just didn't want him to play the spousal role.

It was a terrible blow, the image of his child in another man's arms. A cutting pain that only blanketed him in greater despair.

"But we don't even know anything about this Emerson!" Peter cried.

Sebastian bristled. "Emerson?"

Peter nodded. "The butler said Lord Emerson had called on the girl, that the couple had dashed off together. He witnessed the two running across the green, hand in hand."

A great upheaval in his brain, Sebastian tried to recall a scene from the Hellfire Club. It was a bleary scene, though. But he was sure there had been a rousing row between him and Emerson—over Henrietta.

Hand in hand? A lovers' elopement? Not bloody likely. Emerson had dragged her away—by force. The villain was not the sort of man to settle down. He might have charmed Henrietta, tricked her into thinking him a respectable sort, but he was nothing of the kind. He was a dastardly son of a bitch—and he had a taste for Sebastian's blood.

The letter! The rumor in the paper! It had to be Emerson's doing. All of it. Sebastian had been reading the letter when Emerson interrupted him. The fiend must have snatched it from him after the fight, then aired it all over the city to get even with him. And according to the butler, Emerson had attended the engagement party. If he'd overheard Henrietta's confession, that she wanted a marriage in name only, *he* must have spread the tale in the society papers.

With brisk and determined strides, Sebastian thundered toward the door.

He could feel it, deep inside his gut. Emerson had taken Henrietta, hauled her out of the house to get back at him for some foolhardy quarrel. Sebastian couldn't even remember what they had squabbled about, but he knew Emerson a craven knave bent on petty retribution—and Sebastian knew just where the bastard had taken Henrietta.

Outside, the winter winds nipped.

The viscount couldn't deny it anymore, the throbbing panic in his breast, the compulsion to tear off Emerson's limbs . . . Sebastian loved the chit!

"Where are you going, Seb?"

Peter had to sprint to keep up with his brother's long strides.

"To fetch Henrietta back," said the viscount, snatching the horse's reins.

"Thank God!"

Sebastian mounted the great beast. "*You* are not coming with me, brother."

"The devil I'm not. You can't go after the couple alone. You might need me, Seb."

"No!" Sebastian twisted the reins around his palms. "I want you to fetch the magistrate, Peter. Bring him to the Hellfire Club."

Peter paled. "Oh, good God. Seb, you have to let me—"

"No! It's too dangerous, Peter. You have a wife. I don't want you to come with me; I don't want you to risk your neck."

"Oh, blast it! Here, then." Peter reached behind his back. "You're going to need this."

A pistol appeared.

Sebastian eyed the piece. "Where did you get that?"

"From the baron. I figured Emerson might put up a fuss if we tried to bring the girl home. But I didn't think he was *that* dangerous."

Sebastian tucked the weapon into his waist.

"Be careful, Seb."

But Sebastian was already pounding down the drive at breakneck speed.

It was cold inside the abbey. Dank, too. Tears burned in Henrietta's eyes. Blood seeped from the wounds at her wrists, trussed with rope. But she didn't care. She thrashed against her dastardly captor, bit him, too.

Emerson hollered, "You bitch!"

He licked the wound at his finger, slapped her soundly for imparting the injury, then grabbed her by the hair and shoved her through the dark passageway.

Bruised cheek throbbing, she gritted, "Why are you doing this?"

"Quiet, you little whore!"

It was clear the man loathed her, considered her

a harlot. She didn't care for his good opinion of her, but she did care to know his motivation.

Oh, what a fool she was! It was a stinging hurt in her belly, the truth. She had failed to see Emerson's true nature. Well, that wasn't entirely accurate. She had sensed his nefarious ways, but she had ignored her misgiving. Fearing her heart was a poor judge of character, she had convinced herself to listen to reason. But it was her *heart* that could spot a rogue at ten paces. And since Emerson was a rogue . . .

"It was *you* who flaunted my letter all over London, wasn't it? It was *you* who spread that dreadful rumor in the paper?"

"It was indeed."

"But why did you do it?"

"To avenge myself on Ravenswood."

There was a terrible ache in Henrietta's ear, a sort of buzzing sound. "How do you know Ravenswood? And how do you know about the Hellfire Club?"

"Don't feign innocence with me," he sneered. "We all three frequent the club."

Henrietta gasped. Another cold chill gripped her. And this time it was not the winter air making her shiver.

"Oh yes, I know what you are, you strumpet," he snapped. "I saw you with Ravenswood in the catacombs . . . right after you stomped on my foot."

Her mind spinning, memories filled her head: a man in a purple mask, wanting to strap her to the banquet table for an orgy . . .

Henrietta had a profound urge to retch. "So you're a member of the Hellfire Club, too?"

"*Was* a member before your dastardly lover humiliated me in front of the friars. But Ravenswood will pay for what he did to me. He took my pride from me . . . so I'm going to take something from him. *You*."

She shuddered under his biting words. "What do you mean?"

"Stop yapping!"

An arm strapped to her throat, Henrietta was forced down the stone steps into the catacombs. She trembled. The brisk air nipped at her nose. It was dark inside the catacombs: a torch here or there. It was noisy, too, the rowdy din of merry "friars" echoing throughout the tunnel.

She closed her eyes to bring her thundering heartbeats to a steadier canter. "If you're a former member of the club, what are we doing here?"

"I'm going to avenge myself on Ravenswood *and* win back the respect of the friars. And you are going to help me do it."

"Like hell! You can go to the devil, Emerson. I won't help you!"

She jabbed her elbow into his ribs.

He grimaced—and tightened his grip.

"I've never met such a fussy slut," he growled.

Emerson tore the neck cloth from his throat and gagged her.

Henrietta choked on her tears, her shame. Why did she keep associating with members of the Hell-fire Club?

Torchlight flickered, casting the statues in the tunnel in a fiery glow. She stumbled through the chilling channel, pushed to the arena's threshold.

Henrietta paused.

Inside the banquet hall, she spied the notorious banquet table—and the shackles at the table's edge.

Her heart shuddered.

"Emerson!" the friars jeered. The room was filled with heckling villains, wenches, too, all foxed and loving it. "Did you run off to get married?"

The cackles must have burned Emerson's blood, for Henrietta could feel him bristle behind her.

Emerson growled, "She's not my bride, brothers . . . she's ours."

The inebriated friars piqued at the implication.

Emerson pushed her toward the table. Henrietta screamed against her gag and kicked, letting loose a savage tantrum. But it was futile. The drunken carousers grabbed her wrists, her ankles, and hoisted her onto the banquet table.

Her tears smothering, she swallowed a sob. She kicked again, but Emerson gripped her ankles, spread her legs apart. He secured the manacles at her boots. Some other foul oaf wrested her bound wrists and clipped the heavy irons above her head.

There was a throbbing pressure on her breast

as her heart pumped hard and fast. She flicked her eyes across the room in dashing strokes, searching for help, for some way out. But she was trapped.

Emerson moved to the head of the table. He looked at her with venom, and whispered, "Once the friars feast on you, *I'll* be accepted back into the club, and Ravenswood will be devastated. Your pain will be his." Emerson stepped back and smiled. "Who has a knife, brothers? Let's tear this dress to pieces and enjoy our bride."

A glittering knife appeared.

Henrietta thrashed against her bonds.

"Don't fight too much." Emerson winked. "It'll only hurt more."

A pistol cocked.

Henrietta bristled . . . but then her heart throbbed with unfettered joy.

Ravenswood!

The earth stopped spinning. The sickness in her belly went away. One look at the most sinfully handsome man in creation, and everything in her heart and soul was put to right.

The viscount stepped into the catacombs, covered in snow. He was a wonderful sight! Breath ragged, the exertion of a pounding ride was clear in his body. He had come for her. Hell-bent to get to her. She wasn't alone in the chilling darkness of the abbey anymore, trapped with a band of devils. The relief inside her was overwhelming. The joy almost crippling.

With ominous strides, Sebastian approached, murder in his eyes. "Let her go."

The friars slowly backed away.

A flabbergasted Emerson quickly gathered his wits and released her.

Trembling and sweating, Henrietta yanked the neck cloth out of her mouth and let out a sob.

"Come here, Henry," Sebastian ordered, gun still trained on the dastardly Emerson.

She took one shaky step, then two. But before she could reach the viscount, Emerson yanked a pistol from his coat.

Eyes wide, heart fluttering, Henrietta demanded, "What are you going to do with that?"

Emerson jerked her roughly against him, coiled his arm around her throat, and placed the pistol to her temple.

"I'm going to have my revenge on the viscount," he whispered.

Henrietta could feel the earth spinning again. Revenge? On Ravenswood?

"Stop right there, Ravenswood," cried Emerson, "or I'll kill her where she stands!"

Sebastian stilled.

"Drop the pistol, Ravenswood!"

Emerson clearly didn't want to give the viscount an opportunity to shoot him. And Ravenswood didn't hesitate.

Cold metal hit the stone floor and resounded throughout the catacombs.

Henrietta wanted to scream, but Emerson's grip across her neck prevented the outcry. Unarmed, Ravenswood was a clear mark. She thrashed instead.

"Hold still!" barked Emerson. "Do you want me to squeeze the trigger by mishap?"

"Be still, Henry," Sebastian snapped.

She went very still.

Something snagged on her heart at the sight of Sebastian, an ache so profound, she gasped for breath. She didn't know what the sentiment was; she had never felt such a crushing pressure before. But to see him standing there. To know that he was in danger . . .

"You just had to take everything from me, didn't you?" said Emerson, his voice croaking.

Even though Ravenswood was defenseless, Emerson still trembled. Henrietta could feel him quivering against her back, the sweat from his palm against her neck.

"Don't be a fool," growled Sebastian. "I didn't take anything from you."

The villain snorted. "I suppose my pride is nothing to you?"

"What the devil are you talking about?" Sebastian said darkly.

"The friars all think me a coward."

Sebastian looked confused. "Why?"

"Because you chased me under the banquet table when I suggested we have this wench for our next banquet. I was a laughingstock! Don't you remember?"

"I was foxed, Emerson."

"Well, I remember," he spat. "I was going to make everything right tonight, but you had to take *that* away from me, too. Well, I'm going to make you suffer for what you did to me."

Emerson lifted the gun from Henrietta's temple and pointed it at Ravenswood instead.

With a startled gasp, Henrietta kicked back her boot and slammed it into Emerson's shin.

He yelped and tossed her aside.

She hit the ground.

Sebastian started toward her, but Emerson regained his balance and steadied the pistol. He aimed the weapon once more at the viscount's chest.

With a desperate cry, Henrietta grabbed the pistol Ravenswood had cast aside. In a sweeping gesture, her wrists still bound, she cocked the gun, aimed, and shot the gun clear out of Emerson's grip.

Both men looked stunned.

Sebastian quirked a brow at her. "You really are a good shot, aren't you, Henry?"

Henrietta let out a half sob, half sigh of relief.

Emerson screamed.

The coward hit the ground, frantically searching in the shadows for his pistol: his only means of protection against Ravenswood's wrath.

But it did no good.

Ravenswood grabbed him and trounced him soundly: a solid jab to the midriff.

Emerson keeled over, coughing.

"I'm going to let the magistrate deal with you," said Sebastian between seething breaths. "I'm going to enjoy watching you hang."

Ravenswood picked up the villain's gun and walked away. There was no reason to hurt the feeble creature anymore.

Blinded by stinging tears, Henrietta scrambled to her feet and rushed out of the banquet hall.

Sebastian shouted, "Henry!"

But she didn't stop. She had to get out of the catacombs, away from the abbey. She stumbled up the winding stairs, darted through the dark passageway, and burst out into the cold night air.

She tossed Papa's pistol into the snow, brought her shivering fingers to her face—and wailed.

"Henry, are you all right?"

A warm and hard set of arms wrapped tight around her.

She stuck out her wrists. "U-untie me."

Sebastian unfastened the knot at her wrists, kissed her bloody wounds before he bound the injuries with strips from his neck cloth.

Something thunderous resounded in the distance.

"Wh-who's that?" she said with shaky breath.

Two figures on horseback were fast approaching, the horses' hooves kicking up snow in wild stomps.

"It's just Peter and the magistrate, Henry. You're

safe." With a gentle caress, Ravenswood touched her bruised and tender cheek. "That miserable bastard!"

She jerked her face away. "I-I'll be all right. Please take me home."

Sebastian glowered. "Henry, what is it?"

Wretched tears! It was so hard to find her voice amid the sobs in her throat. "I just want to forget about everything that happened today."

He looked stricken. "Henry . . . did Emerson force himself on you?"

"No!" She wiped the briny drops from her eyes. "Stop being so wonderful, Sebastian! Stop acting like a gentleman! I can't take the lies anymore."

He grabbed her by the shoulders, rankled. "Devil take it, Henry—"

"I know you went to see a doxy while I was away," she cried. "You haven't changed one little bit!"

He let her go then, brushed a shaky hand through his unkempt curls. "You're right. I did go to see a prostitute."

She shuddered. "You're not even going to try to deny it?"

"I went to see Madam Jacqueline, you foolish chit!"

Henrietta hiccupped. "The courtesan? But why?"

"Because I needed her advice. I didn't know how else to get you to trust me." He sighed. "You're bloody stubborn, Henry. When are you going to re-alize that I'm not the same man you stumbled upon in the Hellfire Club?"

Henrietta looked deep into Sebastian's eyes: warm, even under the ghostly moonlight.

Amid the cold and dead of winter, he breathed and radiated a noble strength . . . a truth.

He grouched, "And Madam Jacqueline has a message for you."

Disarmed by the intensity of what she was feeling, Henrietta squeaked, "What is it?"

He growled, "She wants me to tell you that she's proud of you for so thoroughly bewitching me."

For some absurd reason, Henrietta simpered at the words.

"Henry." Sebastian lifted his hand and traced his forefinger softly across her cheek. "You vixen, I—"

"You son of a bitch!"

Henrietta gasped.

A weak Emerson staggered out of the abbey, eyes burning with an unquenchable hatred for Ravenswood. He snatched the pistol Henrietta had discarded in the snow, lifted it—and aimed it straight at her. "I want you to live with pain, Ravenswood."

Ravenswood twisted his body around her and roared, "*No!*"

The shot ripped through the quiet countryside, echoing.

Henrietta screamed.

Ravenswood hit the snow, so still.

"Sebastian!"

On her knees, a tearful Henrietta hovered over the wounded viscount.

The snow was steeped in blood. She could feel the sticky liquid between her gloved fingers. Sebastian had stepped in front of a bullet to shield her. He had saved her life—again!

Frantic, Henrietta patted his body, searching for the wound.

The magistrate appeared, Peter fast on his heels. The men dismounted and quickly tackled Emerson to the ground, confiscating the weapon.

But it was too late to help Sebastian.

Cheeks stained with tears, Henrietta pounded on Sebastian's chest. "Wake up!"

But Sebastian didn't move. He wasn't breathing, either.

A tremendous grief swallowed her heart and spirit then. A boundless misery that sucked her into a chasm of darkness.

She crumpled on top of Sebastian and let out a sorrowful sob, wanting to die right there beside him. He had changed his wicked ways for her. He had told her so himself, but she hadn't believed him.

The guilt nestled in her throat. It was bitter to taste. She was going to suffer for her stubbornness. She was going to spend the rest of her days alone—without Sebastian. Oh God!

"I knew you loved me, Henry."

Henrietta bristled.

Slowly she lifted her head and looked down at Sebastian.

Even through her tears and jarring hiccups, the

fuzzy smile across his sensuous lips was easy to see.

"Why you miserable"—she struck him—"wretched"—she struck him again—"rogue! Did you just *play* dead?"

Sebastian grabbed her and hoisted her until she was straddled across his lap.

"Tell me you love me, Henry."

"I would rather eat worms!"

He grabbed her cheeks and yanked her to his lips—or a hair's breadth away. Oh, sweet heaven, it felt so good to be this close to him again!

"Tell me you love me, Henry."

Henrietta inhaled the spicy scent of rosemary and lemon, looked deep into the rogue's dashing blue eyes—and kissed him. She crushed her lips over his until he couldn't breathe.

"I love you," she whispered. And kissed him again. "I love you. I love you. I love you."

Sebastian chuckled between kisses and gave her a tight hug. "I love you, too, Henry. I don't know when it sneaked up on me, the sentiment, but I think I've loved you for a long time . . . And I always will."

Henrietta was weeping again. But for a whole other reason. The fear in her heart was gone. She trusted Sebastian. She *loved* Sebastian. Really loved him. For years she had nursed a girlhood fantasy. She had been smitten with a dream. But now she knew Sebastian's true nature . . . and it was more wonderful than she had imagined. He wasn't per-

fect—neither was she—but he was her *im*perfect
hero. And she loved every bit of him.

"Uh-um."

"What the devil do you want, Peter," growled Sebastian. "Can't you see I'm engaged at the moment?"

"Yes, well, I was going to offer to dress that wound
in your arm, but if you'd rather bleed to death . . . ?"

Henrietta gasped. "Your wound!"

She quickly groped along his arm and fingered
the thick moisture, oozing.

"It's nothing," said Sebastian. "A mere graze."

"Still." Henrietta struggled to get off his lap. "We
have to get you to a doctor."

But the mulish man wouldn't let her go. "Do
we have to go? I'd rather stay right here with you,
Henry."

"Yes, we have to go!" She staggered to her feet.

With a sigh, Sebastian rolled and stood up, too.
He was all covered in snow from their tussle, and
looked like a whimsical snow angel.

Henrietta quickly stripped the scarf from her
throat to wrap around his injury.

"I see I'm not needed." Chuckling, Peter returned
his attention to the magistrate and Emerson.

"Well, Henry, I suppose there's only one thing left
to do," said Sebastian.

Henrietta was busy ministering to the viscount's
injury, so she furled her brow and said, "I'll have the
wound stitched up in a second."

"Not that, Henry." He took her by the hands and

kissed her knuckles. "You still have to consent to be my wife—in every way."

A brow lifted. "Oh, do I now?"

"Henry," he growled.

With a wicked smile, Henrietta slipped her arms around Sebastian's midriff and arched on her tip-toes. "Kiss me and I'll think about it."

And he did kiss her: a wild, sensuous, heart-stopping kiss.

As if she'd ever give *that* up for the rest of her days.

Epilogue

~~~⟨⟨⟩⟩~~~

Henrietta dandled the baby on her knees.

"He has Peter's nose," she said, inspecting the infant's profile. "Don't you think so, Sebastian?"

The viscount shrugged. "I suppose so."

Henrietta looked at her husband, sprawled in an armchair, legs stretched and crossed at the ankles. He was like a lazy cat, perusing his surroundings.

"Something else on your mind, my lord?"

He grinned at the appellation, a term of endearment now. "I'm just admiring the sight of you, my lady."

Henrietta snorted.

She lifted the baby to her lips and kissed him on the nose. "What a rogue your uncle Seb is. How shall we punish him, Frederick?"

Frederick gurgled in his aunt Henry's arms.

"Lock him out of the bedroom, you say?" She grinned. "What a wonderful idea."

Sebastian chuckled.

Peter sauntered into the room just then, and beamed to see his son. "How is the dear boy?"

Henrietta handed the fussing babe over to his papa. "A darling, Peter. As ever."

The proud father settled into the settee and propped the infant across his chest. "He is a dear, isn't he? Handsome, too. Although I think he has your nose, Seb."

Sebastian rolled his eyes.

Henrietta fell back in her chair with mirth. It was such a warm family gathering. She was so very happy for her sister and Peter. Little Frederick was a much sought-after addition to the family.

Henrietta sighed, content with the idle autumn day. The family had gathered again at Baron Ashby's country home. Poor Papa had been very sorry to see the last of his offspring marry and leave the nest. But Henrietta had kept her promise to visit often. The whole family had made the same vow, much to the baroness's displeasure. Mama was not one to suffer a house filled with noisy children. But for the sake of the baron's good cheer, Mama reluctantly endured the reunions.

Henrietta nestled in her chair and gazed at her husband with love. How she adored the man! It filled her heart with such joy, being with him, her reformed rogue.

The dastardly Emerson had been exiled to Australia. His father, the Earl of Ormsby, happened to wield enough clout to spare his wretched son from the gallows. Even though the earl did not get along with his son, he couldn't let the villain hang. Blood was blood. Or so Henrietta had heard. She did not trouble herself with such details. Life in a penal colony was a much more fitting form of punishment, she was sure. All she really cared about was her family—and her darling husband.

The butler entered the room.

"A letter for you, Lady Ravenswood."

Henrietta took the letter from the silver tray. "Thank you, Wilkes."

With a curt nod, the butler departed.

Two sets of curious eyes then settled on her.

"Who is it from, Henry?" said Peter.

"I shall soon find out." Henrietta broke the red wax seal and scanned the missive. She smiled. "It's from Mirabelle."

"And how is the Duchess of Wembury?" said her husband.

"In very good health, I'm happy to report. We are invited to a christening, my lord, for baby Alice."

Sebastian sighed. "Too many babies."

Peter chuckled at that. "And when will *you*, dear brother, become a father?"

Sebastian made a moue in jest. "Why the devil would I want to do that? Now that you have a son, Peter, I don't need an heir."

Peter chortled. "I think your wife might have something to say about that."

Sebastian looked at his wife.

Henrietta quirked a brow. She had yet to have a babe . . . but she was determined to change all that.

"No babies, my lord?" she said.

Sebastian pretended to think about it—then a slow and wolfish smile touched his lips. "Well, maybe one brat."

Peter cradled the babe and pounced to his feet. "Come along, Frederick. I don't think you need to hear this."

Father and son quickly vacated the room.

Alone with her husband, Henrietta put all her seductive training to good use, and crossed the rug with very sensual strides.

Sebastian followed her every move with avid interest.

She settled very comfortably on his lap and traced her forefinger along the ridge of his masculine jaw. "Just one babe, my lord?"

He wrapped his arms tight around her waist. "Well, maybe two."

Henrietta giggled and kissed him with passion. Breathless, she said, "And when will we start to try for this babe or two?"

"How does right now sound?"

She nipped at his lush lip. "It sounds very agreeable. Shall we go upstairs?"

"I'd rather not, Henry."

She pinched her brow. "But—"

Sebastian wagged his brow. "Billiards, Henry?"

She let out a hearty laugh. "What a wonderful idea, my lord."

Avon Romances

the best in exceptional authors and unforgettable novels!

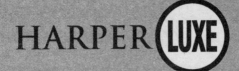

Avon Romantic Treasures

Unforgettable, enthralling love stories, sparkling with passion and adventure from Romance's bestselling authors